Kevin
For a goo

CW01084559

BALTIC INCIDENT

Charles Smart

Marang Publications
Beech House
Thorold Gardens
Barkston
Lincolnshire NG32 2NR
Tel: 01400 251503

Baltic Incident by Charles Smart
ISBN 0-9551776-0-X
13-digit ISBN: 978-0-9551776-0-6
© Charles Smart 2005

Cover photograph: Charles Smart
Author photograph: Mary Auckland
Book production: Into Print - www.intoprint.net
Printed in the UK by Antony Rowe

FOR PATRICIA

PROLOGUE

RUSSIAN TRAWLER SUPPLIES HOLIDAYMAKERS WITH DIVING POOL
(Radio Sweden's 'Panorama' English language broadcast to Eastern Europe)
Holidaymakers on the south coast of Sweden are delighted to find that the Russian fishing fleet has supplied them with a new diving pool this season. In February, the Russian trawler SHISHAK went aground only thirty metres from a holiday beach bordering on the international golf course at the small village of Falsterbo.

When the SHISHAK was towed off five days later, it left behind a large hole twenty-five metres in diameter and about three metres deep, an ideal place for diving and swimming in an area where the water is normally little more than ankle deep.

By Easter, a family of seals found the deep water near the beach and for about a month used it as a playground. Taking a hint from the seals, the local Swedish commune last week anchored a floating diving-board near the centre of the pool and now visitors to this south west corner of Sweden can enjoy an unexpected swimming pleasure – by courtesy of the foundered Russian trawler.

BALTIC INCIDENT
Chapter One

The SHISHAK rolled heavily in the storm-lashed narrow strip of sea between Rødvig in Denmark and Falsterbo on the south west tip of Sweden. The Russian captain was under strict instructions to ground his ship in a way that would look unquestioningly accidental. The small trawler, festooned with aerials running from forward to stern masts and cluttered with multifarious detection devices, had wallowed slowly westwards for the past two days, waiting for the low pressure weather zone to arrive from the north Atlantic. There was no threat from the royal Swedish navy coastguard cutter, mainly because visibility was bad with rain clouds at sea-level obscuring most lights beyond three quarters of a mile, but also because the movements of the single-gunned boat were known in detail. The cutter had last changed crews at the small fishing harbour of Skanör at 18.00hrs and would not be back for another six hours. Time enough for the drop.

Boris Stavrinsky stood protected from the worst of the gale by the forward control cabin, his hooded, dark-blue greatcoat covering all but the prominent features on his square-jawed face. He held tightly to the stanchion near the door and strained his eyes against the cutting rain and the darkness to watch the flash of light from Falsterbo lighthouse, almost directly ahead. The light flickered on for four seconds at a time before dying to a glimmer, showing for only brief moments the white tops of the low waves rushing shorewards. Facing him, to the right of the ship, he imagined more than he could see the grey-black mass of Falsterbohus, the only building of size near the beach. No lights showed. Nor did he expect to see any at three o'clock on a stormy night in late March.

He had been thoroughly briefed and knew exactly what lay across that short strip of racing shallow sea. It would be an easy landfall, Stavrinsky reflected. At forty-eight years of age and trained by masters in the international game of agent-planting, Stavrinsky had entered countries in more ways than he cared to remember. He'd gone into the Shah's Iran as a diplomat on a first-class air ticket. Easy, but exciting enough for a first mission. The United States had been not only easy, it had been disconcertingly popular among the minor politicians and anti-communist league members of Philadelphia where he had gone on a goodwill visit as a member of a West German Ukrainian expatriate group. On that occasion 'M' section of the Leningrad-based KGB had surpassed itself in providing him with authentic documents proving that he had fought as a Ukrainian patriot against the Russians in 1944. Which was true. What the documents did not mention was that the retreating Germans had put a rifle in his hands and a revolver in his back, along with four hundred other teenagers. Other entrances were less comfortable. Submarine landings were nauseous and claustrophobic. Even worse was the parachute method used in Greenland. Parachute jumps were unusual as well as dangerous for amateurs like himself. But they were sometimes necessary when a committee decision had been made at the last moment and the information urgently needed, as in the case of the Greenland operation. For Greenland happened to be the focus, at the time, of American, Canadian and British manoeuvres for the practice of north Atlantic blocking exercises against the USSR's northern fleet of nuclear submarines.

BALTIC INCIDENT

But the really rough leg-work was behind him. As his most recent promotion to colonel indicated, Stavrinsky now had a more important role to play as chief coordinator and liaison officer to younger operatives in the field. Physical dangers were less; responsibilities greater.

The trawler rolled more heavily to the right. Stavrinsky felt a shudder under his feet that indicated more than just another wave. The ship came upright again, but he knew that the first ridge of sand had been smoothed away by her keel. He turned and looked through the window into the dimly lit, cramped wheelhouse and saw the captain move to flick a switch. A spot of red appeared on the control console, duplicated, Stavrinsky knew, in other parts of the ship as a signal to the crew for the last phase of the beaching operation. The throbbing of the engines died away. They were close enough for the wind and waves to do the rest. Stavrinsky opened the door and went inside for the last time. No one spoke. For the captain, the two electronic technicians and the agent himself it was just another job. The three seamen, their work over for the moment, stared through the starboard ports and watched the dark beach lurching closer. They all knew that within ten minutes SHISHAK would be held fast by the sand in the shallow waters. For Stavrinsky the action was about to begin. He bent to a locker and took out his leather briefcase. The ship keeled heavily on another sand bar, throwing the stooped agent off balance. The briefcase slithered and spun away from him across the floor to fetch up sharply against the metalled leg of the radio operator's table. Stavrinsky recovered himself and picked up the briefcase, swearing softly as he saw the circular scuffmarks scratched deeply into the smooth black leather. He straightened up and joined the others at the ports, mentally preparing himself for the last wet and cold thirty metres' trip by rubber dinghy across the breaking waves and on to yet one more alien shore.

'Check' said Jessup. He sat back in the cushioned chair and looked up at Dorn. His partner studied the move. Both men sat comfortably at the fireside. Not that a fire was needed, even on the coldest winter night. The room, like the rest of the house in which Dorn lived alone, was centrally heated and the treble-glazing kept the heat where the designer had intended it to be – inside. Luxury surrounded them, from the thick rugs strewn on the solid parquet flooring to the heavy pale-blue drapes that covered enormous floor-to-ceiling windows. Jessup knew that the six-bedroomed pine built house was similarly appointed. Not at all like the mini one-bedroomed apartment he shared with Carol on the other side of the woods in Ljunghusen.

'You play a good game' Dorn said, breaking into a smile, 'but just a little more attention to detail would help you win more often.'

Jessup watched as Dorn confiscated, with a long-range bishop uncovered by a pawn two moves earlier, the knight that had threatened his king. With a sigh Jessup toppled his own king in resignation. He grinned his acknowledgement and picked up his whisky glass. 'Perhaps you're right. But I really don't get enough practice.'

'Fiddlesticks' returned Dorn. 'I get no more practice than you. Where else in this cold climate could I get a friend to drop in casually for a drink?'

Not for the first time Jessup noticed how well the German could use English colloquialisms in the right place and at the right time. He looked towards the four-seater divan, an authentic comfort in sea-blue velvet, placed under a magnificent landscape painting in riotous greens and yellows of a south Swedish spring countryside. Martina was curled up in the middle of the plush sofa. She looked up from the novel she was reading.

'Finished?' she asked brightly.

'I'm finished' returned Jessup, pulling down the corners of his mouth in a grimace of affected hopelessness. 'Your man here always seems to win when he's on home ground.'

Dorn turned towards her and she transferred her smile to him. Jessup could almost feel the electricity between them. They were as well matched as the original Adam and Eve, though better dressed. Martina's long, fair hair flowed like rich cream to below her shoulders. And when she moved her head her hair floated, light as ripe corn in the breeze of an Indian summer. She uncoiled a shapely pair of legs from the sofa and glided, shoeless, into the kitchen to fetch coffee.

Only a week before, Jessup had believed Heinrich Dorn to be just another expatriate making a rather more plush living than himself. For over a year they had been friends, after that first casual meeting in the local supermarket, calling in on one another for a chat over drinks and the occasional game of chess. Jessup had believed Dorn to be a successful thirty-five year old West Berliner sent by his company, the private German passenger and freight airline Air Germanic, to expand the business into the Scandinavian market. But that was a week ago.

What Jessup now knew about Dorn was enough to upset anybody's game.

Then Jessup had received a telephone call. It had been from a professor Stanley Derringer. Jessup knew him slightly as head of a small section within the department of International Relations at Lund University. When Jessup had first arrived in the country he had talked with Derringer for about an hour. Derringer was of east European origin, probably a Serb, and they had talked about his work for British intelligence during the Second World War. Derringer seemed to enjoy the few occasions when he could again speak English with an Englishman. Jessup had soon forgotten the incident. There'd been no opening for him in the department, anyway.

So he had been surprised and pleased to hear from Derringer that there might be some work. 'Come up at about 17.30 on Wednesday' Derringer had suggested. He had obviously adopted the Swedish habit of using the twenty-four hour clock timing. Jessup was getting used to it. 'You remember where I am?' Jessup had wondered at the timing. He'd been in Sweden long enough to learn that the Swedes were creatures of strict social habit and, in particular, paragons of punctuality. All offices normally closed at four o'clock, including those in the university. Everybody in the country, so it seemed, had to sit down to supper at precisely six-thirty. Of course, Derringer was no doubt excused the ritual since he was a foreigner. Foreigners were expected to behave strangely.

The spring sun was lowering itself between the twin towers of Lund's medieval cathedral by the time Jessup arrived. He had found the outer door of the building open. The shapes and positions of the room showed that this section of the department had once been a private house, built at the beginning of the century. Across the small entrance hall was the secretary's room, once a dark kitchen, now a neon-lit office. It was empty. Staff had gone and the caretaker had not yet arrived to turn off lights and set alarms. Only the outer door had been left open, presumably by Derringer. The house was silent. Jessup turned left and started up the wooden stairs to the first floor where the academics had their studies. He knocked on the door of Derringer's room. A man's voice bade him come in. It must be the wrong door, Jessup thought. The intonation of the invitation came straight from southern England with no trace of a foreign accent. He opened the door.

'Sorry' he began 'I thought this was Dr Derringer's room.' He stopped in some confusion. The man in the room was sitting behind Derringer's desk and waving him in. It was certainly not Derringer.

'Don't apologise. Please come in. You're not in the wrong place.' He smiled and pointed to an upright armchair near the desk. 'Take a seat. Afraid it's I who ought to be apologising. Dr Jessup, isn't it? Name's Goddard. James Goddard. How do you do?' He stretched a hand across to Jessup.

Jessup guessed Goddard to be about thirty three years of age. He was slim and pale-faced and his fair hair dropped in a limp wave over his left eye. He wore a tweed jacket with a brown nylon tie. Jessup felt he had made a particular effort to look casual. He tried to find a slot for Goddard. Perhaps he was a misplaced Inland Revenue officer or a successful IBM salesman. Surely not an academic. Jessup was puzzled. He sat down. 'Dr Derringer said something about my teaching here' he began cautiously.

'Bit of an excuse to get you here, actually.' Goddard smiled apologetically. 'Dr Derringer was just doing me a favour when he rang you.'

'Interesting.' Jessup faced the self-assured Goddard and, with some deliberation, took out a meerschaum-lined Plumb briar and began to fill the bowl from a black leather tobacco pouch.

'Well, yes. And I owe you an explanation. I hope it will become clear when I tell you why I'm here. Bit of a funny approach, I know.' Goddard paused and looked appraisingly at Jessup. 'There's something we'd very much like you to do for us.'

Jessup noticed the 'we' and, through the flame he held to his pipe, looked with raised eyebrows at Goddard's lean features.

'First' Goddard continued, settling himself more easily in his chair, 'I hope you'll let me tell you something about yourself. I assure you it does have a point.'

Jessup pocketed his lighter and made himself more relaxed. 'My favourite topic. Who's the "we" , though?'

Goddard ignored the question. ''We know you're an independent sort of chap, not in the normal run of academics. Bit of a maverick, that sort of thing.'

Jessup winced at the choice of nouns. But it seemed to fit with Goddard's slight tendency towards clipped sentences. In his experience, that usually meant one of two things. Either the speaker was a self-made millionaire with no patience for the niceties of intellectual stimulation, or had a military background where full sentences were regarded as just a waste of breath. Since Goddard was certainly not the former – the lacquered manner was part of his nature, not grafted – he was probably army. Not quite that either, though.

Goddard leaned back in Derringer's upholstered armchair, fingers bunched against his chest. 'Your name is David Jessup, second son of a factory foreman. You left elementary school at the age of fourteen and your application to become a postman was turned down.' The smile he gave Jessup didn't quite reach his eyes.

'Bad health.' Jessup touched his thick lensed spectacles with the stem of his pipe.

BALTIC INCIDENT

Goddard went on. 'For the next eight years you drifted from job to job. Never settled into any one of them.'

Jessup interrupted. 'I didn't fancy spending the rest of my life on a factory floor.'

It wasn't at all a sore point with Jessup that he'd had eight different jobs in as many years before the idea of teaching was put to him. What needled him slightly was the barely veiled value judgement Goddard seemed to be making, as though it were necessarily a weakness in a person's character not to have secure and satisfactory employment from school to retirement. It was the sort of unreflective comment he'd heard more than once, years ago, when he'd started to collect academic degrees. Only that time it had come from narrow-minded schoolteachers.

'Quite. Just wanted to look at the facts first.' Goddard had suddenly stopped smiling. 'By the time you were twenty-one you still didn't know the difference between a verb and a noun. Correct?'

That did startle Jessup. A number of acquaintances could have known the precise facts of his inadequate early education, but it was a shock to realize that a total stranger could supply this quite meaningless historical titbit.

Goddard went on. 'Just over a year later, and after some effort, you were offered a college place. You began to train as a teacher in history. It seems you ran faster than most after that. Within a few years you'd collected two university degrees in England and a doctor's title from Melbourne, and from then on stayed teaching in universities.' He paused for a moment, then offered the nearest thing to a fixed smile Jessup had seen since he'd looked at the face of the head doorman outside the Ritz in Piccadilly. 'Not bad, I'd say.'

CHARLES SMART

If the man had a point to make, Jessup felt sure it could have nothing to do with his unorthodox educational indefatigation. But by now he was seriously curious to find out what more Goddard had unearthed and where the strange interview was leading.

'You eventually took up a post in the university of the South Pacific and returned to Europe three years later. Since then, you and your wife, Carol, have lived in a flat owned by a rich Swedish friend down in Falsterbo. Made the best of it. Still swimming while your colleagues in Britain are being prematurely retired.' Goddard finished with a little flourish of his hands, outstretched as though to embrace all the potted history he'd just outlined. 'Covers the main points, wouldn't you say?'

Jessup had turned sideways in the wooden-armed chair opposite Goddard and was looking through the tall window at the corrugated angles of the student union building, starkly printed on a background of darkening blue sky. There was something very unusual indeed about this little, one-sided, chat, Jessup thought. And it hadn't escaped his notice that Goddard was in full command of the facts without having to refer to notes. A quick brain? A photographic memory? 'Main facts, perhaps', he replied carefully. 'But what's all this about? Why the special interest?'

'Quite right.' Goddard was quick to come back, as though he did not want to lose Jessup's complete attention. 'But consider, you've carved out a minor name for yourself here, even though you're a foreigner. In five years you've become completely accepted at the university. Respected, and so on. A fair representative of that oddball the English academic. Different – but accepted. And that's the point.'

BALTIC INCIDENT

Jessup stared at him, puzzled. 'I'm not quite with you. I'm sure you didn't ask me to come just to help me write my memoirs. So why the analysis?'

Goddard had developed the habit of smoothing his brow with a rather feminine-shaped hand, ending the movement in a sweep that brushed his hair deftly back into place. He did so now, but instead of giving Jessup a direct answer, Goddard leaned forward and clasped his fingers together in front of him on the desktop. Then he said 'What happened when you last visited the police in Malmö?'

It was about then that Jessup began to feel doubtful vibes from Goddard. As far as he knew, it was absolutely none of Goddard's business what dealings he had with the police. Jessup nearly forgot the golden rule he'd learnt from hard experience, not to show his feelings too soon. He answered mildly, 'I shouldn't have thought that was anything to do with you.' Then he added, letting a malicious smile crinkle his brow 'Unless, that is, you're thinking of the time they called me in for questioning on the charge of smuggling cocaine.' He didn't much care whether Goddard took him seriously or not. His blue eyes twinkled. The image of the young Jamaican had come to mind. It was while he and Carol were travelling back to Europe via the West Indies, in Port Antonio that Joshua had offered him the white powder. It had amused Jessup to reject Joshua's glib salesmanship, in the embarkation shed, so close to the Italian cruise liner, not on the grounds that it was cocaine being offered, but because Joshua swore it was sixty per cent pure. Jessup had told him, in the same conspiratorial manner, that he was only interested in ninety per cent.

Goddard was bred to smile indulgently. He did so now. 'Something a little more prosaic, I think. Let me tell you. You were told you could stay and work indefinitely. Future applications for residence and employment would be granted automatically. Went through their files like a dose of salts. Right?'

The question was rhetorical. Jessup said 'Obviously I'm a supernumerary in this conversation. Could we come to the point? I'm sure I'll beat the rush-hour from this metropolis if I go straight away.'

'We've reached it, Dr Jessup. The people I represent could use someone with precisely your background. Someone above suspicion in public and private. And' Goddard paused slightly, as though for emphasis, 'a little out of the ordinary.'

Jessup uncrossed his legs and turned full-face to Goddard. 'If I understand correctly, you, or whoever the "we" are, think I can help in some unspecified work on the grounds that I'm a typically English cultured nobody.'

Goddard held up his hand in protest. 'No, please.' His face became serious as though to give point to his sincerity. 'Hear me out.'

Jessup wasn't really annoyed anyway. It would take a great deal for him to doubt his own worth, whatever others thought. But he did want Goddard to speak his mind and stop beating about the bush.

Goddard said 'You're a foreigner with all the oddities the Swedes expect, and you hold the respect they often have of the English. You're accepted and trusted. You've managed to remain quite different while being beyond suspicion. You're exactly what we're looking for.'

Jessup didn't respond immediately. A bright street lamp, slung across the road outside, flashed on and was reflected in his horn-rimmed spectacles. Deep down he knew there was something important in this strange interview. He didn't think Goddard was unintelligent, so the biographical background had to have some special meaning for him. Goddard, or somebody behind him, had gone to considerable trouble to get at those details. His curiosity was growing. It was worth finding out who this man was. He said 'Very well. What do you think I can do for you?'

Goddard brought out a wallet from his inside breast pocket and extracted a small green folder. He walked round the desk and handed it to Jessup. Jessup opened the folded plastic. He expected to see something like a continental identity card, full of dates, computer numbers and signatures relating to a badly taken photograph. Instead, he found what looked like a very ordinary business card. Printed neatly in the centre was Goddard's name. Under that it simply stated 'Director, Dunn's Radio Equipment, Hounslow.' On the bottom in each corner there was a telephone number, one marked 'Office', the other 'Home'. Nothing else. Not even a bad photograph.

Jessup handed back the folder and looked up at Goddard. 'What's this supposed to mean?'

'Does look rather simple, doesn't it? And if you telephoned to either of those numbers you'd be able to make an appointment to have your wireless or television set mended without the slightest trouble. What's more, they'd do a good job. The firm's genuine. The telephone operators are not.' Goddard walked to the window overlooking the rear courtyard of the university house. The room was quite dark now, they hadn't bothered to put on the lights. The pale blue of the sky was still tinged with the sun's afterglow. The first stars were yet feeble. He was almost a silhouette to Jessup. 'You must be aware of the many different departments in British defence organizations. Well, this is one of them. Doesn't have an official name, just a number. So we call it "Squawk". The nickname stuck about fifteen years ago when it used to specialize in de-briefing field officers from overseas trips. Before my time, that.'

Jessup already knew that Derringer had been with MI6 during the war, so why hadn't he made the connection sooner? Perhaps World War 2 was becoming just another piece of history to him. He was getting old. He'd not given a second thought to Derringer's minor boast about how he'd got his job as a lecturer in politics on the basis of his work with British intelligence in Moscow and East Europe. It had sunk to the bottom of Jessup's mind without trace; an older man's experiences often did this to their listeners. But it fully explained why Goddard was able to use Derringer as well as his room at the university. So Derringer had remembered him. He could have been the source for much of Goddard's assessment of Jessup's work and standing with his Lund colleagues.

A quick mental adjustment was needed to absorb the fact that he was actually being approached by a representative of the British secret service. Or was he? Jessup went through the mental shift without a pause as he responded to Goddard.

'So how does this card identify you?'

'Very simple. You ring one of those numbers. An operator will answer in the normal way. Incidentally, if you ring the "home" number, it won't be my wife who answers. Not the marrying type. If you say anything but the right thing in the first sentence, you'll probably get your television repaired. On the other hand' Goddard turned on his smile again 'if within that first sentence you mention a Nordiska radio – the company doesn't exist so it's quite safe, just identification – you'll be put through to a rather different office in another part of

BALTIC INCIDENT

London. All you have to do then is ask about me. It'll be safe to talk.'

Jessup emptied the dead ash from his pipe into the heavy glass ashtray on the desk. 'How could I be sure it wasn't all a hoax and they'd confirm anything I asked about you?

'Fair question. Tell me, do you know the number of your passport?'

'Not without looking at it.'

'And it's a fair bet your acquaintances or even your closest friends wouldn't know it either, what?'

'No.'

'The second telephone connection will be able to tell you precisely what it is and, if you like, quite a lot of other information about yourself as well. Like to give it a try? A lot more efficient than a photograph with an identity card.'

Jessup turned away from the silhouette at the window with something of a sigh. Why did he feel that this conversation was running away from him? In the gloom he shook his head slowly, 'You know, all this sounds a bit silly' he said at last. 'What could possibly be so important for you to go to all this trouble just to get my help? Let's suppose I accept your credentials for the moment. What is it you think I can do?'

Goddard dropped the smile with the bombshell. 'Yes. Well, there's something else you ought to know first. We learned some months ago that your friend, Dorn, is a Soviet agent. He's not a West but an East Berliner. His company, Air Germanic, is under suspicion, too. But that's being looked into by the West Germans. The fact that you two have become friendly is one of the main reasons for our asking your help. Sorry I had to put that item last. Just thought you'd respond better if I went the long way round.'

'Why do I get the feeling that this is some elaborate hoax? I think I know Heinrich well enough. He's got a regular routine. I know his home and I've seen him in his Malmö office, he appreciates a good joke, does some of the food shopping as I do. What you say is inconceivable. And if he's an undercover agent why should he want to befriend me?'

'I have to say we believe he's cultivated your friendship as part of his cover and routine employment is part of the deception. Let me show you something.' Goddard opened a manila folder and took out several eight by twelve-inch black and white photographs. Jessup walked round the desk to stand at Goddard's shoulder. Goddard handed him the first print. 'Do you recognize anyone?'

Jessup took the picture and studied it for a moment. He was looking at two men standing near the double doors of a large multistore in a busy city street. He said hesitantly 'I don't think so.'

'Look carefully at the younger man.'

Jessup looked again. 'Could it be Heinrich? This person is too thin.'

'So he should. It is Dorn. The picture was taken ten years ago when he was starting out with Air Germanic as a trainee manager. That was his cover at the time, of course. Look at the other shots.' He handed Jessup five more prints showing the two men from slightly different angles and at various distances. Jessup took the pictures and moved back to his chair to face Goddard across the desk. He removed his spectacles to look more closely at the photographs. He could see the moustache more clearly now, incipient but visible. The six different perspectives of the younger man made it almost certain, to Jessup, that it was indeed Heinrich

BALTIC INCIDENT

Dorn, but he wasn't prepared to make things easier for Goddard.

He replaced his glasses then, with the stem of his pipe, tapped on the pictures in front of him and looked with a frown at Goddard. 'Let's assume this is Heinrich Dorn. What's so significant about these photographs? And why show me old ones?'

The shadow of a smile crossed Goddard's features. It didn't touch his eyes. 'To answer your last question first, they're old pictures because the men have not been seen together since that time. And the significance of the photos is to show you the connection between the two. You see, the person we were really tracking on that occasion was not Dorn. He entered our files at that point for the first time. It was the older man. His name is Viktor Karjagin, one time first secretary at the Soviet Embassy in London. He was expelled from Britain in 1971 for espionage. A top KGB officer.' Goddard paused before he made his final point. 'Karjagin now heads the Soviet mission here in Sweden. We think one of his main agents is, once again, your friend Heinrich Dorn.'

Jessup didn't want to show his emotion, but he felt fingers of ice touch his spine. His pipe lay as cold on the desk in front of him as he listened to Goddard. He rubbed a hand across his brow. He began to feel that the times and confidences he had shared with Dorn were as paltry as a fairground plastic duck. The figure of Dorn in his mind had suddenly lost its substance; had become a featureless silhouette. He was careful in his response; needed time to think. Jessup got up, began to fill his pipe again and walked round the back of the chair he'd been sitting on. If Goddard had wanted to surprise him, he had. Jessup was astonished. He leaned on the back of the chair for a moment, then walked to the door and flicked on the light switch. The cold neon tube flashed twice in the ceiling before it decided to flush out the deep shadows of the faded day. He turned to face Goddard. 'I suppose you want me to check up on Heinrich, or something like that?' There was a brittleness to his voice Goddard had not expected.

'Well, yes. As a matter of fact there's something quite specific we'd like you to do. And it's rather urgent.'

'You've done quite a lot of talking in the past half-hour. Perhaps you are who you say you are, but I'd like to think about the whole thing before we go any further.'

'Be my guest. And when you're satisfied we'll go into details. Alright?'

Goddard moved from the now darkened skyline and handed Jessup one of his cards. 'I'd be glad if you'd keep this under your hat. And, er, do remember to mention the Nordiska radio, won't you?'

Jessup suddenly felt dreadfully tired. He wanted to go home and make himself a good strong cup of coffee, to sit back and reflect with somnolent pleasure on the thriller he'd just seen at the cinema. Only it wasn't a film. He forced himself back into Derringer's study and tried to look brightly at Goddard. 'Can I reach you here?'

'Not at this point. It may be necessary later.' Goddard shook his head. The lock of hair fell again to touch the tip of his nose. 'There may be only a strip of salt water between Sweden and Denmark but as far as I'm concerned it might as well be three thousand miles wide. Sweden's very neutral. Denmark is a member of NATO. There would be a nasty diplomatic exchange behind the scenes if the authorities here knew what I was doing. The nearest point for the moment without unnecessary risk is Copenhagen. Best if we meet there.'

BALTIC INCIDENT

It was much later that Jessup would remember God-dard's slightly contradictory thinking. In the first place it would appear that he was trying to help the Swedes by exposing Heinrich Dorn. In the second place it would apparently provoke a row if the Swedes knew he was working as a British agent within their borders. Long before he learned of the first fatal consequences he'd become too involved to back away.

CHARLES SMART
Chapter Two

Jessup knew he generally gave the impression of being a 'grey' man, a pleasant but colourless academic. It amused him to remember the occasion when that description had actually been used. They'd been about to move house and Carol was busy in the kitchen. He'd forgotten his key and his front door had been opened to him by somebody from the removal firm. The man had said nothing. Leaving the door open for Jessup, he'd gone off to report to Carol that there was a 'grey man' at the front door. It was a fairly accurate description since Jessup had been wearing a grey overcoat and grey deerstalker. He even had grey eyes. Of course, it was a cover. Some people displayed competence and notable success like Joseph's coat. The grey man remained unnoticed, invisible. Jessup revelled in its disguise. Under cover of greyness Jessup had developed a core of ruthlessness that had surprised even himself. He was a natural anarchist. Not the formal sort that would join a society of the like-minded but one who would follow no rule just because it was there. The choices he made were his own and for his own reasons.

He recalled the first time he'd been made aware of the value of being invisible. It was during his stint as a reporter for the Wolverhampton Star newspaper, before beginning an academic career. A well-known married businessman had suffered a heart attack while in a compromising position with his secretary. He had warned the nurses in Ward A of the Birmingham Accident hospital, where he'd been taken, to keep at bay the juicy scoop-hungry journalists. The visiting doctors were recognizable but nobody noticed the young porter wearing a regulation brown dustcoat. It had been as easy as a dog snatching an unguarded meat joint from the kitchen table. With brush and dustpan the young man was able to literally sweep his way into the private ward and poke his broom under the recovering businessman's bed. That brought his head within six inches of that of his quarry. The businessman was first astonished and then amused at the young man's cheek. Jessup got the story and made his first byline.

Jessup gripped the leather steering wheel of his Jaguar 420S and prepared to drive home to Falsterbo. He swung the car from under the birch trees and across the sandy parking area that lay in the more solid shade of Lund's cathedral. Goddard had got the facts right enough, but his company mindset hadn't penetrated to the substance and there was certainly a significant gap in his recital. Jessup couldn't repress a chuckle. Could it really be that Goddard had failed to discover Jessup's connection with Tommy Falk?

Falsterbo was a very small, isolated village crowded during a few short summer weeks with Swedes seeking the traditional sun-tan on the wide white sandy beaches. But it was practically deserted from August until May, the private luxury apartments empty. Except, that is, for David and Carol. Jessup's student contact time at Lund University was light, often in the evenings, while Carol went off each day to teach English at a school in Trelleborg, twenty miles further up the coast. Lengthy walks along the foreshore and sand dunes and in the nearby pine woods were ideal for Jessup's research and writing preparation.

If he had read – which he hadn't – a recent copy of Jane's Fighting Ships, the international manual of military shipping, he would have been aware of the imminent threat to Sweden's defence capability. But the Swedish government didn't need to read it. They already knew at first hand the danger posed by Soviet submarine activity. The newly formed Ubåtsskyddskommission (Submarine Defence Commission) had held a crisis meeting under the chairmanship of the Prime Minister himself. The commission had become seriously alarmed at the increased number of Soviet submarine violations of Swedish territorial waters off the coast of Karlskrona in the south east of the country. Targets of the spying raids by elite groups from Russia's naval base at Kronstadt included air, naval and communications bases, fixed artillery and mine defences and beach exits, as well as the easiest routes from the Stockholm area to the south Norwegian border. The combat groups were equipped with miniature submarines and trained in techniques of raiding, sabotage, reconnaissance and political murder. What he knew was only what he'd read in the Sydsvenskan newspaper of U137, the Russian submarine that, with malfunctioning air-conditioning, had been forced to the surface inside Swedish waters. It had been a national story. Even so, he had been surprised at Tommy Falk's proposal.

It had been five months before Derringer's 'phone call. Jessup had been walking close to the lapping wavelets of a calm Baltic sea on a deserted beach, lost in thought on the problems raised by the logic of Wittgenstein's 'family resemblances' analysis of knowledge. To Jessup Tommy Falk had appeared from nowhere. But Falk had been watching Jessup's movements for the past fifteen minutes from behind the eight-foot high grass-tufted sand dunes. In fact, Falk, an officer with Säpo, the state security special intelligence police, had monitored Jessup's quiet beach walks for over a month. Today it was time to reveal himself.

It had seemed to Jessup a mild enough request; nothing arduous, or even time-consuming. Just a simple service to a state that wished to maintain its neutrality. Tommy had merely asked him to note and report any kind of sea-going vessels he might observe as he walked along the beach each day. Tommy had shown him his Swedish ID card and suggested he confirm his identity with the Malmö police chief. All Jessup needed was a Stockholm telephone number so that sightings could be checked and monitored. For weeks on end Jessup had seen nothing of interest out on the grey waves. On clear days he could see the passenger 'planes on their approach path to Denmark's international airport at Kastrup some fifty miles to the north west. It was an unobtrusive activity that nicely balanced the more mundane challenges of academia. He had found Tommy Falk to be an agreeable character, friendly and reasonably forthcoming, and had enjoyed the occasional telephone conversations he'd had when Falk rang to keep contact. But there had been no shipping of significance to report.

Then came the night of the big storm. For twelve hours wind and rain had lashed the meticulously kept lawns and flowerbeds of Falsterbohus communal gardens. By eight o'clock in the morning the storm had passed. Carol had driven off to school. Jessup sat on the high stool in the kitchenette and drank a third cup of coffee. From there he could look across the sitting room through the large plate glass window to the sodden grass outside. The wind had dropped and across the lawns he could see the drenched fabric of the three Swedish flags on the crenellated walls of the main building clinging to their flagstaffs like unwrung dishcloths. He concentrated for ten minutes on his partly prepared seminar notes, food for thought on his walk, wrapped himself into a scarf and overcoat, tied the tapes of the Russian style fur hat under his chin and trod the eighty yards' track that ended in the sand dunes.

In the thick and dampened sand he passed between the last two shoulder-high mounds. As he had expected the beach stretched deserted to left and right until lost in the sea haze. Beachcombers searching for valuable nuggets of amber – the fossilised resin from the long lost forests of the southern Baltic – would arrive in the next few days, as always after a storm. The sea was as grey as a slate roof in the Rhondda Valley. There was little swell, in these shallow waters, to indicate the strength of the previous night's storm. But there was something out there. He couldn't have seen it as he trudged among the dunes but as he emerged onto the beach he saw the ship; a little to his right and not more than fifty yards from the shoreline. It was so unexpected and so close that he stopped for a moment and gaped. He could tell from its size, its rigging and general outline that it was a fishing trawler. It must have been blown into the shallows during the night. Three or four manned rubber dinghies fussed around her stern. He could hear crewmen calling to one another. The ship was clearly grounded and sat on the waves solid and dark like a huge misshapen rock. Screwing his eyes to tight slits for clearer focus behind his spectacles he could just make out the name on the ship's starboard bow: SHISHAK. He hurried back to the apartment deciding to call directly to Tommy Falk. Barely a minute later, having reported the stranded trawler, Jessup slowly replaced the receiver. He was puzzled. He sat down on the edge of the bed and searched his overcoat pockets for his pipe and tobacco pouch. It was probably nothing of significance but Jessup mused on the fact that Falk had taken the news so quietly, perhaps too calmly, and with no comment other than to say that Säpo had heard of the situation an hour earlier and were sending out vessels to haul the SHISHAK into deeper waters when the tide was right. Two days later Jessup had seen that the trawler had been dragged off the sandbank.

- - - - - - - - - - - - - - -

As he drove back to Falsterbo from Lund, taking the dual carriageway by-pass around Malmö, Jessup had felt a mild form of shock when he'd first understood what Goddard had revealed about Dorn. It was mainly instinct that had made him stall for an answer. Even Goddard's casual use of Dorn's surname had sounded unreal. Jessup had to remind himself that it was his friend, Heinrich, Goddard was referring to. One of his first reactions was to consider confronting Dorn with this bizarre story. The sheer incredibility of the idea had made Jessup momentarily certain that Heinrich would just laugh at him. But if what Goddard had said were true, then Heinrich might still laugh, and how would he be able to interpret that? After all, he could hardly expect Dorn to slap him on the back and congratulate him as though he'd just scored a home run. Much as he wanted to, Jessup had to acknowledge that that approach could be a dangerous mistake. No. A direct approach to Dorn was out of the question. Yet Jessup could not quite overcome the feeling that, even if Goddard turned out to be a genuine government agent, he had not been entirely honest. That smile, a bit mechanical, a salesman pushing slightly inferior goods. He could check with Tommy Falk, of course, but that would be an extremely delicate matter and one best left as a last resort. Then another thought struck him. If Goddard was a bona fide agent then he, or his 'squawk' department, would almost certainly expect Jessup to ring the coded number.

For Jessup not to make contact in this way would surely be taken as a sign that Jessup was not cooperating. It would be a first positive response to the beginning of some action or other. They needed to know that the operation – whatever it was – had got off the ground. Whatever else he did Jessup had to make that call.

Next morning, after Carol had gone off to do some food shopping, Jessup did a check with a local newspaper office and found that there had indeed been a Nordiska company which had made pianos but had gone out of business twelve months earlier. It made sense to use a genuine name, Jessup decided. Then, to reinforce a negative, he rang the British Embassy in Stockholm. He drew a blank. Not unexpectedly no one among the puzzled Embassy secretarial staff had heard of Goddard or of a Nordiska radio repair shop in Hounslow. He still couldn't get rid of the other lingering thought, that the whole story was a complex joke, engineered by some of his more playful colleagues or some imaginative student. It could do no harm, after all, he thought, to ring the Hounslow number. He could dial direct and no one would know he was calling from Sweden – unless Goddard was on the level.

It was eleven o'clock in the morning, ten o'clock London time, when Jessup dialled the number printed on Goddard's card.

'Dunn's Radio.' A male voice with a marked London accent answered brightly. 'Good morning. How can I help you?'

Jessup didn't find it easy to sound casual from a thousand miles away. He experienced a melting sensation in the pit of his stomach and his palms began to ooze an unnatural sweat. 'Ah, er, good morning. I should like to know if you are able to repair my Nordiska radio.'

BALTIC INCIDENT

His throat had gone dry. He knew he sounded stiff and unnatural.

'Very sorry, sir, would you care to repeat that?'

'I said Nordiska radio.' Jessup decided it did not matter what he said as he fitted in the meaningless phrase.

'Yes sir. Just one moment, please.'

Bingo! Jessup found himself nervously biting the inside of his cheek. There was a pause from the earpiece. He knew the conversation was being recorded.

A warm female voice came on the line. 'Good morning. Would you mind repeating your request?' Jessup did so.

'I must ask you to wait. Please don't replace the receiver.'

Thirty seconds later the voice introduced itself again. 'Your name is David Jessup and you're ringing from Sweden?'

Jessup's hand shook slightly as he held the handpiece to his ear.

'And you wish to know whether a certain James Goddard is a member of the "Squawk" department?'

'That's correct. You seem to have answered my question before I've asked it.'

'Glad to be of some service, Dr Jessup. Is there anything else?'

''As a matter of fact, there is. I assume you know the number of my passport, would you please tell me what it is?'

The operator did so without hesitation. She was obviously waiting for that one.

'There's something else.' Jessup wanted a little more than his passport number. He asked for the name of his eldest son and, after what was probably a computer consultation, was told he had no children, either by his first or his present wife.

Jessup wasn't sure whether he was pleased or not at having Goddard's credentials verified. After only a moment's hesitation, he said 'I'd like to meet Goddard in two days' time in Denmark. Can you arrange that?' Now it was done. And Jessup felt he was on the way to satisfying his intense curiosity.

- - - - - - - - - - - - - - - -

The passenger ferry Hamlet took fifty minutes to cross between Limhamn, a southern suburb of Malmö, and Dragør in Denmark. Jessup had parked the Jaguar in Limhamn at nine o'clock in the morning and had enjoyed the fresh breeze and fine weather of the Öresund crossing. The London operator had simply taken his instructions concerning the time and place of meeting and Jessup had no doubt Goddard would be waiting, pleased that he had made a successful recruit. Jessup had specially chosen the village of Dragør rather than Copenhagen. A lingering suspicion had forced him to make it a place of his own rather than Goddard's choosing. A token show of independence, Jessup thought, could do no harm, even if Goddard was on the side of the angels.

The small fishing harbour of Dragør presented a delightfully old-fashioned scene. The fish, caught during the night by the busy little boats, were held captive by nets in the water below the harbour wall. Jessup passed a woman carrying a plastic shopping bag from which a large fishtail protruded, still flapping in life.

He walked across the cobbled quayside and opened one of the double doors of the Royal Restaurant. He saw Goddard almost immediately. He was sitting next to the wide picture windows facing the yachting basin and slipway, a silver pot of coffee and two cups lay at his elbow. On a warm summer evening there would be dozens of locals and some of the more discerning tourists enjoying a quiet evening stroll. Just now there were few people in this part of the village and, as Jessup had planned, the restaurant was empty but for the man from Squawk. In the peacefulness of that village quay-side rendezvous, with an early spring sun beginning to warm the cobbles outside, Jessup learned of a scheme that was intended to shatter the delicate balance of territorial dispositions tacitly accepted by East and West since the end of the second world war.

Goddard had relinquished the tweed look and now wore a narrow-lapelled dark blue business suit. It made him look thinner, the grey eyes that much colder. Or should that be more calculating? Jessup couldn't decide. But he greeted Jessup warmly enough before launching into his explanation.

'What we're talking about' Goddard began 'is a plan conceived in outline some twenty years ago by top Soviet military advisers and generals in their reaction to Kennedy's victory in the Cuban missile crisis. It's been on the shelf since then. But certain military and political situations in the past five years have made the plan not just more attractive but, in Soviet eyes, a necessary part of their overall strategy.' He paused, still looking at Jessup. His eyes gave nothing away. Goddard went on. 'Let me fill you in on the background. In 1980 the Russians built the largest consulate in Sweden. It's in Gothenburg. The Swedes ask, Why are so many Soviet diplomats needed in Gothenburg? It's the wrong question. What the Swedes seem not to know is that the Russians have built up a large stock of electronic and computer equipment, sophisticated enough to direct inter-continental ballistic missiles. They need highly trained technicians to operate it. Those technicians all have diplomatic status and many of them live in luxury flats specially built within the grounds of the consulate itself.'

Goddard picked up his coffee cup, sat back in his chair and turned to look through the large plate-glass window. Beyond the yachting pool, now quietly in repose awaiting the summer's activity, lay the open sea, looking eastwards towards Sweden. He nodded Jessup's attention to a grey Danish frigate steaming north.

'They pass all the time' Jessup commented. He looked back at Goddard, trying again to assess the enigma and the intentions of this British undercover agent.

Goddard ignored the remark. 'There are two people in charge of every ship.' He gave Jessup a quizzical look as though the statement had been a question.

'Is that supposed to mean something?'

Goddard did not respond to the touch of intended irony. Perhaps, thought Jessup, he thinks the honeymoon's over, now that I've checked him out. He allowed a smile to stay on his face. If Goddard wanted to keep his impression that Jessup was a naive outsider whom he had a momentary use for, so be it. For now.

'There are the captain and the chief engineer' Goddard went on, again ignoring Jessup's comment. 'Neither can work without the other. What the Russians had in Sweden until 1982 was a "captain", a full blown ambassador, like other countries. In the case of the Soviets it was one of their top KGB men, based in Stockholm. Now that the Gothenburg consulate is fully furnished they have their "chief engineer". That means the powerhouse of the Gothenburg technical community is able to plot every military movement in and around the south part of the country. His name is Viktor Karjagin. Karjagin operated as a KGB agent in Britain before he was thrown out in 1971. Anyway, any navy man will tell you that one other key figure is needed in a warship. That's the gunnery officer. The man who trains the guns on the correct target at the right distance.'

Jessup couldn't help smiling at the slightly pompous lecturing manner Goddard had assumed. He hid the smile behind the match he held to his pipe.

'You know' Goddard went on 'those submarines you've been hearing about, the Russians in Swedish waters?' It was Jessup's turn to keep his thoughts to himself. He merely nodded. 'Most of them decoys, just a psychological ploy.

'These military movements had two effects. The first was expected, the second a bonus. In the first place, the incursions of the submarines drew the biggest cry of "We are neutral" ever heard from Sweden. The Russians had calculated this. It is, as you could guess, impossible to tell one potential enemy that you are neutral without also telling the rest of the word, otherwise it's meaningless. The Swedish government's reaction was easy to predict. In its efforts to convince the Soviets of their neutrality the Swedes had to warn off the west as well.'

'What else could they say?' Jessup asked rhetorically.

'Absolutely. By the rules of neutrality there was nothing else they could say. But what NATO heard, loud and clear, was the message that Sweden would not, could not, turn to the west for protection in the event of a problem. Their help would have to be refused, whatever the Russians did.' Goddard paused for the waitress to pour fresh coffee from two silver containers. He fastidiously waved away the milk.

'And the bonus?'

'That came directly from the Swedish Prime Minister. By secret meetings between his United Nations ambassador, Anders Ferm, and a member of the Soviet Communist Party's Central Committee, Georgi Arbatov, the

PM wanted to make it known to the Russians that the strong language used in the official protest notes to Moscow over the incdents were little more than a formality demanded by certain conservative sections of the population.'

'Has he ever heard about the long spoon and the devil?' Jessup said.

'It's damn dangerous but, for what it's worth, that's the background. Believe you me it's not been easy for intelligence departments in Britain and the States to come to terms with what appears to be the final phase of the Russian operation.' Goddard picked up his cup and drank the remains of his coffee. He eyed Jessup over the rim of the cup. If Squawk's head of department was correct in his evaluation of Jessup's character, Jessup would follow a very ordinary line of thought and play the ball exactly as they wanted him to. It wasn't every afternoon of the week squawk could pick its actors so easily and so central to its purpose.

Jessup's spectacles reflected the bright daylight as he looked out over the sea. He turned back to Goddard. 'Are you suggesting that Russia is preparing to move in on Sweden, in a west-style Afghanistan?'

Goddard brushed his left hand across his forehead in a characteristic gesture. 'Not in the same way, but substantially that's what our information leads us to believe. With Finland "neutralized" by its defence pact with Russia, the recent strengthening of its air defences against even trials of cruise and Pershing missiles based in West Germany, paid for by Russia of course, Sweden is the next logical step. And, as Russia has recognized since Kennedy's time, it would be the most effective move since Stalin persuaded Roosevelt not to advance beyond the Elbe in 1945. With Sweden under Soviet control, they would have a gun pointing straight down on West Germany from the north.'

Jessup felt the first tinge of apprehension. He hadn't expected to be part of such a vast enterprise. He'd read the newspapers and had decided that the sabre-rattling politicians sounded much as they did ten years ago. But the fingers on his back were too cold, and the man opposite him was too real. Maybe he ought to back out. No. That wasn't good enough. It was too easy. He knew the shivers would pass, given time. He'd felt the same when he'd been in Belfast. July 1972. He'd arrived after one of the earliest IRA bomb attacks. The vaulted but now shattered dome of Queen's Road railway station had showered glass shards around him. And in the city centre the soldiers with their automatics on street corners, wearing grotesque bullet-proof vests, eyeing without looking at the heavy suitcase he carried. Others, sitting patiently behind muslin curtains on the upper floors, their sights trained on his heart, fingers on the trigger, ready to squeeze if he so much as moved away from his luggage in the crowded street. But it took no more than an hour for the shivers to pass. Like the citizens of Belfast he could shoulder the everyday threat and breathe a certain air of indifference. He could do that again. He asked 'Why at this particular moment in history?'

Goddard made his answer sound like a dull university lecture. 'Three things point in that direction. First, there's the background I've already outlined. Second, we believe Russia is more worried than they care to show about the west's ballistic missile capability. They desperately need to prove that they've not lost any military ground. Finally, we believe the "gunnery officer" is now in position and that his specific task of feeding

the final items of information into the Russian "guns"
– to use that figure of speech – is nearly complete.'
'You're referring to Heinrich Dorn?'
'Partly, yes. And that leads us to another conclusion. If
any military operation were to take place, it would be
in the south west of the country. To be precise, in the
west of what Swedish military maps refer to as MILO
S, short for "Military Area South". So you can see why
there has been no Soviet activity in that particular part
of the country. They don't want the Swedes rushing
equipment down there.'
Goddard decided it was time to haul on the line. 'So
what we want now, and we want it fast, is to know exactly what Dorn is doing, what he's already uncovered
and how much there is left for him to do. We want to
put him out of the way as soon as possible. Hand him
over to the Swedes with no fuss and in such a way that
British intelligence cannot be said to be involved. Never do for neutral Sweden to be seen hob-nobbing with
one of the blocs. That's where you come in.'
'So Heinrich and I are good friends. But you don't expect me to be able to walk up to him one evening and
ask him where he keeps his secret maps, do you?'
It was Goddard's turn to smile. He had had plenty of
time now to study his man. The squawk file on Jessup
had just about everything in it. Average intelligence,
stolid, jingoistic enough, would play ball because it was
right, not for the money. The original innocent. Tailor-
made for the department and no surprises. 'We've done
some of the background work, of course. All we want is
for you to get something concrete and to be able to support it honestly to Säpo. Not too difficult, I think.'
'What exactly am I supposed to do?'
'There should be something in the house – and you're
the one with the access. A file, some plans or notes.

Anything you can spot for yourself. You'll recognize it when you see it.'

Jessup felt that, even now, he could back away from Goddard's persuasive proposition. And what if he decided there was nothing worth reporting? He still wanted to keep his options open. 'I suppose I could try. What do I do with anything I find?'

'Right.' Goddard leaned forward, showing more eagerness. 'In the first place, don't disturb anything more than you have to. Make sure you leave everything as you find it. That way we can hope Dorn won't notice anything's gone wrong and do a disappearing act. All we want are a couple of items, enough to attract the interest of the authorities; they'll do their homework, too. Then you contact me straight away. Telephone the Hounslow number and tell them where and when I am to meet you.' He thought for a moment. The reins had to be tightened at this point. Jessup might just get it into his head to suggest some cloak and dagger place that could be compromising. 'No. When you get through to the London office they'll want us to go back to Derringer's room in Lund for the next meeting. Be simpler that way. Alright? Just give me enough time to get there.'

He looked around at the other tables. In the past fifteen minutes four other people had entered the restaurant, evidently for an early lunch. 'I think we've been here long enough.' He took out his wallet and offered Jessup three one-thousand Swedish kronor banknotes. 'Would you be good enough to pay the bill with this? I understand they take Swedish currency here.' He was smiling now. The die was cast and he had no doubt Jessup would be as conscientious as his file indicated.

Jessup smiled in return and carefully knocked out his pipe in the ashtray. 'I don't think coffee is that expensive, even Danish coffee.' Goddard had just handed him the equivalent of £280.

'Probabably not. But keep the change anyhow. Just expenses I managed to wring from the department. I'm sure your Jaguar isn't all that economical.' His lean face crinkled into the boyish grin Jessup remembered from their first meeting.

As they walked towards the restaurant exit Goddard brought up his hand to stay Jessup. 'One other thing.' His grey eyes took on a serious look, assessing the chances of this raw but necessary recruit. 'Try not to get physical with Dorn. He's had a good East German training. Armed and unarmed combat, that sort of thing. Could probably hurt you if he had to.'

It was almost noon when they separated outside the Royal. Jessup walked slowly back past the fishing harbour to catch the first ferry of the afternoon for Limhamn. He had two lines of thought. First, he was highly amused that he had become a freelance agent for two governments on opposite sides of a single operation. Did that make him a double or a triple-headed spy? Goddard had missed it! Had not known about Tommy. Not too surprising. Not even Carol knew of the tall dark-haired Swede Jessup had spoken with on the beach. And on his own admission Goddard – and behind him squawk department of SIS – was avoiding all unnecessary contact with Swedish government agencies. Second, and the thought furrowed his brow as he looked down at the fish held by the net in the sea, not knowing they'd already been caught, did Heinrich know nothing of the net closing over him? The fresh sea wind ruffled his thick hair. He unconsciously pulled the collar of his old grey English overcoat more tightly round his neck.

- - - - - - - - - - - - -

BALTIC INCIDENT

Jessup could hardly believe that it had been barely three weeks since the trawler incident and his two meetings with Goddard. Events seemed to be tumbling over one another at considerable speed. He glanced again at Heinrich over the whisky glass. Dorn was a big man, not over-tall but powerfully built. He sported the thick and slightly drooped moustache common among German men of his generation. What Goddard had said about Dorn had shaken Jessup. Like anybody else who can read between the lines of an average daily newspaper, Jessup knew there were such people as professional spies. No doubt they would
look very ordinary people indeed. They would surely appear to have ordinary jobs. But it was disturbing to think that he himself had an agent as a friend, and from the other side, as well. A person he played chess with. Dorn was a confident and friendly talker; sometimes over-confident in the German manner, about business, holidays and the small-minded provincialism of the Swedes. Ordinary expatriate conversation. Jessup could have expected a certain restraint or an indication of falseness. But Dorn was an open-hearted, downright friendly individual. Jessup had begun to wonder whether Dorn kept a gun in a drawer in his bedroom, then realized how incongruous that would be, how out of character. Or was it?

'That wine you told me you get from your German consulate client.' Jessup thought he'd made a tentative probe forward. 'You said it was cheap. How does he get it past Swedish customs?'

'No problem, David. He collects it himself. All he has to do is show them his diplomatic identity card. Customs don't inspect diplomatic parcels. I simply pick up the crate when I go to give him my sales talk about every three months. Of course, I let him have half a dozen bottles of the best Kaiserstuhle. He's happy enough with the arrangement.'

Jessup came back carefully 'You mean you buy the wine wholesale in Germany and simply address it to him in Sweden?'

'There's nothing special about that. We do a lot of business together. I give him special rates for himself and some of his staff on the passenger side of the company. A little extra freight traffic for the consulate is not worth anybody's notice. Another game?'

Jessup couldn't concentrate on the second game, either. He was wondering about the wine shipments. If the large boxes that arrived in Sweden every so often were immune to normal customs inspection, wasn't it just possible that the deliveries contained other things, too? But what? Dorn had proudly shown him his wine cellar for the first time over a year earlier. Jessup decided that the cellar would be worth looking at again, without Dorn's cheerful company.

Martina joined them in the entrance hall to say goodnight. The cloakroom was not a room at all; it was a small vestibule. At one side there was a door marked 'Gäster', on the other two walls there were racks and coathangers. As Jessup reached for his overcoat among a variety of Dorn's own outer garments, he accidentally kicked over an object standing near the wall and half hidden by the longer coats.

'Sorry, Heinrich. That whisky must be as good as your chess.' He laughed and bent to pick it up.

Dorn was quicker. He grasped the handle of the bag Jessup had knocked over. 'It's just an old overnight case I keep handy.'

It didn't look old to Jessup. Quite new, in fact. It was a shiny, black, expensive-looking leather briefcase closed with two silver coded locks. It was marked on one side

BALTIC INCIDENT

with big circular scratches, as though someone had swung it around like a spinning top on an abrasive metal surface.

43

CHARLES SMART
Chapter Three

The door closed behind Jessup. For a moment Martina said nothing. She knew the briefcase did not belong to Dorn. She took it firmly from him, placed it at the foot of the stairs and turned her face up to him. She put both hands on his shoulders, a slight frown on her attractive features. 'Now tell me, Heinrich' she said gently 'why do we have to put up with that man?'

'One of the nicest persons I know. Plays a good game of chess, too' said Dorn, playfully misunderstanding.

'Be serious for a moment' she chided. 'You know who I mean. That Stravinsky man.'

'Stavrinsky' he corrected with a smile.

'Alright, him. He's so cold. Gives me the shivers. And why on earth do I have to hide every time he's here? If he's a Russian agent, just somebody from the other side you have to cooperate with, what's our relationship to him?'

Dorn responded by smoothing Martina's long blonde hair to the back of her head, his hands coming to rest on her soft ivory neck. Slowly he slid his left hand acros her shoulder, smoothing off the thin material holding up the top part of her dress. He leaned forward and pressed his lips lightly below her ear. He knew the goose pimples rising on her upper arm were not brought out by cold. 'You, darling, have the two flaws I adore in women.'

Martina pouted at the plural.

'You are illegal and you're a biological mistake.' Dorn lifted her head to see her suspicious expression. 'I've told you, my love' he went on, caressing her neck. 'My masters expressly forbid their minions to have serious romances. And for that reason alone you're out of bounds. Besides' Dorn was unable to resist teasing 'I like to live dangerously.' He was still smiling and, with his other hand slipped off the second shoulder strap. 'As for your biology...' he brushed the soft skin above her nipples with his lips, 'not even Bonn has been informed that God had tired of creating plain women the moment before he made you.'

Martina lifted his head with a forefinger under his chin and searched his face. 'You prepared to prove you mean that?' She was still disturbed by the lightheartedness with which he sometimes treated her.

For a moment longer they held each other's eyes. Then Dorn took her hand and led her up the wide, carpeted staircase. She didn't seem to care, if she had noticed at all, that Dorn had picked up the briefcase with his free hand.

Two evenings later, Jessup saw his chance to look around Dorn's cellar in the near certain knowledge that he would not be disturbed by his friend's unexpected appearance. He was nervous, but hardly needed a cover story on this occasion for he had left Dorn in his flat to work out the next complicated chess move he'd contrived. And Carol was there with him suffering the chore every teacher of English had to face: a pile of exercise books lay on the kitchenette counter in front of her. He also knew from Dorn that Martina would not be there.

The early evening was bright with stars. Their light filtered through the thick pine-wood branches. Avoiding the surfaced tree roots that protruded from the thick, soft layers of old pine needles, Jessup stepped quickly along the path that led to Dorn's house. It hadn't been difficult to tell Dorn that he was going to nip out to buy more beer from the local late night store. When he visited Jessup's flat, Dorn usually deposited his house key on the small table near the front door of the flat. Jessup had simply picked it up on his way out. He had given himself twenty minutes to get to Dorn's place, look around, then get the beer on the way back.

He came out of the wood and on to the edge of the golf course that ran for over a mile next to the sea. Looking to the right he could see the club house angularly silhouetted against the brighter sky. As he looked, there was a brief flash of white light from far away along the curve of the coastline. Then he heard the sound of the heavy coastal guns used regularly for military training. Red lights streaking seawards warned that live ammunition was being used. Turning away from the club house, the dirt road went past Dorn's property and Jessup quickened his pace.

The hall light Dorn always left on at night shone from the big house. Jessup let himself in the front door and closed it carefully behind him. He walked to the end of the long hallway, past the winding staircase on his left and the curtained entrance to the large sitting room on his right and opened the door to the kitchen. He risked the main light then turned to reach the door he knew opened on to the stone steps leading to the basement. He fumbled for the lightswitch at the top of the steps, feeling the cooler air reaching up to him from below. A naked light-bulb at the bottom of the steps lit his way, casting its glare to the dimmest corners of the cellar. Jessup paused. A minute and indistinguishable sound came to him from somewhere in the house. A creak of the wooden structure, he decided, or mice. It was unlikely that Martina would have come and stayed in the house alone, even if she had a key. At the bottom of the steps he looked swiftly around. The stone and concrete-built cellar, larger than the average sitting room but with a low roof, was not cluttered with the rubbish of a lively household. Five neatly placed boxes of crockery and kitchenware lay open on the floor at the far end of the room. Standing in the centre of the room was a half-filled wine-rack, four yards long and ceiling high.

Against the wall to Jessup's right there were three cup-board-like boxes. Each was about three feet in height and over half that in width. He crossed the floor for a closer look. All three boxes had been opened, their front panels taken off and stacked on the ground nearby. Wood shavings and sawdust littered the area and Jessup caught the fresh aroma of recently cut pine. The boxes appeared to be empty. He kneeled to exam-ine one of them more carefully. The space he could see would hold about a dozen bottles of wine in two layers. It occurred to him that the outside depth of the box was twice that needed to hold twelve bottles. He felt the back of his neck wrinkle in a spasm of coldness that did not come from the chill of the cellar. The box was fitted with a panel, he realized, fixed at a point about half the depth of the whole box and constructed to hide the oth-er half of the box's contents. Whatever lay beyond that, Jessup thought, almost certainly would not be wine. He shuffled on a foot and a knee to check the other two containers. The second had its panel in place like the first. The third had had its panel prised loose. Very gently, Jessup pulled the panel back further and tilted his head to look inside. The panel grated along the saw-dust at the bottom of the box. There was enough light for him to see that the secret space was empty. There was no hint of what might be inside the unopened cases or what might have been in the opened compartment. There was not enough time to open the panels now, he decided. Besides, he wouldn't be able to cover traces of

his interference. They would have to wait for another opportunity. He felt a pang of
disappointment at this failure of his first clandestine foray. Still, he'd have to tell Goddard. Perhaps Goddard could make sense of what seemed to be secret compartments in the crates. He checked his wristwatch and was surprised to see he'd been in the house for less than five minutes.

As he stood up again he saw the old work desk. It was half hidden under the stone steps and he had missed it in his hurry to look inside the wine crates. The desk might be old but Jessup could see at a glance it was still used. An anglepoise lamp was fixed to one corner of the desk. Various papers were strewn on top. A letter typed in English caught his eye. It was addressed from a firm in the middle of Sweden and had an undecipherable signature. He scanned its contents. It seemed to refer to times and dates of deliveries. There was nothing strange in the fact that the letter was in English. It was the language often used in commerce between Swedes and Germans. What did appear peculiar were the addresses for the deliveries of what the letter simply termed the 'merchandise'. He made a mental note of the two addresses and replaced the letter in its original position. The desk held three drawers on its right side. None appeared to have a lock. He pulled open the top drawer. Nothing but writing material, pens, writing paper of different sizes and a pocket Swedish-German dictionary. The second drawer was empty. With the third drawer he hit the jackpot. First there was a photograph of what Jessup identified as the south west area of Sweden. A satellite picture? Then he saw the points, each marked by hand with a cross on the photograph. There were three of them; red, white and green. The red cross marked a village on the Danish coast named Rødvik; it lay across the sea almost opposite Dorn's own house. The green cross appeared to make the house he was in, at Ljunghusen. The white cross marked a spot near the beach and close to the old Falsterbo church.

By the side of the photograph, and half hidden by it, was a chart. On a larger scale than the photograph, the chart showed not only the south west of Sweden but also an area of land and sea further to the east. Three broad arrows, each with a number beside it, were boldly drawn in red from east to west and were pointed towards the south west tip of Sweden, the area Goddard had said was designated MILO S on Swedish military maps. There were other marks on the chart but Jessup had seen enough to confirm what Goddard had suspected. The chart, to Jessup's untrained eye, appeared to mark what could well be an invasion route, together with the figures relating to the size of an invading force. That it was a Russian force could hardly be doubted. All the names on the chart were in Cyrillic script. Jessup felt the throb of excitement as he studied the chart and photograph. He hadn't felt such elation since he'd received the formal letter from the Registrar of the University of London informing him that he'd passed his first year's exams with the highest marks of all the candidates in classical Greek, his first foreign language. A banal comparison, he thought, but now he was able to put his skills to work again as he carefully memorised the addresses and details of the information he'd found.

Had Jessup not been quite so absorbed with the desk and its contents he might have heard the slight movements above him. Infinitesimal sounds came from footsteps in stockinged feet. From the moment he had passed the foot of the stairs in the hall Jessup had been expertly followed to the cellar. Now, as Jessup searched the desk, all his movements were watched from the angle where the steps rose to meet the ceiling, less than two yards above his head. The watcher waited for Jessup to open the lower drawer and was satisfied that Jessup was engrossed in studying the chart. Then, as silently as before, the muffled feet returned to the upper reaches of the house.

Jessup closed the drawer, switched off the table lamp and took a final look round the cellar. Ten minutes in the house was all the time he could safely spare. Quickly he went back up the steps to the kitchen, turned out lights and closed doors as he had found them and began to jog along the dirt track towards the road and the shop. He was not to know that his silent observer had again descended to the cellar and taken away the contents of the desk that had interested Jessup so much.

- - - - - - - - - - - - - - -

He knew he ought to contact Goddard at once. But he found it hard to be a mere messenger boy. Questions and possibilities crowded his mind as soon as he had said goodnight to Dorn. What sort of reaction would there be from the Swedes to what appeared to be a plan of military action against their country by Russia? What would they do about Heinrich? Put him on trial? Cover up the whole thing by sending him back to East Germany without publicity? And how could they make a public or private protest without Dorn and some pretty conclusive evidence? The more Jessup thought about it the weaker the evidence seemed to be. Surely, more proof would be needed than a photograph, a chart and an ambiguous letter. The mysterious boxes could have contained anything. And would his mere verbal report mean much to Goddard?

Jessup, his pipe unlit, slumped in an armchair for two hours after Carol had gone to bed, wondering what sort of sense anybody would be able to make of what he'd found. Finally, he realized he was wasting his time. He didn't even have the photograph to show Goddard. A bit strange, actually, that Goddard had told him to leave everything as it was. Either the photograph or the chart would have told him something. Perhaps Goddard had said that to protect him.

He thought again about the letter, then sat upright, suddenly, struck by the connection that obviously existed between the letter and the satellite picture. Three deliveries were mentioned in the latter, but only two addresses were given – and one of those was in Denmark. Why should Air Germanic receive merchandise in Sweden for delivery in Denmark? Jessup remembered the two addresses. Now he knew what was odd about the letter. He saw in his mind's eye again the three crosses on the satellite photograph. If Dorn's house was included, the place marked with the green cross, then the two addresses mentioned in the letter corresponded exactly with the white cross near Falsterbo church and the red cross on the Danish coast. And there had to be some connection between the deliveries mentioned in the letter, the satellite photograph and the sea chart with those menacing arrows. Almost certainly the contents of the secret compartment in one of the boxes had already been delivered, no doubt to one of the two addresses given in the letter. If so, it intrigued him to think there were two possible courses of action he could take. Either he could wait for another occasion to get into Dorn's house alone, or he could take a closer look at the other two addresses. Why not both? It was too soon to expect to be able to make another clandestine sortie into Dorn's house, so why not nose around the other two places first? He knew that the problem of getting inside the other properties might be a lot more problematic than getting into Dorn's house. If Dorn owned or rented the other properties how could he be sure that Dorn would not arrive at the wrong moment? It occurred to him that the only address he could investigate with a measure of safety was the one in Denmark.

--- --- --- --- --- --- --- ---

It was eleven thirty at night. The quay at Dragør held a multitude of gloomy shadows cast by bright floodlights. It was deserted except for a customs officer and a few late workers. Two giant lorries on their way to Holland, four or five cars and the regular bus carrying passengers from Sweden to Denmark's international airport at Kastrup were the vehicles to roll off the ramp with the Jaguar. Jessup had reasoned that since Rødvig – marked as the red cross on Dorn's photograph – was about a twenty minute drive from the centre of Copenhagen, then Dorn's visits to the Danish house would normally be made by car. The other main car crossing was between Helsingborg in Sweden and Helsingør in Denmark, but that meant driving almost an extra two hours north up the Swedish west coast. Jessup knew that if he caught the last boat, sailing at ten-thirty in the evening from Limhamn, there was little chance that he would meet with Dorn, unless Dorn were already at the house.

It had been about four in the morning when Jessup had made up his mind that he would have to get rather more information about Dorn than he had before contacting Goddard. The other decision he had made was to bring Carol into the picture. Whatever Goddard thought about secrecy or security, Jessup believed that Carol's common sense could only help. Over a late morning pot of coffee and toast Jessup had told Carol everything. From Derringer's telephone call to his search of Dorn's basement. Carol had sat opposite, her straight form against the back of the dining chair, listening without interruption.

Carol had been even more sceptical than he when she heard Goddard's improbable story. Finally she had agreed that it couldn't do any harm for Jessup to check up on the house in Denmark. She had kissed him playfully on the top of his mouse-coloured hair and said 'So long as it's Heinrich you're investigating and not Martina, give it a try.'

Jessup was soon speeding through the silent village streets and on to the main road towards Copenhagen. Skirting the city to the south he found the narrow road that led directly to R›dvig. The address he had memorised contained no number. Just the name 'Stranden'.

Beyond the double beam of the Jaguar's powerful headlights Jessup detected the black emptiness that could only be the sea. Fifty yards ahead there was a small, winding lane off to the left between the trees, obviously used for serving the frontages of the houses facing the sea. It was a secluded area. Even in the darkness he could see the large and expensive-looking villas, each one almost hidden by its screen of pine and birch.

At half past midnight the only lights came from a small sea inlet a hundred yards away, at the end of a low sea wall. Jessup saw the outlines of launches and fishing craft bobbing gently on their mooring ropes. The name of the house, cut into a wooden plaque, had faded, but by the light of a torch he had brought from the car Jessup picked out the letters 'Stranden'. He pushed open the small wraught-iron gate. The hinges screeched in rusty joints and Jessup froze. Everything remained silent and he carefully picked his way along a coarse stone path partly overgrown with grass and weeds towards the double fronted doors. He had prepared his story. An English tourist who'd lost his way would not be uncommon in this part of Denmark. But he already had the feeling his story would not be necessary. The gate, the path, the state of the drive that came from the side of the house to end in a sandy clearing in front of the doors, all indicated that the place was not regularly occupied. Jessup tried the doorbell anyway.

At least the electricity was connected. The bell rang hollow through the house. He gave himself a margin of sixty seconds then picked up a large stone and wrapped it in an old towel – one of Carol's contributions. With his leather driving gloves it was sufficient protection. To the right of the doorway there was a narrow, opaque window. He looked around once more, listening for sounds of human movement. Only the surf breaking on the rocky coastline hissed through the silence. With his right hand well muffled against splinters Jessup hit the windowpane he thought would be closest to the catch on the inside. He succeeded only in cracking the glass and he was reminded of the fact that homes in Scandinavia commonly used triple glazing for decent insulation. He hit the pane harder. The glass shattered and this time the stone, much of the towel and half his fist went through the window. He brought his hand carefully away and dropped the stone then, after re-wrapping the towel round his gloved hand, reached gingerly through the broken glass and grasped for the catch halfway up the length of the window. There was a handle held fast by a press-stud lock. It clicked open under pressure from his thumb and he brought the whole window partly open before extracting his hand. He thrust torch and towel inside his overcoat pocket and climbed awkwardly into the ground floor guest lavatory.

He opened the door and found himself in a short hall-way, the double front doors on his left. He used the torch with great care, making sure its beam should not illuminate any of the windows of the house. The hall-way led straight into a more spacious circular-shaped vestibule; three doors and a staircase led off the area. Moving slowly Jessup tried the three doors in turn. Two opened on to living rooms, a smaller one facing the front of the house and a much larger room at the rear. The third door opened into an empty kitchen, electrical fittings hanging loosely from different parts of the walls. There was no sign that the house was lived in. He began to climb the dogleg flight of stairs, broken by a square shaped landing that led from the hall to the first floor. Three doors confronted him. The first two rooms contained nothing but scraps of rubbish such as a previous owner might have left behind. The third, larger room proved more interesting. Lying on the floor in the centre of the room was an enormous saucer-shaped object.

Jessup had no idea what the technical terms were for such a piece of equipment, but it wasn't difficult to guess that the object was a dish antenna of the sort used for receiving satellite TV pictures. It was about twelve feet in diameter with a wave collector in the middle. The saucer – clearly not completely fitted, for there were tools, wires and various metal rods scattered over the floor – was made up of two-foot long shiny metal rectangles overlapping from the outer rim to the centre of the dish. A small pile of panels lay to one side ready to be fitted into place. If his imagination wasn't running away with him Jessup decided that those panels had recently been inside certain boxes of wine he had seen in Dorn's basement.

- - - - - - - - - - - - - -

Dorn whistled a snatch of song from HMS Pinafore softly to himself as he pushed wider the garden gate

Jessup had left open. It grated noisily on its rusty hinges. He fumbled under his warm sweater and blazer for the house key in his trouser pocket as he crunched over the unkempt path to the front door. It closed heavily behind him and he felt in the darkness for the hall light switch. Without pausing Dorn continued along the hall to the stairs and began to climb the uncarpeted wooden steps.

Unable to stop a sudden trembling in his knees, Jessup stood behind the open door just inside the bathroom. The creak of the iron gate had given him time to step across the landing. The heavy tread on the stairs had to be Dorn's. He couldn't help thinking of Goddard's warning about tackling Dorn physically. Not that a warning had been necessary. Jessup knew well enough he could not hold his own in a brawl. He didn't think he was a coward, but he certainly didn't wish to face a heavyweight. Better to make a dash for the front door once Dorn had entered the room where the metal dish lay, as he surely would since the house appeared to be otherwise empty.

Dorn was not obliging. He turned into the bathroom, intent on more basic labours, and went straight to the john without bothering with the light switch. The glow from the hall was enough. Jessup knew it was now or never. He stepped from behind the door with the intention of slipping out before Dorn turned round. Unfortunately for Jessup about the only article of furnishing left in the house was a large mirror fixed to the wall above the wash-basin. Dorn could hardly fail to catch a fleeting glimpse of the movement behind him. He turned in astonishment, lips pursed in mid-whistle, as Jessup disappeared through the doorway. Dorn's well-trained reflexes worked at lightening speed. For all his weight there were no flabby muscles and no surplus flesh on Dorn's six-foot frame. By the time Jessup had reached the foot of the stairs Dorn had poised himself on the landing half way down and leapt the gap of the final eight steps to land with his full weight on Jessup's fleeing figure.

Jessup went down as though the roof had fallen on him. His glasses flew into the air, bounced off the wall and slithered, unbroken, to the floor. Only an involuntary buckling at the knees with arms instinctively stretched out cushioned the blow and prevented a number of broken ribs, or worse. Even before he hit Jessup, Dorn had recognized the intruder. He could hardly mistake the ancient overcoat and Jessup's way of moving, but by that time he was already in the air. Both men were spread flat on the floor, the breath crushed from Jessup's lungs and Dorn, on top of him, apparently intending to keep it that way.

'What the hell are you doing here?' Dorn was far more surprised than Jessup, but that did not stop him from twisting Jessup's arms from front to back in a swift movement that made Jessup feel like a trussed turkey. He was in no condition to talk back, his face thrust hard to the floor. Without releasing his grip on Jessup's arms, Dorn kneeled to one side to allow Jessup to get into a sitting position. Dorn was hardly out of breath. 'I'm waiting, David. This is no place for you.'

Jessup was inclined to agree. He had checked that Dorn was at home in Ljunghusen by telephone without identifying himself, minutes before he had driven to Limhamn harbour.

Dorn gave a sharp twist to Jessup's arms. 'We're not playing games now. How did you find out? Who told you?'

Jessup knew he was in a mess, but he wasn't ready to tell the truth just yet. How far would Dorn go? 'Heinrich, let me get up and talk. This is no position for a conversation.'

Dorn had been trained to be hurt, physically and painfully. And he had been trained to kill, ruthlessly and in cold blood if necessary. Had Jessup been naive enough to think he could involve himself to this extent without getting hurt? He released Jessup's arms and stood. For a moment longer Jessup lay still, unable to move his cramped shoulders. Slowly he eased his arms into a more natural position. He raised himself on hands and knees, groped for his glasses and sat on the floor with his back to the wall. He looked up at Dorn, desperately trying to come to terms with this new predicament. He made an effort to keep his head and cursed himself for placing it in a noose that did not belong to him. It was one thing to find evidence showing your friend to be a spy, but quite another thing to be confronted with an immediate and hostile situation.

'Look, Heinrich. It was all a bit of an accident. About a week ago, at your place, with Martina and Carol. Remember? I went to get some ice from the kitchen and you called after me to bring another bottle of wine from the cellar. I just couldn't help seeing those papers you'd left lying about. I got curious. I just wanted to check things out.' It was a terrible explanation, but he couldn't think of a better right now.

Dorn spoke quietly, he didn't know if it would be convincing, but he had to play Jessup along, at least for the moment. 'You're lying, and I don't know why. There's nothing in my cellar, or anywhere else in my house for that matter, to make you take off in this damn stupid manner. What the hell are you talking about?'

'Game's up, Heinrich. I know you're working for Russia on a plan to invade Sweden.' Jessup took the bold way and just hoped it would work. 'Might as well let it go. How do you think I knew about this place? You've got no future, Heinrich.'

Dorn had leaned back against the wall opposite Jessup, his blazer open, the single silver button had been torn off in his leap from the stairs. He folded his arms and looked down at Jessup, shaking his head slowly. 'So let's say you didn't dream whatever it is you're talking about. How did that bring you here?'

Jessup ignored the question. 'That antenna upstairs. Part of a guidance system, isn't it?'

Dorn towered over Jessup. "Operation Searchlight" was more important than Jessup could guess, and he already knew too much. Jessup's arrival in Denmark could be a severe complication. Dorn moved another pace away from him and motioned the older man to his feet. It was time to bait the hook with a more delectable titbit. 'I'll not deny I'm making a few investigations for a certain government, but maybe you would know that's practically legal in Sweden. Both sides do it, and very few get chased away by Säpo.'

Jessup saw the old smile hover around Dorn's eyes. Dorn must be made of steel to be able to stand there in utter confidence, knowing the Russian plan was no longer concealed. Nothing had been said between them about a third party, yet Dorn must know his cover had been blown. And it was either a childish denial or the truth for Dorn to tell him there were no incriminating papers to be found in his house. Jessup felt Dorn was speaking the truth. What was wrong? He said 'So what happens now?'

'You've seen my homework upstairs. I'll just have to keep you under wraps for a while. We're going back to Sweden. Come on, into the kitchen.' Dorn hustled Jessup to his feet and took him by the arm. This job was turning out to be a little more complicated than he had bargained for. The problem now was to get Jessup back as quickly as possible and point him in the right direction before he got more fancy ideas. The Rødvig house would have to remain as it was.

Ten minutes later, Jessup with his wrists bound behind his back with wire torn from the kitchen walls, they were on the deserted road outside. Dorn directed Jessup to walk towards the harbour lights.

From the deep shadows behind them a more solid figure emerged. Stanley Derringer kept close to the dark hedges and overhanging trees of the gardens. Thirty yards in front of him Jessup walked clumsily in his overcoat, his hands behind his back. On Jessup's left and slightly behind Dorn kept in step. Derringer smiled to himself at this touch of professionalism. Both men were clearly visible against the lights of the harbour.

Derringer, hunched in a short driving coat and ready to melt into the trees at any sign that Dorn might turn round, watched as the two men crossed the narrow road to a gap in the sea wall, just short of the main harbour. They disappeared from his view as they took to the steps leading to the water, Dorn guiding Jessup by the elbow. Derringer crouched low, crossed the road without a sound and peered into the dark beyond the wall. Ten yards away and below him he saw the interior light of a small cabin cruiser. Jessup was seated near the rail in the well-deck. Dorn emerged from the miniature cabin, climbed the four steps to the helm and began to manipulate the controls.

Keeping low and close to the wall, Derringer now moved fast and silently towards the lights of the harbour proper. There was a chill in the air. It was the darkest and most vulnerable part of the night, but it was also the best time to fish for the succulent silver herring whose grounds lay ten miles south of Rødvig.

BALTIC INCIDENT

Now the sport of rich holidaymakers and yacht owners, the silver herring had once been a major item of export from Rødvig to other members of the ancient economic federation known as the Hanseatic League. For all his sixty-eight years, Derringer could still teach a few tricks, mainly crude ones, to the younger field operatives of the various secret services he had been associated with. It was the main reason why he was still on the books of MI6, and had been offered to squawk as a 'useful if temperamental communist ideologist of the old school', a euphemism which meant to the initiated 'use, but do not present him with a spinal view.' If he was to keep Jessup in sight he had to do something fast. He would have to rely once again on his long practised ingenuity.

As Derringer had guessed, at least one visitor was preparing an early breakfast in the spacious suite of a luxurious motor launch for an early start to the herring shoals. A narrow beam of light shone from a partly opened curtain on the other side of the basin. Derringer went into his act. Now that he was well within the lighted area Derringer quickly took off his driving coat, pullover and tie without pausing in his stride to reach the launch. The ruse had worked before, in a hospital in allied occupied Berlin in September 1945. On that occasion, working for Moscow and with the tacit approval of MI6 – the thought had made him smile – he had managed to draw away the German security guards from a private room and give himself sufficient time to squeeze the life out of a particularly unpleasant Nazi colonel. On the best Russian and British information the colonel, a specialist in chemical experimental murder in Buchenwald, was about to be spirited away by an American Central Intelligence Agency snatch

squad, from the certainty of war crimes charges and almost certain execution.

Derringer noticed with satisfaction the West German
flag limp against the mast of the boat and that it was
registered in Kiel. After a final check that no one else
was about he slipped off his shoes and, leaning under
the boat's guard rail from the stone quay, pushed those,
his coat, tie and pullover quietly on to the deck and out
of sight behind the stern air-conditioner intake. Then
he stood upright and began breathing very deeply and
rapidly. No more than three minutes had elapsed from
the time he had looked over the wall at Dorn's cruiser.
Now, as he stood next to the German boat, he heard the
roar of the cruiser's engine as Dorn opened the throttle
and headed towards Sweden.

Derringer began to feel light-headed as the blood
pounded swiftly through his veins. The colour left
his cheeks. Blood was leaving his head and rushing
to the lungs and heart. He knew he had not lost all his
old skill and had timed it to the second. He also knew
that oxygen intoxication could be dangerous if it led to
complete unconsciousness, but it had to look convincing first go. Within seconds, large rings of bright light
began to blot out his vision. He stepped unsteadily on
to the stern of the boat, allowing himself to fall to his
knees, and crawled to the lighted window. He banged
on the window with his fists. He knew exactly what he
looked like – death, and deadly cold in the crisp, clear
air, without coat, pullover or shoes.

Conscious, but only just, he heard the cabin door open
and footsteps on the companion way. Someone bent
over him. He heard a man's voice. 'Mein Gott. Er ist
tot.'

Derringer fluttered his eyelids. 'Mein Herz. Bitte.
Schnell. Ein Arzt!' His breathing was becoming normal

again. The red and white circles began to fade from before his eyes, but he maintained enough of the pose to frighten the yachtsman. He saw, through partly opened lids, the man was alone. The young German stared at him, not sure what to do and completely disarmed at hearing his own language spoken in apparent desperation. No fool like a young fool, Derringer thought. 'Doctor' he breathed wheezily again. 'Gehen Sie sofort.' The yachtsman, freed of inaction by the second appeal, stood up at once, sprang for the rail and sped off to look for the nearest telephone.

As soon as he was sure the man had crossed the small square, Derringer got to his feet, stepped carefully down the steps into the cabin and saw straight away where the man had placed his wallet. It was quite a large one, the sort commonly carried by fastidious Germans who hate to see a bulging pocket and prefer to pack their cash into an even more bulky purse. Swiftly, Derringer picked it up by one corner and a keyring fell from the centre fold. It took thirty seconds for him to get on the deck, up the short flight of steps and into the canopied cockpit. A few more seconds and the right key fitted snugly into the ignition. Although the early morning was cold, the automatically choked engine caught at once.

- - - - - - - - - - - - - -

While Jessup sat huddled in the stern of the cruiser, Dorn studied the glowing compass, checking with the lighthouse on a tip of Denmark to the right and behind him. Other lights from the Danish coast had disappeared. Morning mist covered the slight swell of the Östersjö, but within the next twenty minutes Dorn expected to get the first glimpse of Falsterbo lighthouse on his front left and the orange and white glow of the town of Trelleborg far to the right.

Jessup shivered uncontrollably in the fast flowing cold air as the craft sped across the calm sea. He kicked himself mentally once again for not realizing that if Dorn were indeed seriously organized then he would certainly have the means to get directly from Sweden to Denmark by sea. From the moment Jessup had been able to collect his thoughts after being knocked down by Dorn he had tried to work out how he could get away. It was obviously imperative, now that he was sure, to get his information to Goddard. Yet his mind, or, rather, his emotions still refused to accept Dorn as a deadly enemy. In any case there was absolutely nothing Jessup could do with his arms bound tightly behind him and Dorn so completely in control of the situation. He began to wonder what the hell he was doing to get himself into such a plight. Then he realized it wasn't really Goddard's fault. Perhaps the evidence from the cellar would have been enough. Goddard hadn't asked him to go haring off like this; it had been his own idea. But what to do now? Ruefully he remembered that almost exactly twenty-four hours earlier he had been wondering how to get conclusive proof of Dorn's spying activities to present to the Swedish security police. Now, he had all the proof he needed – and wished he hadn't.

The engine was being throttled back. He looked up at the dark shape of Dorn as he lashed down the steering wheel. The boat slowed perceptibly and Dorn turned towards him. With some difficulty Jessup stood up. 'What's the trouble? Don't tell me you've planned to guide half the Russian fleet here and lost your way already.'

'Stow it, David. I never wanted to get you mixed up in this. Your own bloody curiosity seems to have taken you too far anyway. Why couldn't you mind your own

business? Now, give me a hand with this fishing gear.'
He went to the stern locker, unbolted the lid and began to bring out the tackle. 'Got to make it look legal. We've in Swedish waters now.'

'Sure, I'll give you a hand. What would you like me to do, trussed up like a Christmas goose, nod the nets over the side for you?'

'Turn around' said Dorn shortly. Jessup turned to face the sea across the low rail. A crawling sensation covered his spine in the realization that he was utterly at the mercy of the man Goddard had warned him not to tangle with.

What happened next could always, in Jessup's memory, be associated with somebody else's nightmare. The shock of the icy water hit his face and snatched at his feet and hands practically obliterating the flash and noise of the explosion. Pieces of Dorn's cruiser splashed into the water around him. A bright flame of fire rose from an exploding fuel tank. The boat's roof landed with a heavy thwack on the water yards in front of him. Debris seemed to be everywhere, yet still the cruiser, its stern blazing furiously, remained afloat.

Jessup was momentarily stunned and only mechanical movements of his legs and stiff arms kept him above the water. Miraculously, he still wore his glasses. Some ten yards separated him from the stricken craft and he could see, by the light of the flames, Dorn's apparently lifeless body stuck between the guard rails near the centre of the boat below the remains of the wheelhouse.

In the first seconds Jessup knew there was little hope of survival for any length of time in that freezingly cold part of the Baltic. Twice in succession he went completely under the swell. He choked violently, then from sheer reflex called for help. With a great effort of will he overcame some of the suicidal panic that had made him struggle so desperately to keep his head above water. He must try to float on his back. He threw his head backwards, keeping only his face clear of the water. He forced himself to paddle slowly in an effort to bring the centre of gravity to the middle of his body. His overcoat, not completely saturated yet, helped to keep him afloat. For a long moment he fought off terror, refusing to believe he could die like this. He managed to push off one shoe after another, keeping his toes just above the water for balance. He moved his arms sideways, trying to reach the cruiser's canopy. Then he felt the weight of the coat. No longer buoyant with minute air pockets, it began to feel like a leaden casket pulling him down.

He'd been in the water for all of three minutes. It seemed like a life sentence already served. The numbing cold had gone through his bones; even his thoughts had become slow and incoherent. He saw other red lights arcing through the sky above the still burning wreck of the cruiser, but they made no sense to him. All his weakened thoughts were concentrated on reaching the canopy before the waterlogged coat could finally drag him under.

Another beam of light, white this time, cut through the darkness. It searched for a moment then rested on Jessup's sinking body. Derringer gently nudged the motor yacht towards him and lowered a life-belt attached to a rope. He stopped the engines and called out. The voice finally penetrated the cold and Jessup groped for the floating ring, at last realizing someone was there to help. With an effort, he lifted the ring over his head and squeezed one arm through the inside of the ring. It was enough. He clung to the life saver, one arm over and the other under the ring, as Derringer heaved on the rope.

BALTIC INCIDENT

Once out of the water and sprawled on the deck, Jessup began to live again. He'd suddenly remembered Dorn had cut away his bonds a second before the explosion. Dorn may not have known it, but he had just saved Jessup's life. Jessup pushed aside Derringer's proferred arm and croaked through salted lips 'Get him out! Get Dorn. The boat's sinking.'

'Are you mad, man?' Derringer had not expected to be given orders from the half-drowned man. 'That's live ammunition they're using. Don't you know you've just driven that wooden boat into a battlefield?' He glared down at Jessup. 'Listen, youngster, those Swedes are training seriously and their aim's not too good and you're not taking a bloody landing craft on to Omaha beach.'

Jessup struggled to sit up and pointed to the now more than half submerged cruiser, still flickering flame. He stared at Derringer, his eyes black and cold and crazily insistent, 'Do it!' he said, and there was steel in his voice.

Derringer hesitated only for a moment. He knew a case of shock when he saw it. Then he turned away, released the clutch and slid the yacht through the flotsam to the dying wreck. The deck of the German boat was slightly higher than the cruiser's safety rail through which Dorn still hung, head down. Together, Jessup and Derringer reached for Dorn's shoulders. If they had left it five seconds longer, Dorn would have been carried down with his boat. Even as the two men clung to Dorn's arms, the boat rolled away from them on to its side and sank, hissing white steam, beneath the waves, leaving Dorn's feet to dangle in the sea before they could drag him aboard. Jessup, the last of his reserved strength gone, passed out on the deck beside Dorn.

CHARLES SMART
Chapter Four

Derringer, with Jessup helping as best he could, carried Dorn into the cabin and placed him on a bunkbed. Dorn had been thrown from the stern to the middle of the boat by the explosion and there was a large bruise where he had hit his head. Derringer diagnosed concussion and shock. Leaving Jessup to get himself and Dorn warm again with a bottle of kirsch from the drinks cupboard, Derringer hurried to open the throttle and head away from the target area. To the east, a brightening of the sea mist suggested dawn was not far away.

Twenty-five minutes later Derringer ran the yacht aground on the deserted sands within yards of Dorn's house. Derringer, with Jessup's help, carried Dorn up the beach and, opening the door with his own key, took him into the sitting room.

'How did you manage to find us?' Jessup asked Derringer. It had to be more than coincidence for Derringer to be in such an unlikely place at the right moment. 'Are you in this, too?' He was rapidly revising his image of Derringer as the don-cum-secret agent.

'Only on the fringe.' Derringer seemed reluctant, hesitant to fill in the details. 'I told you, I used to work for British intelligence during the war. They sometimes ask me to do the odd job now and again and Goddard asked me to keep a close watch on you.' He spoke as though he had decided Jessup would be satisfied once he had that useless bit of information. ' Look, the Danish police are going to put two and two together – the yacht and the two cars over there. I still have friends in Denmark.' He indicated the kirsch bottle and nodded towards Dorn who had begun to recover, 'Pour the rest of this stuff down his throat while I get on the blower.'

BALTIC INCIDENT

Derringer was on the 'phone for ten minutes. When he returned he told Jessup that his car would be back in its Ljunghusen parking space later that night.

Dorn was fully conscious now, still weak from the knocking about he'd taken. He looked up at Derringer, 'Stalin's sidekick', he said with a grimace. 'I hear you dragged me from a watery grave. What made you so generous?'

'You seem to know one another' Jessup said with surprise.

'Practically blood brothers, you might say' said Dorn with heavy sarcasm. 'Only Derringer has a convenient coat of many colours.'

Derringer glowered at him, too slow to return the wit, but fast enough to field it without any grace whatsoever. 'I didn't save your neck. That was his idea.' He indicated Jessup with a half turn of the shoulders. 'I decided to go along with it just to see what the Swedes would make of you. And if they don't do a proper job of it, just make sure you're not in my way in future.'

Dorn ignored Derringer's final comment, but turned his head to look more thoughtfully at Jessup.

Jessup had no idea what was going on between them, but whatever it was he didn't want to get any further involved in their agency rivalry, if that is what it was. 'Can you two cut the in-fighting. I'm whacked.' He turned to Derringer 'Let's get him below.'

Jessup watched as, in the basement, Derringer bound Dorn's hands firmly behind his back then connected the thin strong rope – a handy nylon clothes line from the kitchen – to his feet as well. They cleared a space on the floor, laid Dorn on an old matress and Derringer insisted on attaching him by a three-foot lead to the water-pipe system.

Twenty minutes later Jessup had telephoned Hounslow and made an arrangement to see Goddard on the following day. Then he left Derringer to keep watch on Dorn until the Swedish security police came for him. He made his way, drooping with tiredness, through the woods to the apartment. It was still before eight in the morning and he was able to relate the night's happenings to a sympathetic and relieved Carol before she went off to her teaching job. She made him have a hot shower and saw him into bed where he eventually slept in exhaustion.

He had somehow sunk to the bottom of the sea. The water was hot. Fight as he would, he could not break free of the seaweed. Then he began to rise. The black underside of an enormous ship blotted out the surface light. Its engines pounded in his ears. He swam into wakefulness to find himself sweating and fighting the bedclothes. The knocking continued and he realized there was someone at the door. The front door opened directly into the bedroom of the small flat, only three feet from the end of the bed. He glanced at the digital bedside clock and saw it was four in the afternoon. He had slept for nearly seven hours. Had Carol forgotten her key? He threw on a bathrobe, scrabbled on the side table for his gasses and opened the door.

Martina almost fell into his arms as she again prepared to hit down with the heavy brass fish-head knocker. She was not distraught; she was not that sort of girl. But she was certainly agitated. She took in Jessup's dishevelled and haggard appearance. 'Oh, I'm sorry if I disturb you. I think something has happened to Heinrich.'

Jessup cut her off with a gesture, recognized her distress. Martina could not know it, but he was extremely anxious to hear what she had to say. 'Come in, Martina. We have to talk.' He hurried her through the bedroom area, his Englishness forcing him to over-apologise for the unmade bed. He sat her on an easy chair then moved to the kitchen area. 'Coffee?'

Martina replied abstractedly, her long slender fingers twisting the strap of a large handbag.

Jessup leaned on the counter that divided the kitchen from the small sitting room. He wanted to find out Martina's reactions before he could explain Dorn to her. 'Go ahead. Tell me what's happened.'

'That's the problem, I don't really know.' Martina's English pronunciation was even better than Dorn's. Only his colloquial ability and humour were missing. Jessup pulled up a stool to the separating bar-top, hands cupping his rough chin dark with a two-day bristle growth, and looked attentive.

Martina hesitated again, nervously and unnecessarily taking a handkerchief from the jacket pocket of her exquisitely cut light grey suit. She looked up at Jessup, recognized an understanding soul and began in a rush. 'You know we had a certain understanding, Heinrich and I? His work. It was not possible for us to have a very regular meeting.' She stopped and drew her eyes down, wondering how much she should say.

'Go on' Jessup encouraged, and poured out coffee for both of them.

'Well, he had suggested I drove down from Malmö at about three this afternoon. I don't have a key and I rang the bell as usual.' She glanced up, the shadow of a smile reached her big blue eyes and she looked much younger than her twenty-eight years. 'We have a special signal so that he knows who's at the door. It was opened by a stranger. An old man. I'm not a fool, but I knew Heinrich was sensitive about our relationship so I pretended to be a sales representative in cosmetics. I asked if I might call back to see this old man's wife. I don't know why that idea came to me.'

Jessup's face creased in a wide, friendly grin. 'More apt than pretending to be the postman.' In the short time he had known Martina he had come to recognize her impeccable taste in clothes. Nothing like the heavy, practical stuff he had come to associate with the women of old Barvaria or the Hoch Deutsch au pair frauleins in the better parts of London suburbia. She could certainly rival the salon beauties of Berlin. He wondered – he persuaded himself it was purely academic curiosity – how long she spent in front of the mirror each morning.

She went on 'He was not very polite in his reply and he was foreign. You know, not Swedish or German. But that's not what worries me. What he said was "My wife's away and we're about to sell the house." He said it very roughly and when I lifted up my handbag to put it under my arm he mistook my movement. He probably thought I was about to give him a free nose-puff or something, and angrily waved me away, saying his wife didn't want any samples.' She paused and, having released some of the tension by talking, flopped both hands on the arms of the chair and sat back. 'What could it mean, David? Did Heinrich tell you he was going away? Could he be in trouble?'

She was not the dumb blonde type. She was sophisticated to her fingertips and could certainly look after herself in normal circumstances. But Jessup could see she was unusually put out by the episode. There was a touch of bewilderment in her look that he would certainly not have normally associated with the poised hostess of one of Dorn's quiet foursome suppers they shared. He decided he would tell her what he knew about Dorn. It might be a shock. That couldn't be helped. If Dorn was not 'away' already, he soon would be, and for a very long time, when the Swedes knew of his precious function in the Soviet service. 'Listen, I think I know who that man is. And you're right, what he said about the house and his wife is sheer nonsense. He just wanted to get rid of you.'

'Whatever for? What's going on?' Martina's eyes widened.

'Perhaps you could tell me something. Why do you think Heinrich's so cautious about showing you to his colleagues and friends? I think it's important we put our cards on the table.' He sat back, took a pipe from his bathrobe pocket and began to fill it slowly, giving her time to think.

'You and Heinrich' she said. 'I know you're good friends. He's told me you can be trusted.' She regained something like composure and curled one slim leg over the other. Jessup was not too old to smile at an imagined crack Carol might make if she entered the room at this moment, seeing Martina and knowing he was naked under the bathrobe. 'Heinrich works for the West German secret service. Air Germanic is just his business cover. I've no idea what's happening at the moment, but I do know he sometimes cooperates with Russian agents in Sweden. Perhaps he's somehow in trouble with them. Or perhaps he's been called back to Bonn. I hoped he might have left a message with you. I think he would not disappear without telling you or me something.'

It was time to tell her much of the story as he knew it himself. He said, flatly 'Heinrich doesn't work for West German intelligence. He works for Moscow and has been given a rather special assignment. One that we have to put a stop to.'

Martina stared at him with widened eyes, as if Jessup's face had fallen away and she was gazing with horror at the face of a madman. 'It can't be true' she whispered.

'I'm afraid it is.' Jessup told her the essential details. When he had finished, Martina sat quite still for a long while. She had believed Dorn to be genuinely in love with her. Did the new story change all that? Would she ever see him again? Heinrich, a communist and a Soviet agent!

'He actually admitted to being a spy for the Russians?' she asked incredulously. Jessup nodded. Martina grasped at straws. 'Yet he denied being foolish enough to leave those documents where they could be found?'

'Strange thing is' said Jessup 'I'm inclined to believe him. He has no reason to say he'd seen them safely on their way to Moscow. But', he shrugged 'we all make mistakes.'

Martina tried again to find a miniscule item of saving information. 'You say he knew this man, this Derringer, and they fought together on sight?'

'They'd apparently met before.' Jessup tried to be nonchalant about it. Did she have the same misgivings about Derringer, just from what he had said?

'Do you trust Derringer?' she asked.

'Well, he saved my life, didn't he?' Even as he spoke, Jessup realized he was not answering her question. Why had he, lying there on the deck, felt so angry with Derringer?

'And you didn't get a chance to speak with Heinrich alone, after the accident?' she pursued him relentlessly, as though he, personally, had split them up.

'No, I didn't. He was very groggy. Although, I don't see what difference that would make to anything.' And as soon as he said it, he knew he was looking at Dorn from a wholly masculine point of view. The woman in front

BALTIC INCIDENT

of him was a woman in love; and that made one hell of a difference. She was determined to find the smallest glimmer of hope. He doubted there was any.

'So' she said 'you left him tied up in the basement until you've seen this man Goddard?'

'That's right. Heinrich's not a private person any more. I know it's a shock for you. It is for all of us. But it's a fact nevertheless.'

Martina obviously didn't share the same view. She said thoughtfully 'I think he would want to see me if he could. Would it be possible for you to talk to him tonight and give him a message?'

'Nothing easier. As far as I'm concerned Derringer is only around for additional security. Apparently he used to be a professional at this sort of thing. What do you want me to say?'

'Tell him' she hesitated as she lowered her voice and looked away. 'Just tell him I miss him.'

Carol came home half an hour after Martina had left. Jessup told her about Martina's brush with Derringer. He had now had a breathing space and was beginning to think more clearly. Events had happened so fast in the past thirty-six hours. There just had not been time for him to digest and reflect on what had happened. Now he began to bring some perspective to the drama. He peered short-sightedly through the shaving mirror as Carol entered the dwarf-sized bathroom to bring him a clean towel. 'I'm not happy with this damn thing.' He patted the warm towel to his cleanly shaven chin and turned towards her.

'What, in particular?'

'For starters, I'm not convinced Goddard is on the level. Then again, I'm the obvious choice for Goddard since I've come to know Dorn so well. And thinking about all that stuff in Heinrich's cellar, wasn't it a bit too obvious?

There's an awful lot I seem to be in the dark about, and I'm not sure I like it.'

They moved into the sitting area. Carol poured him an extra full helping of his favourite Italian dry vermouth, a sherry for herself. It was their usual pre-dinner drink. She looked across the table at her husband, now rested but still looking ravaged about the eyes. 'What are you going to tell this Goddard person?' She had caught his mood about the man from squawk.

'You know me, sweetheart.' Jessup grinned back at her. She was always able to pick up the signs of his quiddity; she responded with a smile.

'So what's that egg-brain of yours hatching now?'

'I'll tell him what he wants to hear, of course. The truth. He's not interested in my opinions, so I shan't offer any. He's just using me. Probably doesn't care a rap about the Swedes, either. That's his profession, just another political stooge. Maybe it's the only way he knows of surviving in that crummy underworld of his.'

Despite the mixture of levity and seriousness, Carol knew her husband could always get his glasses steamed up whenever he felt strongly about something. She loved him for it.

- - - - - - - - - - - - - - - -

Jessup rested his foot lightly on the accelerator of the Jaguar as he turned on to the Malmö by-pass that swept in a wide curve east of the city away from the sea and towards Lund. He had been glad to see the car again outside his flat that morning. He rarely raced it but still enjoyed the power throbbing quietly under the bonnet. He brought his thoughts back to the visit he'd made to Dorn last evening.

It had been nine by the time Jessup had arrived back at Dorn's house and pressed the bell signal prearranged with Derringer. Derringer had obviously made himself comfortable. There was a recently emptied bottle on the table in the corner of the kitchen. The remains of a red wine stained the bottom of a glass set next to a partially finished supper. Derringer had opened the door to Jessup wearing a dirty blue shirt, sleeves rolled to the elbow, neck open and trouser braces that looked as though they had survived 1939. The dirty shirt was understandable; the atmosphere moving around Derringer was more puzzling. He seemed to have reverted, with some reminiscent pleasure, to the farmlands of his East European origins. Jessup thought it incongruous in Dorn's modern house and under the circumstances. The Lund university professor had shed his academic air as he might have done his gown. From the bonhomie of the seminar room to the belligerent shadows of the spy world. Little wonder Dorn had said he had a coat of many colours. Jessup wondered just what colour this one was.

Derringer had said he had been asked by Goddard only to help out in case of trouble, but Jessup had the feeling that he had somehow taken over. He had merely nodded towards the cellar door when Jessup said he wanted to check on Dorn.

After the first greeting, there was an awkward silence between the two men in the cellar. Jessup felt almost embarrassed. What the hell was there to say to an enemy spy you had befriended and who had seemed to return that friendship and at the same time was bent on destroying the whole structure of the society you believed in? Strangely, Dorn had seemed equally sensitive, as far as he could show any feeling at all other than acute discomfort, since he was still bound tightly to the mattress. Jessup had passed on Martina's message, feeling awkward and clumsy doing so. Dorn responded by expressing his concern that she might be wrongly implicated.

In the five minutes he had spent with Dorn, Jessup had time to notice that the desk top was clear and the boxes containing the metal panels for the radio transceiver were as he had left them forty-eight hours earlier. Dorn had made no comment when Jessup looked in the desk drawers and found them empty. Jessup felt caught in a web of a particularly sticky sort. It hadn't helped one bit when Dorn had come out with the flat statement that if Jessup intended to go to the police, then he should do it as soon as possible and leave him to his fate. What the devil was that supposed to mean?

He left with the unsatisfactory feeling he ought to have said more to Dorn; that there was some unfinished business between them. Well, sheer speculation would get him nowhere. This meeting with Goddard might help.

- - - - - - - - - - - - - - -

Jessup could see, as he drove to the cathedral parking spot, that the university town was denuded of students. Today was a public holiday, one of the saints' days Swedes meticulously name in their calenders and diaries, as well as an academic vacation. So Goddard and he would be free of prying office staff, too.

Goddard's smile did not seem to have changed since Jessup had seen it the first time in Derringer's room. Perhaps it had been cunningly fixed with foreign office sellotape. And his hair still hung loosely, drooping occasionally towards a narrow nose. He occupied rather than sat in Derringer's chair. Jessup had not appreciated Goddard's proprietorial air on that previous visit. The confidence of Eton, or perhaps Rugby since the nose was definitely an Arnold feature, was now marked. He greeted Jessup with some enthusiasm; he was sure Jessup had something he wanted.

BALTIC INCIDENT

Jessup told him straight away that Dorn was being held by Derringer in the Ljunghusen house.

'I know about that.' Goddard's smile broadened. 'The contacts in Denmark, and Derringer himself.'

'Did your contacts also tell you Dorn practically admitted he was putting the final touches to a Soviet plan to invade Sweden?'

'By God, but they did not. What did you do to wring that from him? Offer him a seat next to Gromyko at the next Party Congress?'

'It wasn't a confession.' Jessup was not responding to Goddard's smile. The man was over-eager, too confident. Despite his exclamations he seemed to know everything already. 'It was an admission of what we already know' he said pointedly. Jessup went on to tell Goddard of the findings he'd made in the cellar and the letter that had sent him to Denmark to discover the antenna.

Goddard's left hand strayed to hold back the lazy forelock as he leaned forward to listen. The smile slowly disappeared as he heard of Dorn's unexpected arrival at Rødvig and the events that followed. The coldness Jessup had noticed before reappeared in Goddard's expression.

Jessup finished his narrative and sat back to light his pipe. It was, he felt, his turn to appear casual. Perhaps one learnt fast in the spy trade. Perhaps one had to.

'You've done a great deal more than we expected. Taking a bit of a chance, there, weren't you? Best stick to the script, old man.' Goddard spoke lightly, but Jessup got the impression he was not altogether ecstatic. 'Not to worry. At least Derringer was there to get you out of the scrape.' Then, as though all that was in the past, he cheered up again. 'I do believe you'll be the star witness if the Swedes ever bring this to open court – which I doubt, by the way.'

Jessup grunted an acknowledgement through the stem of his pipe, and puffed smoke towards the partly opened window. A strange habit; Jessup disliked a smoky atmosphere. He said 'What happens now?'

'You've done your bit. At least the leg work. Now it's time for us to make a move. First I shall let my contact – unofficial, you understand? – know where Dorn is, and give him your address. He'll take it from there with his chief. I should think their special branch'll pick up Dorn within a couple of hours. They'll certainly go over the house with a fine tooth-comb. Very efficient, the Swedes, with things like that. I'll pull Derringer out first, of course, he's unofficial, too. Säpo will want to see you as soon as they have Dorn inside. Probably sometime tomorrow.'

'What about the yacht? The one Derringer followed us in? It's still on the beach as far as I know.'

'Ah, yes, the yacht.' Goddard frowned and tapped a slightly protruding tooth with the end of a pencil. 'Can't imagine how the devil he picked that up so easily in the middle of the night. I'll get word to the right place. Have it back in Denmark in no time. Make up some cock and bull story for the police there. A nod and a wink from the right quarter should do it.'

Goddard stood, the smile was back on his pale face. He stretched out his hand. 'Splendid work, Jessup. I think you'll find an acceptable cheque in your post one day soon. Undoubtedly the repayment of a loan you made to the owner of a small radio business in Hounslow.'

This time Jessup returned the smile. He could hardly forget it was the extra cash he'd come to Derringer's study to earn in the first place. Carol certainly wouldn't forget it. But did Goddard have to be so damn patronising about it?

Moments after Jessup had left the building, a bulky, black-browed man wearing a traditionally cut navy-blue suit and discreet light-blue tie, entered Derringer's study from a connecting room. He had been listening to the conversation. His heavy face reciprocated Goddard's own smile as they shook hands.

'Your little operation appears to be on schedule,' Goddard said to Stavrinsky.

'I find it refreshing to do business again with the British. Sometimes even stimulating.' Boris Stavrinsky's dark eyes glowed. His American accented English was faultless. 'Perhaps we don't always show it, but we do have a high regard for that extra polish you people add to your work. The CIA can never quite make it. They think results are all that count.'

'Very kind of you to mention it, Colonel. But your own charm doesn't altogether escape us.'

The pleasantries, not totally insincere, over with, Goddard went to look out of the window facing the street. A fair haired, straggly-bearded young man wearing the regulation uniform of dirty sweater and wooden clogs, lounged against the gateway pillar, an open book held languidly in his hand. He looked up and made a single wave motion, palm outwards, towards the window. Goddard turned back to Stavrinsky

'Our professor has gone. Go out the back way, through the courtyard gate. There's a red mini-car by the kerb. Sit in the passenger seat. Peter will drive you to Gothenburg. Not as comfortable as your Mercedes, but safer.'

Goddard had not exactly welcomed the idea of working hand in hand with the Russian. Unlike some of his contemporaries at Cambridge he had never had any sympathy for the views of the left. Born to the wife of a banker in an extremely respectable part of Watford, he had grown up, alone, in passable luxury and with none of the hang-ups that often curse an only son. Nurtured in a safe home, moulded into the correct moral shape at Rugby, Goddard had grown up without the slightest feeling for, or understanding of, the underdog. Like some unenlightened Buddha, Goddard did not know about poverty or failure, about weaknesses of the flesh or excesses of conscience.

As in cricket, his sense of fairness extended only to his equals, the others playing the game. As he understood Brooke's poem, there had to be some English corner of every foreign field. His superiors in the intelligence section of the Foreign Office had never divined this as a fault. They could not. For, to them, he was the epitomy of what they believed of themselves. Which is why, at an exceptionally early age, he had been asked to 'umbrella' the whole of the Scandinavian operational area. It had helped that he kept himself in fine physical trim and, despite his narrow shape, could always muck in with the lads on the ground if the need arose.

Ten minutes later, Goddard had left the building and was easing with the traffic along Dalbyvägen in a rented Volvo towards the Vipeholm area, just outside Lund. Vipeholm was a red brick horror of four storey apartment blocks, squarely planned and stolidly built to the satisfaction of its dull town planners. It was a neat development, created totally without imagination or character, for functional purposes only. Many of the flats were rented, with state subsidies, by university students. An ideal spot for invisibility.

Peter Svensson, Goddard's lounging lookout, was ostensibly a post-graduate exchange student from Yale studying the growing peace movement in Sweden with the strangely balanced title Peace and Conflict Research. The yellow-haired lanky American of Swedish parents was, in fact, one of the CIA's more recent recruits. It was his first overseas posting and he was on trial. Sweden, especially the universities, was a spot beloved by the United States' intelligence service for the initial field training of budding agents. As one recruit had told Peter, back in New Haven, 'They like to lower you gently into the soft soil, brother.'

Many of the trainee agents sent to Sweden over the years were given the comparatively easy task of forming organized or casual culture groups, made up of as many different nationalities as possible. Agents had a primary and secondary objective. Collecting information about people, places and the internal moods and movements within the foreign student's home country was the first. The second objective was rarely achieved but was even more valuable whenever it succeeded. It was to actually hook a non-Scandinavian student for possible intelligence work in their own country on behalf of the CIA. The follow-up pressure to be continued by more experienced Agency staff. Such a catch by the home-bred novitiate agent was almost certain to result in an Alpha-plus grading on his or her file.

It had been the glowing report of his initial training tutors in far-off Seattle, particularly about his ability to act, that had decided the masters in Washington D.C. to loan Peter Svensson to the British for what the British called 'a deuced delicate little thing.' Svensson could put on a 'super Oxford accent', said his Seattle sponsors, without a thought that that in itself might be offputting to a Cambridge man.

It was to Svensson's second floor apartment that Goddard now drove. For the remainder of the time scheduled by the Russians for the completion of "Operation

CHARLES SMART

Searchlight" – wit for coded operations was not encouraged by Moscow – Goddard had arranged to stay with Svensson. It was convenient, inconspicuous if one wore the right clothes, and had the necessary private telephone, as well as several computerised items. Goddard made two calls. The first was to Derringer, the second to his Swedish säpo contact.

BALTIC INCIDENT
Chapter Five

Jessup sat forward on the wooden, straight-backed chair and concentrated on the questions that came at him in a mixture of Swedish and English. The room was a drab shoebox, eight feet by twelve. The door on his left, at one end of the room, opened on to a corridor. Behind him was a waist-high bookshelf full of dusty legal tomes and neatly labelled files. On top of the bookshelf stood an ornately hand-drawn sign, like a Christmas card somebody had forgotten to move. 'Rökning undanbedes' it said. Jessup wondered if anyone would want to stay in the cell-like room long enough to light up.

What the Swedish security police lacked in scope and manpower it often made up for by copying its bigger foreign brothers, usually the CIA. Within the limits of a small and notoriously passive population, and often hamstrung by a political leadership which, when it tried to act fast was clog-hopper clumsy, and when not clumsy took on the speed of a group of democratic bovines, säpo was never too far behind its more powerful brothers in information-gathering. In the best international security force traditions, säpo, in Malmö, had managed to hide its operational base within a busy conglomeration of innocent commercial activity.

Not far from the centre of Sweden's third largest city lay Frihamn. A Swedish joke if ever there was one, for it was the country's closest port of entry from the continent for goods on which all manner of peculiar and expensive taxes were imposed. It was from within the cluster of customs buildings inside the perimeter of Frihamn that south west säpo conducted its covert craft. To ordinary customs officials, police and the general public – all of whom at various times thronged the area since international passenger ships also berthed there – the two-storeyed old red brick building was just another cluster of offices. A grimy notice fixed to the wall near the front door alleged it to be a central government department with special responsibility for classifying dangerous cargo, medicine, drugs and ferti- lizers. It was enough to make the health-phobic Swed- ish citizen keep his distance. And, in truth, some of the säpo agents did specialize in drug detection.

At seven o'clock that morning Jessup had received telephone instructions from the Frihamn agency head- quarters. He was to park the Jaguar in a service alley behind the Hotel Anglais. He had smiled at that, but knowing the cool Swedish temperament he doubted they were aware of the humour of placing a distinc- tively English car, complete with GB sign and plates, outside that particular hotel. From there he was to walk the twenty yards back down the alley to Stortorget, the main square, and get straight into the passenger seat of a bright yellow builder's van that would be parked at the kerbside. A seven minute drive would have been enough to get them to the Frihamn area. Instead, they took fifteen minutes, with an extra turn around the city centre, giving him time to climb into the back of the van and cover up his green suit with a discoloured builder's overall. The precaution was not for his benefit, he was informed by the driver, but a routine safety measure for the agency. The faded pink overall had come complete with a plastic pass and photograph, identifying Jessup as a member of the customs authority works depart- ment. The photograph, he realized, was the twin to that on his Swedish Identitetskort issued by Sparbanken.

His questioner, sitting opposite him on the other side of a utilitarian pinewood desk and fiddling now and again with the papers in front of him, answered to the name of Karl Sorbron. He was the head of Sweden's south west region – MILO S west – säkerhetspolisen, säpo for short. Sorbron finished writing something in longhand then looked up at Jessup. 'Mer kafffe?' The question was asked with more of a grimace than a smile. Not because he was bad-tempered, but because he had few other ways in which to let the world know how pleased he was. He was fiftyish, below medium height with grey stubbled hair and had a face whose furrows showed he more often frowned than smiled. His abruptness indicated a short-fused temper and from the moment they had met Jessup had felt he was a man with a grievance; perhaps passed over for a post in Stockholm, despite his rank as a four star colonel, grade one. After two hours of being subjected to Sorbron's laborious quizzing and bored by his even more laboured scribbling, Jessup felt he knew why. Jessup politely refused the coffee.

The unobtrusive alert from Goddard by way of his undercover contact had produced a turbulance among an inner core of MILO S security agents not known since a mysterious West German businessman had disappeared, together with the secrets of computer equipment earmarked for transit to East Germany, from his summer house near Falsterbo at the end of 1983. Not that säpo headquarters in Stockholm had been informed yet about Dorn. At least not officially. Sorbron was determined to get the whole story before he claimed a triumph from Lars-Erik Stenberg, the national säpo boss.

A gloating quiver that some might have mistaken for a smile had touched Sorbron's slightly bulging eyes as he told Jessup that an immense amount of material had been found in Dorn's house during the night. The paper evidence was neatly piled on the desk. The author of that evidence, Dorn himself, had been shut away with four alternating interrogators somewhere else in the building. Jessup felt fagged after only two hours. He wondered how Dorn was standing up to the pressures of an all-night performance. Sorbron was positively fawning over the Englishman, seeing in Jessup's testimony and eyewitness evidence a first class ticket to higher office and the extra time off to spend in Tenerife that would go with it.

Jessup had to admit the evidence was impressive. As well as diagrams and photographs there were ten notebooks and four folders of quarto sized paper. Much of it in German, some in English and Swedish, but all the written material was either in Dorn's handwriting or from a typewriter found in his house. All this, in addition to the chart, photographs, pseudo-delivery note and the two unassembled aerial parts discovered by Jessup. He was prepared to believe what Sorbron was saying, but he was intrigued and curiously disturbed to learn of the sheer volume of documents he had apparently missed when he had visited Dorn's cellar.

The notebooks contained the facts Dorn had collected during nearly two years of travelling throughout Sweden, ostensibly extending the freight volume for Air Germanic. His survey had been thorough. Among the most sensitive items in the notebooks were the locations of five out of ten secret arms dumps dug deep inside the mountains of central and northern parts of the country; the positions and defensive strength of primary and secondary computer control centres in mid and south parts of Sweden, and the possible number of military reserves available to MILO S west in any twenty-four hour period. Among the facts that appeared to be more innocuous Dorn had listed the morale of the civil population, the type and conditions of beaches along the south west coast, and a graph of estimated statistics on wind speed and direction, and average wave heights for all the spring months. The folders contained Dorn's assessment of the facts in relation to a seaborne attack from the south.

But for most of the two hour period it was Jessup who found himself the centre of attraction. Sorbron studiously avoided questioning him about why he had searched Dorn's cellar in the first place. There were some things it was better not to know, especially in the secret service of a country that was supposed to be neutral. Sorbron didn't want a repetition of the 1974 "I.B. affair" in which the super secret Swedish Intelligence Bureau had been uncovered and accused of cooperating with western agencies. That had cost his predecessor his job.

Jessup had been asked to describe every meeting he had had with Dorn. All the details of their social contact were assiduously noted and appropriately grunted over. From the beginning, Jessup had planned how to avoid all reference to Martina, but it had not been easy when the pencil had paused at the occasional 'we' in the narrative and Sorbron had suddenly noticed he had no names at that point. By the end of the interview Jessup had become hypnotized by the slightly aggressive application of pencil to paper. At times he fully expected to see Sorbron lick the point of the instrument before writing down the next word, like a retarded schoolboy trying to write a composition. At one point Jessup had pulled out his pipe from under the borrowed overalls and begun to push tobacco into the bowl absentmindedly. The writing had stopped in mid-word as, with an apologetic facial movement, Sorbron had looked up and nodded to the no smoking sign.

Finally, Sorbron was satisfied. 'Herr Jessup has been very helpful' he said, using the polite Swedish of the old days. Then he dropped into the vernacular, feeling more at home with the familiar 'du' that had, in the last twenty years, reduced all Swedes to the lowest common level. 'You have brought us information that is of great service to Sweden. Of course we shall want to see you again, but first you will understand we must act on this knowledge immediately.'

Jessup agreed to make himself available.

'There is just the matter of formal identification' Sorbron added. He stood, buttoned his uniform jacket and, with some old Swedish courtesy, gestured for Jessup to lead the way to the door. He leaned forward to open the door first. 'Var så god' he invited. He had the air of a man who had just finished an expensive meal and who was anticipating the accolade of the finest dessert.

The säpo offices boasted no lift and the two men passed along the featureless corridors of the top floor to reach the stone steps leading to the basement. There were few signs of life. If the service employed a clerical staff they worked behind closed doors in soundproof rooms. Jessup got the impression it was a strictly operational building.

On the ground floor it was different. A clamour of hammers hitting bricks and mortar jarred their ears as they turned a corner. The use of a builder's van to screen his entry into säpo's haunt was not as implausible as it had first seemed to Jessup. At the head of the steps continuing downwards, two powerful looking labourers were busy knocking a hole in the wall. As he passed them Jessup noticed the workers give him a double-take look. They wore overalls identical to his own, and he supposed that it must appear strange to them that he was treated with extraordinary deference by a full colonel of säpo.

Dorn's big frame seemed to have shrunk. He sat on a wooden stool, arms thrown out in front of him across a deal table, his head motionless between them turned away from the door. The concrete, bunker-like room had no windows; contained no furniture but the stool, a chair and the table between them. Silently, the uniformed säpo policeman rose and left the room as Sorbron, followed by Jessup, entered. Dorn did not raise his head. He was breathing deeply. He seemed to be asleep. He made no move when Sorbron sat on the vacated chair.

'Herr Dorn'', said Sorbron. His voice was harsh. 'There is someone you must see.'

Dorn moved his head, chin still on the table, and raised his eyebrows to the colonel. From the movement, Jessup knew at once Dorn had not been asleep. It was the attitude of one conserving engery. Dorn's normally soft brown eyes glinted at Sorbron as though waiting for the next attack.

Sorbron bent his head towards Jessup. Slowly, without removing his chin from the table, Dorn rolled his head over and looked. There were deep shadows under his eye sockets. His face was grey and lined with dirt. Derringer had obviously not allowed him to wash and the security police had been concentrating on other things. The stubble of beard looked a week old. He wore only dark trousers and a dirty white short-sleeved shirt. The blazer he had lost in the explosion on the motor launch. His eyes showed a flicker of interest as he recognized Jessup. He was dead tired, Jessup could see that, but he was by no means beaten. His tough training was paying off. The Swedes had not touched him bodily. The defeat of their pro-German feelings in 1945 had long-term effects, particularly on the Swedish police forces. Physical contact with prisoners who needed persuading was forbidden. It said so in the rules governing police behaviour. The fact that Sweden had actively assisted in Nazi German concentration camp medical experimentation into the question of racial purity lay deep in the sub-conscious of their political leaders. Only a handful of citizens knew of the well-documented skulls, thousands upon thousands of them, that had provided their pre-war researchers with proof that the Nordic race was a superior human species. Hitler had shown his gratitude by not invading the country provided, of course, the Swedes maintained the flow of high quality steel to the Third Reich. But all that was now hidden in the socialism they pointedly refused to call 'national' in the post-war years and, with the aplomb of complete self-deception, embraced the other arm of Hegel's philosophy of power.

The question that passed briefly through Jessup's mind was: who had won the first round? The relay of all-night inquisitors, or the Russian-trained spy? But he knew the answer to that before the question had finished forming itself.

Sorbron spoke to Jessup, the harshness in his voice hardly muted. Perhaps for Dorn's benefit. 'It is necessary for you to say if this is the man you have been speaking about, Heinrich Dorn.'

It was not so much a question as a statement to which assent was all that would be necessary. The linchpin in the case against Dorn; the vital but already accomplished step towards promotion. Jessup felt the unlikely affinity between this uncouth, officious colonel and the smooth man from squawk.

Jessup ignored him. 'Hello, Heinrich.'

BALTIC INCIDENT

Dorn lifted his head from the table, slowly sat back and folded hs arms. 'They said you'd be coming.' His voice cracked drily as he spoke. 'Can you persuade these gentlemen to produce coffee? My mouth's as dry as a Swedish comedy.'

Sorbron showed his annoyance at this lack of formality. 'I must ask you to answer my question, Hr.Jessup.'

Jessup, still standing near the closed door, looked at him and produced a smile as false as a well manu-factured rose. 'I just did, colonel.' He had long since learnt that anything short of a straight answer was apt to confuse a Swede, particularly one in uniform. 'And would it be permissible for this man to have a cup of coffee?' There was something he had to say to Dorn and there wouldn't be another chance like this. Jessup said to Sorbron 'And colonel, can I have five minutes alone? It's important.'

Sorbron decided he had all that was necessary for his report, but if there was something more, he'd get it off Jessup later. 'Alright.' he said, giving Dorn a hard look. 'Five minutes.'

Jessup felt no embarrassment at facing Dorn alone on this occasion. Dorn had been his friend and their re-lationship had been perfectly genuine, he was sure of that. But there was something more he could do for a friend in Dorn's position, as he had told a sympathetic Carol late the night before. She had wholeheartedly agreed he should try.

For several moments Dorn and Jessup looked at one another saying nothing. Jessup knew he had done the right thing, damn Goddard! but it had made him feel dirty and for the life of him he couldn't tell why. Finally, Jessup said 'You could have got rid of me on that boat, couldn't you? What stopped you?'

Dorn sighed deeply. 'Let's just say I went a bit soft.'

Jessup knew he was playing the wit.

Dorn said 'Look, this isn't the Mafia. Secret agents don't kill for the sake of expediency these days. I slipped up somewhere and that's all there is to it.' His tired eyes looked wary even now.

'Heinrich, you're in a heap of trouble. Just tell me one thing, are you a communist? I mean, do you really believe in the ideology?'

A veil seemed to come over Dorn's eyes and Jessup had the feeling he didn't want to talk any more. Jessup decided to spell it out. 'I'd say give the game up. Defect. Talk to the Swedes. Tell them everything you know. Perhaps they'll be able to steer clear of this invastion you've been planning. You know, some diplomatic effort or other. What have you got to lose? You could ask for asylum here.' He stopped. He didn't have to say all this to Dorn. Dorn knew what the stakes were. Probably always had, before ever Jessup had come along.

Dorn gave Jessup a frank look, then slowly smiled. 'You know, David, you're an incurable jingoist. Leave it alone and go back to that lovely wife of yours.'

At that moment, Jessup felt deeply sorry for Dorn. Whatever the Soviets had gained or would gain, Dorn had lost his particular battle. Perhaps he'd lost his will, too. He seemed strangely content to leave things as they were. But that wasn't Dorn. He just wasn't the martyr type. And since he'd been uncovered and the invasion plan was no longer a secret, he could hardly expect a hearty welcome back in the East.

Jessup knew he might be touching a raw nerve, but he had to say it. 'One more thing, then, Heinrich. Spare a thought for Martina. She's worried stiff about you. She's a good girl, but she wouldn't be able to live on the other side of the curtain.'

BALTIC INCIDENT

They heard footsteps outside and Dorn said, with a return of humour 'Tell you what, David. I promise to think about asylum if you'll promise to look after Martina.' There was a twinkle in his eye, like the old times. 'Is it a deal?'

He was suddenly smiling from ear to ear when the key turned in the lock. But by the time Sorbron had walked in, the beaten look had come back as if by magic. Jessup was only partly satisfied with Dorn's response. But Sorbron stood by the door, waiting. A younger man came in carrying a tray. Jessup smelled the strong coffee as he followed Sorbron from the room.

Three quarters of an hour later, Jessup was again seated in the featureless office on the second floor, reading through the typewritten version of his statement before signing it. He'd had time to reflect. He'd felt the strength emanating from the exhausted Dorn. And if that was a contradiction then it could only be part and parcel of the strange world Jessup had entered. Dorn was dead tired but he had radiated a purposeful will such as Jessup had not seen in any man before. He wondered whether the security police had felt it, too. Probably not. Policemen were notoriously indifferent to feelings when they were in hot pursuit of the facts. He knew from Sorbron that Dorn had admitted to nothing, except the collecting of information, insisting that that was not illegal.

Jessup would have liked to talk to Dorn again. He hated to let it go. The business felt unfinished. It was not just a question of Dorn's carelessness, nor even the doubts about Derringer. What was more disturbing was Sorbron's confronting him with a mass of obviously genuine evidence that Jessup was told he had missed, even though his search of the cellar had been little more than perfunctory. He felt sure he could not have failed to see it; that it had simply not been there that night and was certainly not there after the boat accident. Yet säpo had found it. Throwing the net over Dorn was one thing; but why did he himself feel caught?

--- --- --- --- ---

An insistent bell began a clamour somewhere in the building. Feet ran loud in the corridor. There were shouting voices but Jessup could not distinguish the hurried Swedish words. He opened the door to find out what was happening. A plain-clothed säpo agent hurried past, fastening the belt of his shoulder holster as he went. Jessup followed. At the bottom of the steps on the ground floor there was a small group of men cluttering the space where the builders had been working on the wall. Sorbron was giving orders, urgently and with some arm-flinging, to three of his men. He had little time for Jessup.

'Coffee!' he spat the word at Jessup. 'That's the payment for being pleasant.' He spoke fast, his face red with anger. 'Wanted the toilet. He said it was only natural. Knocked over two of my men and bolted through there!' He flung a hand in the direction of the hole in the wall.

He was already striding towards the main entrance at the back of the building to organize the searchers outside. He said brusquely over his shoulder 'He can't get out of the customs' perimeter.'

Jessup bent to the hole. The din of confusion had died down in the building. The action had moved outside, now organized, but no one was shouting out there. The chase in public had to be discreet, he realized. Thorough, efficient and, above all, quiet. He squeezed with difficulty through the double-brick wide and three foot high jagged space and found himself in a large darkened warehouse. It was half filled with private cars, each with a foreign registration plate, awaiting assessment of their value before being allowed into the country. The joke about Frihamn, as Jessup knew to his cost, was on the owner when he received the bill.

He stepped out of the Judas gate at the far end. To the left was the high perimeter wall. Two labourers, almost certainly säpo men, he thought, were walking along its length. On his right there was a lot more activity. No panic or rushing, but he recognized two säpo agents among six people close to the main customs goods entrance. That seemed to be sealed off, too. But the major activity was taking place a hundred yards away, between the quay and a large customs shed. He walked in that direction. The eight thousand tonne Thor line passenger ferry, plying between Sweden, Denmark and Germany had recently berthed from Kiel. Passengers were shuffling down a covered gangway from the ship to passport control.

Didn't they say that the place to really get lost was in a crowd? He began to walk towards the throng of disembarking passengers, dockside workers and officials. Sorbron had already acted on the idea. Säpo agents were in place and watching every movement around the exit. Sorbron himself had disappeared, probably to scout the outer side of the customs area where Dorn, impossible though it seemed, might have already slipped through with the disembarking passengers. Jessup leaned against an eight-wheel road trailer and watched.

It was a dead end. For Dorn, too. Jessup did not see how anyone could escape for long within the confines of the guarded area. If Dorn had tried to walk out of the main transport gate he would have been already in the hands of regular customs officials. The ten-foot walls were unscaleable without some preparation. Dorn wouldn't have had time even to raise a casually left ladder. The only other possible exit route was the water itself. But the harbour was wide, bordered on the other side only by a breakwater jetty. Anyone swimming over to that would be spotted as easily as a white rabbit wearing a top hat and sitting in the middle of a green field. In any case, Sorbron had lost no time in contacting the harbour police. The launch, its bright yellow and blue flag snapping in the wind, was already making its second run near the breakwater. And Jessup saw three men walking along the top of the harbour wall. Sorbron hadn't forgotten that, either. The hawk-eyed security police were everywhere.

Jessup felt for his pipe. Instead of a jacket pocket, his fingers clawed at rough material. He still wore the overalls of the customs works department. He looked down and, for the first time it registered that he was in a uniform of faded pink. That was why no one had challenged him as he walked freely round the yard.

The group of workmen loading boxes into the side of the ship were not all wearing pink overalls. It was hot work hefting the crates of food and drink ready for the ship's quick turnaround at Malmö, and at least six of the labourers had discarded them to work in their own open-necked shirts or vests. Dorn was sweating like his new-found companions in the ant-like line of box carriers to the ship's side. Like the others he wore a soft hat with a long peak to shade his face from the sun and, with his dark trousers and dirty white shirt, did not stand out from the other workers. They were all big and muscular and brown.

Had it been a group of dockers in England, Dorn's appearance among the group would have been cause for comment, for each would know the other, either from casual conversation or from the local pub. There was nothing like that in Sweden. There was no such fraternity. A single pint of strong brown ale taken the night before would be enough to lose a man his driving licence. Dorn was accepted because he just looked the same as the others. Overlooked might be more accurate. But even he couldn't haul crates indefinitely. The loading would be finished; the labourers would go on to other jobs, and every worker but Dorn could produce an identity card.

The pile of boxes being loaded was shrinking. Dorn had to do something soon. He picked up a crate in his brawny arms and, hoisting it to his shoulder, headed obliquely away from the ship's side. He aimed for the ramp at the ship's stern down which the last of the private cars was being driven. Two offloading crew members stood at the head of the ramp. Dorn did not hesitate. Wearing the peaked cap and with the box on his shoulder, his features were impossible to see clearly, even if anybody had been interested enough to examine the faces of each sweaty labourer. Dorn had achieved the effect of being as public as possible without being identified as a stranger. To complete the impression, he called out in German. One of the ship's crew replied laughingly in the same language. Few Swedes would have understood the quick exchange in the broad Hamburg dialect, even if they heard it. It could only be one German crew member joking with another.

The metal slope from ship to shore was not a long one. The incident was over in seconds and Dorn was inside, swearing loudly in the rough seaman's manner. The deception and technique worked smoothly. Dorn was away and out of the circle of security police as quietly and effortlessly as a hot-air balloon released from its moorings.

CHARLES SMART
Chapter Six

Dorn struggled up three flights of narrow metal companionway with the heavy box on his shoulder. On the saloon deck he found himself with the last of the boarding passengers and dumped the box casually on the floor outside the cafeteria pantry. He took off his cap and, making sure he was unobserved, placed it deep inside a garbage can. He spruced his hair and made himself presentable. He made his way to the main passenger concourse, then followed the picture signs to the large, first class dining salon.

The sun streamed in from the west through enormous plate-glass windows by which the room was enclosed on three sides. Two dozen tables had been recently laid with bright stainless steel cutlery on snowy white tablecloths. Passengers were already settling in on the window seats facing the bows of the ship. White coated waiters hovered to take the first orders. He felt the soft warmth of luxury as he released the double swing doors behind him and stepped on to the carpeted floor.

A waiter, busy at a salad buffet on his right, stared at his unorthodox appearance. Dorn could do without the attention at this moment. He gave the waiter a short but polite 'Guten Tag', then walked with easy confidence towards one of the tables.

The man already seated was facing the door by which Dorn had entered. He did not look up from the current issue of Time Magazine he held as Dorn sat down opposite him. He was a small, wiry man and wore an open-necked chequered shirt under his jacket. Dorn had no difficulty in identifying Bill McMahon. The lined face made him look about ninety years old. He was, in fact, sixty-five, and even that was too old for his voice when at last he spoke.

'What kept you?' It was a quiet voice with a Newhaven accent mellowed by travel and by the two months he spent every winter at his very private retreat in North Miami. He hadn't raised his eyes. Like the voice, the hand movement could have belonged to a man twenty years his junior as it left the magazine to flick ash into an ashtray from an elaborately long cigar.

'Somebody forgot my size. I nearly lost the skin off my back squeezing between those bricks.'

The American chuckled and looked at Dorn for the first time. 'Nobody's perfect' he said. The smile had reached his eyes and they sparkled with humour. 'At least the acid worked.'

They did not shake hands. The precaution was natural and understood by both men.

McMahon went on 'Listen. We don't have much time, so let me tell you right away. Room twenty-one on "B" deck. Left hand side of the wardrobe. Just make sure the pockets are empty when you throw the damn thing away. Got it?' He slipped a room key carelessly across the table. 'Leave the key in the room and the door on the latch.'

Dorn nodded. He knew he shouldn't spend longer than necessary in the company of the American. Besides, it was less than an hour's sailing time to Helsingør, on the north east tip of Zealand. 'How's Boris?' he asked.

'I'd say he's got the whole operation ticking over very well. We should be seeing some results pretty soon.'

Dorn stood up from the table as a waiter came for their order. McMahon asked for Karlsberg beer and Dorn shook his head to the waiter's questioning look.

The waiter having gone, McMahon said 'Fixed your accommodation for tonight?'

'In a manner of speaking, yes. Not exactly the Waldorf but safe as houses, you might say. Not even säpo would think of looking there.'

McMahon gave a barely perceptible nod and immediately became absorbed again in his reading. To the casual eye he might have just got rid of a plagued nuisance.

Dorn felt the throbbing of the ship's engines as he stepped out of the small passenger lift on "B" deck. The ship had moved from the dockside and, with luck, the säpo agents were still scurrying about on dry land like ants that had just had salt scattered into their nest. What he needed right now was a good night's sleep before the final and most delicate phase of "Operation Searchlight" began in earnest.

He made sure the corridor was empty before opening the door to room twenty-one. He locked the door securely behind him and turned on the light. The cabin was small but contained luxurious fittings, from the red plush carpet to the well-filled glass fronted ice-box. He could do with a drink at this moment, feeling he'd been on the wagon for a month instead of two days. But this wasn't the time. The celebration could come later. The single but ample size bed looked even more enticing. Even the TV set showed a video of a calm Scandinavian landscape to the mellow music of Grieg. He had the mad idea of throwing himself on it and sleeping for about a month, then thrust the thought from him. He went to the wardrobe and slid open the mirrored panel. The photograph and details attached to the lapel of the brown coat identified him as a storekeeper, second class, of Drottning Sylvia, the ship whose decks he'd walked for the past half hour. That was his ticket past any curious immigration busybody. From the pocket of the brown coat he took a packet of Styvesant cigarettes and an electronic cigarette lighter. He pulled off the cellophane wrapping from the cigarettes, broke the blue seal and shook out one of the long white cylinders. Placing the cigarette in his mouth, he flicked the cigarette lighter into flame. He hadn't smoked for years and, although the cigarette was mild, it nearly choked him when he attempted to inhale. 'Scheise', he spluttered. Recovering from the coughing spasm, he again drew experimentally on the cigarette, not taking the smoke into his lungs this time. It was still acrid, and he found himself almost envying McMahon's aromatic cigar. He stubbed out the burning end in an ashtray then looked closely at the silver coloured lighter. The circular indentation at its base was almost invisible but it was what he needed to check. The pressure of fingers in normal handling would not disturb it, but it was vital to test the mechanism. With the edge of his thumbnail he pressed hard into the indented circle. The room lights flashed with stroboscopic effects and the summer landscape on the TV turned to electronic snow. To his relief the micro-electronic pulsator worked perfectly. It was all Dorn needed to know and he pressed again with his thumbnail to cancel the sub-atomic particle stream hoping that the ship had maintained its course. Then he placed the cigarettes and lighter in his grubby navy-blue trouser pocket.

- - - - - - - - - - - - - - -

Eight hundred miles north of Malmö, Pekka Hainnu came on duty at the electricity transformer station near the small town of Hjälta. Hainnu was a fiercely patriotic Finn, working in Sweden, like thousands of other Finns, only because it was difficult to get work back home. He had lived in Sweden for five years and hated every minute of it. He thought the Swedes depressing. He had few Swedish friends. They disliked his outspoken criticism of their cold culture. He missed the Finnish drinking parlours and cafes where a man could really drink, and enjoy a proper quarrel when he felt like it. The inhibitions of Swedish social life he found deplorable.

His objective was to make enough money to pay off the loan he had taken out on a house he'd bought ten years before, near the town of Tampere in the forests north of Helsinki. His job as senior engineer at the Hjälta plant wouldn't pay for that as well as the upkeep of his wife, two children and the commune flat he rented. But part of the reason for moving to Sweden was the black money that could be made. High taxes had made black money into a modern Swedish institution. As a highly skilled electrician, Hainnu never had problems in finding work that he could safely leave out of his yearly tax declaration.

Hainnu had struck a particularly rich vein only nine months earlier. A small but successful computer components testing and sales company, based in Stockholm, had approached him. He had his own ideas on how they'd become so successful within such a short space of time. Industrial espionage, he'd learnt, was common enough in the western world. Not that he'd been asked to steal anything. Research, they'd said, to do with electrically operated medical equipment. What had surprised the Finn was the size of his payment for so little work. All he had to do was place a light metal box, no bigger than his fist, at a high output loading junction, and to change it every three months.

He had no intention of asking what the boxes were for. That was their business. He'd only wanted to be assured he wasn't starting up in big-time crime. They had insisted he should know, just the same. Job satisfaction, they'd said, with a smile. Increasingly sophisticated equipment, especially for internal physical medical examinations, were needed by doctors for finer measuring instruments, they had explained. Electricity was the normal power source and the output had to be refined and measured out for different instruments and often made to correspond to resistance patterns that varied from patient to patient. The Stockholm firm's expertise, said the neatly dressed go-between, was in the collection and codification of the range of fluctuation in electrical discharges of different magnitudes. It was to be fed into a new age computer. A fast growing field, they said. They believed they were ahead of the Americans. No one must know the source of their measurements. A big electricity supply such as the one he worked with was exactly what they needed to keep ahead of their competitors.

The sealed box, the Finn was given to understand, had two functions. The first was to measure the small amounts of variation in the high voltage output. The second was to transmit this measurement by remote control to the radio link from which it could be taken and fed into a computer. All Hainnu had to do was place it inside the main junction box and extend the small aerial for clarity of transmission. For this he was to receive one hundred thousand Swedish kronor every time he fitted a box.

Tonight, Pekka Hainnu was to exchange the box for the third time, and tomorrow he'd be richer by another hundred thousand. Two or three more of these, he wallowed in the pleasurable thought as he pulled on his white overalls and yellow safety helmet, and he'd be able to pay cash for his snug home in the woods of his native Finland, where a man could take a proper drink with his friends.

He would have been less cheerful had he known that the box he was to place in position tonight was not a test sample, as the previous two had been. It was packed with plastic explosive; sufficient to take off the top part of his torso as neatly as an Arkansas farmer could shake off the head of a chicken.

- - - - - - - - - - - - - - -

Goddard sat at the writing desk in Peter Svensson's apartment. He stared, unseeing, at the window-boxes of the block of flats opposite, tapping with lean fingers on the blotting pad in front of him. His long-jawed face bore the faintest trace of a frown and, for fully three minutes the unruly lock of slightly wave hair drooped towards an eyebrow before being brushed back into place.

It couldn't be said he was worried. He would have agreed with his chief, 'Worry' Gerald Dyson, head of Squawk, had once told him, back in the large rambling but secluded house at Stoke Poges, 'is a psychological luxury we can't afford.' Goddard's equivalent to worrying was an increase in his mental output on the problem in hand. He was uneasy. Jessup shouldn't have gone to Denmark at all. Goddard hadn't expected that sort of initiative. Jessup should have been satisfied with what he'd found in Dorn's cellar. There'd been enough stuff there for any amateur to get excited about. It was a miniscule loose end, but Goddard's rapid rise in the service was largely due to his attention to detail. Gerald Dyson had picked him out of a group of three MI6 field agents for just that reason. Dyson fully understood that an agent whose business it was to maintain close contact with Russian and other East European undercover agencies, especially on neutral territory, required more than normal operational skill and diplomacy. In this particularly delicate venture, extreme punctiliousness had been the pivotal quality for selection.

Goddard did not want to over-use Derringer. A hint from Dyson was all that had been needed to caution Goddard that, useful as he had been in the past, Derringer was now a mite passé. On the other hand nobody else was readily available. And Derringer had been good, if a trifle crude at times. Besides, it would be a tactical professional error to introduce a new or untried agent into an operation already half completed.

Goddard picked up the telephone and dialled Derringer's number.

- - - - - - - - - - - - - - -

The door knocker sounded excessively noisy in the little Ljunghusen apartment. Jessup looked at his wristwatch. Ten o'clock at night was late for visitors in this part of the world. He and Carol had dawdled over dinner, talking about Jessup's interview with Sorbron and Dorn's disappearing act. They were still at the coffee stage. Jessup glanced at Carol then placed his pipe on the side table and went to the door.

A subdued Martina stood in the darkness. 'I've been speaking to Heinrich on the telephone,' she said without preamble. 'Can I tell you about it?'

She didn't have to repeat her words, despite Jessup's involuntary exclamation at this astonishing announcement. He felt immediately uneasy but gave no sign of it to Martina.

She must have driven down from Malmö, and that meant half an hour's fast drive. He quickly ushered her inside, giving her one of his warmest smiles as he did so. 'You'd better come and sit down.' He took her coat and placed it on the bed as they went through into the sitting area.

Carol stood up holding out both hands to clasp Martina's in greeting. 'What's happened? David has been telling me about Heinrich.'

Jessup said, speaking over Martina's shoulder, 'Martina's had a telephone call from Heinrich.'

Carol immediately caught his mood of caution, tinged with tension, and concern showed on her face as she looked at Martina.

Martina began to explain. 'He called me. From Denmark.' She looked at Jessup as he came to her side, and it came out in a rush. 'David, what's going on? Heinrich said I was to tell you he understands what you had to do and doesn't blame you for it. He phoned only to stop me worrying.' She was twisting a saffron coloured silk scarf in her fingers in her agitation. Carol led her to the sofa. Martina looked very young and very confused, her long blonde hair clasped with a pin at the side of her white neck.

Jessup shot a swift look at his wife. She understood, and let him do the talking while she went into the kitchenette to make fresh coffee.

Jessup sat on a chair opposite Martina and began gently. 'Martina, you do realize he's a spy working for Soviet Russia, don't you? I told you that the other day.'

Martina looked at him with a show of determination. 'I know that. And I don't care. He's escaped and I think I know where he is.'

Jessup looked up at Carol, then said to Martina 'Did he tell you?'

'Not in so many words. But I'm sure.' She looked across at Carol, including them both in what she was saying. 'I wouldn't have come here just to tell you he rang me. I want you to help me. I mean us. Heinrich as well.'

Jessup said 'Listen Martina. I don't think we're in a position to help. I don't see how anybody could help him now. It's a political matter and my guess is that he's hiding until he can get back to the East, or perhaps to the Soviet consulate in Gothenburg where he might be helped by some diplomatic means.' Jessup knew, even as he spoke, that the words would make little sense to a woman as strong minded as Martina.

She said 'I believe I could persuade him to stay if I could only see him again.'

Jessup didn't want to tell her he'd already tried to get Dorn to defect, but neither had he forgotten his unspoken promise to Dorn.

Carol brought steaming coffee cups to them. She said 'You think it's quite out of the question, David? If Martina knows where he is couldn't we at least give it a try?'

One of the few things Jessup had learnt in his varied career was not to argue against a united female front. The logic, as always, was unassailable.

Carol sat down with her own coffee and turned her soft, liquid, questioning eyes on her husband. 'After all, if Martina were to succeed, it could do nothing but good. This wretched plan of the Russians would backfire, wouldn't it?'

Jessup had a pretty good idea that nothing would affect the Russian plan at this stage. The last few minutes he'd had with Sorbron and, after two hours of fruitless searching for Dorn in the Frihamn area, had convinced him that the Swedes were prepared to fight doggedly against any foe, without help from the West. Sorbron had left immediately for army headquarters in the north breathing fire and carrying with him enough evidence to start a war even if Dorn was never seen again. But Jessup realized that none of this was worth arguing about with Martina, nor could it have any influence on the way her mind was working. Come to that, maybe she was right. It wouldn't be the first time he'd stuck his neck out in a lost cause.

He sighed, picked up his pipe and said 'Alright, Martina. Let's consider the possibilities. First, where do you think he is?'

- - - - - - - - - - - - - -

Martina had left the flat over an hour earlier and it was well after one o'clock when Carol picked up the rubbish bag for tomorrow's collection from the communal bin. She had insisted Jessup should go to bed while she cleared the dinner dishes. She tiptoed past the foot of the bed and soundlessly opened the front door. She stepped out into the covered walkway, deeply in shadow from the bright moon rising above the tall Scots pine trees. Closing the door softly behind her, the plastic waste bag held in one hand, she stood for a moment, savouring the cool, fresh air. The muted lapping of the Baltic Sea on the beach two hundred yards away whispered through the surrounding woods.

The car park faced her across a border of low bushes. An elderly man stepped from the shadow of a mini-van and took the path leading through the trees to the main village road. Carol smiled to herself; a late visitor sensibly walking home to avoid the breathalyser. She went on quietly to the refuse cylinder discreetly placed in the wall at the end of the block.

- - - - - - - - - - - - - -

Kungslottet, near the small hamlet of Karlskuga, was not really a castle. It was a two storeyed compact stone and wood mini-mansion built by king Gustav the Fifth in 1910 and used by him as a hunting lodge especially for the pheasant introduced to Sweden three years earlier. But its twin turrets, bulging outwards from both wings, complete with battlements and archers' slits, had made the name stick from the beginning. The castle no longer belonged to the monarchy. It had been nationalized, with about a dozen others, in 1965, and officially designated as a retreat for members of parliament requiring a few days of concentrated and uninterrupted work on specially important state matters; a sort of communal Chequers. It was perfect cover for the secret military business meetings that were sometimes necessary. The extensive, labrynthine complex beneath Kungslottet was of more recent origin and covered six acres under the main structure. The surrounding thick forest of larch, pine and birch made excellent cover for transceiver aerials and satellite dishes. It was the focal point, the brain of Sweden's defence system. A tame press was willing to accept the official description and left the castle and its doings severely alone.

It was one o'clock and, after nearly five hours of discussions and briefings the senior officers in the defence organization of the realm were talking quietly in the common rooms or walking in the gardens of the spacious and secluded grounds. On the dot of eight that bright morning, Commander Stenberg, chief of Swedish security forces and anti-espionage groups, had given the floor to Sorbron. The Prime Minister was present but, as usual, was to remain silent until his chiefs of staff had presented their statements. The Prime Minister felt vaguely uneasy at Karl Sorbron's ebullient presentation of his case. There could be no doubting the man had all the facts. That had been clear from the moment they'd had their first meeting privately the night before. He felt that something was being overlooked.

Plans, photographs, schedules and a mass of small detail, collected by Dorn over the past two years, were laid out as exhibits on tables at the sides of the room. Sorbron had never had such limelight; he revelled in it. He had completed his review of the facts with the solemn pronouncement that, in his opinion – and he had even made that sound as if it was part of the evidence – it must be concluded that the Soviet Union was about to launch an offensive military operation on the south coast. Säpo's chief computer expert was even now working on a possible date for such an offensive, compiled from the sea and weather charts Dorn had made and which had been checked as reliable. Stenberg had followed Sorbron with a short account of recent subversive incidents aimed against the security of the state. Among the more important he listed the Spring 1982 break-in at the national telecommunications computer centre, where highly expert thieves had not only got into the Stockholm building undetected but had actually made copies, on its own equipment, of the telecommunications' security system. Stenberg cited the dates and possible objectives of the numerous submarine incursions into militarily sensitive Swedish waters since the blatant U137 incident at Horsfjörd in October 1982. He ended his account with a review of the more recent attempts to smuggle into Sweden, for re-sale to Czechoslovakia, highly sophisticated computer systems. These, he emphasised, were only the known incidents.

He had been careful to remind the military chiefs and strategists sitting in front of him that not all of even the known affairs were conclusively proved to be Russian, or Soviet-directed actions. As a political appointee, the youthful-looking forty year-old security head had been doing his best to follow his socialist Prime Minister's directive to the effect that nothing negative should be attributed to the Soviet Union without conclusive proof. The policy of neutrality, the standing directive stipulated, had to be maintained, if necessary at the cost of offending the less sensitive western alliance.

BALTIC INCIDENT

The military chiefs kept their counsel on what constituted 'conclusive proof' and, to them, with one or two exceptions, the evidence for Russian culpability was circumstantially overwhelming.

Intensive debate had followed. Sorbron, smiling confidentially, had successfully parried questions about the missing spy. Dorn, he had answered, was of little consequence; it was the evidence that mattered. Besides, Dorn had been identified personally by Jessup who was himself an unimpeachable witness. That brought the most obvious question from the Minister for Defence, Hendrik Olsson. Who was this Jessup? If he had been on such friendly terms with the spy Dorn, could he be trusted? Had säpo checked him out thoroughly? Stenberg had smiled and nodded to Sorbron. Olsson was handed a dossier. It was a complete file, with photographs, of Jessup, compiled from both the Swedish Foreign Office and the police records of three towns in England where Jessup had lived. Sorbron had been thorough. Even before Dorn's house had been searched by his agents, he had used the intricate west European police tracking system. He had had a complete report from the British Home Office by special telex an hour before he had met Jessup in his office. The minister stopped questioning and became absorbed in studying the report.

Half an hour later the group had split up to study the documents displayed on the tables and, by half past eleven, the plenary session had met for a decision on the action to be taken. Senior officer, Admiral Knut Dahlgren, had felt himself and his service to be under acute political pressure as a result of the constant and tantalizing game of hide and seek he was forced to play with the Russian submarines. It was close to becoming a joke with the rest of the military staff, as well as with half the Swedish population. Dahlgren determined to salvage some of his damaged image. He summed up the mood of the meeting with a step by step analysis of growing Soviet interference in the country. It ought to be observed, he had reminded the group, that the recent and intensified activities of Russia within the country's borders, culminating in the present horrific disclosure of a Soviet plan to attack Sweden, had coincided with an inexplicable diplomatic appointment: namely that of the known and high-ranking KGB agent, Viktor Karjagin, as Consul General in Gothenburg. If we link together the clandestine military activities, Dahlgren had said, with this particularly significant diplomatic move, then we have all the ingredients necessary for a smooth and relatively bloodless occupation. The admiral had concluded that the situation called for immediate mobilization.

The Prime Minister, the säpo chief and Ragnar Nilsson, säpo's computer expert, were probably the only three not to have taken a lunch break. Although he had said practically nothing, the Prime Minister had indicated, more by his silence, the gravity of the situation. No one commented over lunch, or afterwards in the gardens and common rooms, but all knew he would be working overtime in collating the necessary details before making a positive proposal.

A discreet messenger passed from small groups to individuals deep in their own thoughts, in the short interval after lunch. The Prime Minister had called them together for two o'clock. At one minute to the hour the nine military and intelligence chiefs, together with their advisers, were again in the conference room. Nobody was talking. No one was relaxed. No one smoked, and no one fidgeted with the mineral water in front of him. Each person was occupied with his own deliberations on the emergency. If one thought predominated it was the awful spectacle that what had been prepared for and feared for so many years was about to fall upon them. Only the accidental discovery, as it seemed to them, of a key spy had given them the chance to prepare their military defences.

The Prime Minister entered the room. His lined face and rather large mouth, tilted upwards at the sides and giving the impression that he was always ready to smile, which indeed he was, now appeared grave.

He sat down at the head of the long table and began without hesitation. 'Gentlemen. There are three items I wish to bring to your attention.' He looked at each of them in turn as he spoke. Not ever their heads, but straight into their eyes. It was a habit he had cultivated over his thirty-five years in politics; a habit he had deliberately studied in the best public speakers. He also had a tendency, observers noticed, to marshall what he had to say in groups of three.

'First, I have just been speaking by telephone to my colleagues leading the other government parties. They will join us shortly. Meanwhile, they have approved my present course of action in this emergency, provided you gentlemen are also agreed.'

One or two of the military chiefs exchanged glances. They were among the few in Sweden who believed it impossible to operate a serious military operation by means of a democratic vote. The PM's allusion to the other political parties, they thought, was the first sign of weakness in the chain of command.

The Prime Minister went on. 'Second. We have, now, the computer analysis of a possible timing of the offensive indicated in the documents you have studied. It appears likely that the winds, tides, general sea conditions and other data point to favourable circumstances for a seaborne landing on our south coast within the next forty-eight hours.' He paused to let the information sink in.

'We already know that forces of the Warsaw Pact countries have planned major military manoeuvres for a two-week period beginning tomorrow. The question is whether the Russians intend military action against us under cover of this exercise.

You are aware, more than anyone, that the south west part of our coast is very lightly defended. It is possible that foreign submarine and air incursions in the east and south east have been designed to mislead us. On the other hand, as Field Marshall Stig Holmberg explained to us this morning, a conventional type of landing of troops on the south western beaches would be exceedingly exposed to air attack, since even the fastest modern tanks could not get across the shallow water and wide sand quickly enough.' He looked to the Field Marshall for confirmation. 'We cannot, therefore, discount the possibility of tactical deception. The computers are working on alternatives.

When my colleagues arrive we shall draft an urgent message to be sent to the United Nations Secretary General and to the Security Council, and also decide what form of approach is to be made to the Soviet Ambassador. But I fear the time is too short to rely totally on diplomacy. We must at least be prepared to defend ourselves by military means.'

His small audience heard the words 'military means' they had themselves helped to manufacture. Their professional lives had been spent in preparing and refining the means for this exigency. But it was hard to bring their emotions into line with the realities of their profession. Not straight away. They heard the words and understood them, but their feelings could not absorb the sense of physical action the words implied. An enemy of flesh and blood was nothing like the theories they'd worked with.

The sun streamed in through the south side windows and they felt torpid in their well-cut green and blue uniforms. The Prime Minister understood their mood.

The Prime Minister's third point was that, if continuous talks with Moscow produced negative results during the next twenty-four hours, then the military staff should be prepared to go to 'Red Alert'. There were two final steps laid down in Swedish military orders for defensive preparations against an invader. Red Alert was the first. It was practised only every two years. On this order, every man and machine already serving with the armed forces had to be in a state of full readiness, all engines running, at depots and assembly points throughout the country within six hours. But if the movement of personnel and equipment involved in Red Alert was enormous, then the final order, 'Execute', was colossal.

Recognizing the limitations of a total population far less than that of greater London, and trying to defend a large territory in time of war, the Swedish government had planned a policy of total civilian mobilization in the event that the order to 'Execute' was given. The little yellow book explaining the duties and dangers of careful underground resistance for use during the second World War was being constantly revised. Every citizen under the age of fifty – that meant more than a million and a half – had a specific task to do. Most men and women within the age-group would be called to the nearest military or civil defence headquarters.

The Execute operation involved a major national upheaval and the myriad strands of mobilization, with its attendant mechanical and electronic apparatus, amounted to top secret information. For, while every member of the adult population knew, to a greater or lesser degree, his place within the smaller groupings of military or civil defence, the whole picture of its calculated effectiveness, its total pattern of organization, was known only to the Prime Minister, certain government officials, and the chiefs of the military staffs. Even then, they could know the details only by referring constantly to the computer-stored information.

All combatants would move from assembly points to battle stations. Fighter 'planes would take off; warships would slip their moorings and sail out to sea; tanks and armoured vehicles would emerge from their camouflaged positions deep in the forests; strategic bridges and tunnels would have their already-placed explosive charges linked and ready for detonation; police would be rearmed. Field hospitals and equipment would be loaded into aeroplanes and helicopters, the staff would board and wait for news of the first battle area. All radio and electronic devices would be integrated in centralized command posts, the secret codes opened and read. Above all, radio and physical traffic between major military posts and the all-important and top-secret arms supply dumps, hidden in forests and under mountains, would increase to a point never before tested. The whole defence complex of Sweden, its positions, secret codes and communications systems, would be functioning. Nearly eight million people in one of the most advanced of the world's technocracies would be under the strictest of military regulations.

The men sitting at the conference table knew that the Execute instruction would be a national disaster if ordered prematurely. The Prime Minister knew it, too. Red Alert, he said, could be ordered. But the instruction to Execute would only be given if the Soviet Union did not send out the agreed 'Exercise' signal. He reminded them of that agreement.

Under an international treaty, made ten years earlier as a safeguard against mistaken counter-strikes, the Soviet Union and the United States had agreed on the protocol to be observed whenever one of them mounted large-scale military exercises. It took the form of a coded signal to be sent to the opposing bloc and to those countries closest to the place of the exercise, especially in areas of great sensitivity like the Baltic. Decoded, the signal would read 'Exercise' on the monitoring computers. The signal was to be sent whenever an exercising force – usually by sea or air – crossed into sensitive areas throughout the world. For safety reasons, it was sent in triplicate; from the power responsible for the exercise, usually Moscow, Washington or NATO headquarters; from the country under the mock attack; and from the 'attacking' force itself.

One of the greatest areas of sensitivity in the world lay both sides of longitude 13'30" East, in the Baltic Sea. NATO forces were expected to send out the Exercise signal when they crossed from West to East and Warsaw Pact forces on crossing from East to West of the longitude. Sweden had received the signal eight times since the treaty had been signed. The Prime Minister was proposing they wait for the Russian Exercise code for up to half an hour after the Warsaw Pact battle fleet had crossed the 13'30" East longitude – assuming they headed that way – then, if it were not received, would activate Execute.

Sorbron left the meeting elated. It had been something of a coup for him, and his promotion to Stockholm – assuming the army did its bit on the southern beaches – seemed assured. He knew accurate information when he saw it. Above all, he knew that the British agent Jessup had worked for was an impeccable source. Unofficial, of course.

Like her husband, Carol had fallen in love with the big cat purr of the Jaguar's four litre engine. In her battered Volkswagon she was, as Jessup injudiciously pointed out, a devoted clutch-driver. She was prepared to agree. It was pure magic to her to be able to simply press on the gas pedal for a fast, smooth take-off without having to tug at a tiresome lever.

This morning, as she sat at the wheel on the way to Malmö with David beside her, she had other things to think about. She didn't think she had pushed him too far in giving active support to Martina's idea. He'd already seemed receptive, despite his initial questioning opposition. That was only his male method of rationalizing. They had finally decided, the previous evening, that there could be no harm in trying to persuade Dorn to ask for asylum in Sweden, with Martina as the more than willing bait.

They had learnt from Martina that Dorn had found a bolthole in the castle outside Helsingør, made famous as Elsinore in Shakespeare's Hamlet. Dorn and Martina had used the castle as a tryst on a number of occasions. They had loved to lose themselves in the anonymity of the many tourists that the Danish castle attracted. The vestry behind the altar, they had discovered to their delight, was used for religious services that took place in the castle's chapel once every two months. Dorn's unwillingness to be seen with Martina in public they now understood well enough. The castle was ideal cover. In his apparent eagerness to assure Martina of his safety, Dorn had identified their personal hideaway as his temporary refuge.

BALTIC INCIDENT

Helsingør was the closest point to Sweden, immediately opposite the Swedish town of Helsingborg. It was to Helsingborg that Carol now drove, once they had picked up Martina. Jessup had imposed one condition: that he should go to see Dorn alone first, on the slightest chance that there might be complications. But nothing could keep Carol and Martina from being equally insistent that they drive north with him.

Martina was eagerly awaiting them on a drab central Malmö street, outside the tobacconist's shop above which she rented a flat. She was unable to sort out her feelings even now. She didn't know whether to be unhappy about Dorn's arrest or glad he had escaped and the possibility that she might be able to get him to stay in the West for good. For the moment, she was willing to thrust the complications to the back of her mind. The first thing was to see him again.

Helsingborg was just over an hour's drive from Malmö and Carol concentrated on the road that ran along the coast. Even if she had been looking for it, she would not have seen the metalled grey Saab combie following the Jaguar. Derringer kept his distance and was always at least a mile behind. There was no need for him to keep the Jaguar in sight. The small magnetic transmitter, the shape of a delicate pill-box, had fitted snugly and out of casual view behind one of the Jaguar's twin fog lamps where he had carefully placed it the night before. He looked down again at the small box lying on the seat beside him, bleeping evenly once every five seconds.

He had not expected to hear so soon from Goddard. The telephone call the evening before was almost peremptory. It was certainly specific. Keep Jessup away from anybody and anything that might be connected to 'Operation Searchlight', at all costs, Jessup had said. Derringer knew he hadn't meant that literally. He had grown old with MI6 and knew they rarely had thoughts of that kind. But Goddard had sounded fractionally anxious about what Jessup might do next; had even asked Derringer to telephone a progress report at six the same evening. A weak link's a bad link, Derringer had said to himself. Get rid of him if necessary. Well, heavy persuasion, anyway. So Derringer had decided to bring his own form of persuasion with him. It was a memento from the old days. Even the showing of it had often given a certain point to his commands. He felt its hardness in his right-hand pocket now. Quite like old times. Only this time it was impossible to imagine having to use it on an amateur like Jessup.

He had been too far away to see why Jessup had stopped in the Malmö street. But when the Jaguar had moved on and he had slowly passed the spot moments later Derringer had seen the shop. Jessup had obviously stopped for tobacco.

Three quarters of an hour later, Derringer was taken by surprise, and nearly missed Jessup. He knew almost exactly where the Jaguar must be, but he hadn't expected Jessup would want to take a boat trip as well. Perhaps this wasn't routine after all. Derringer felt the old hunting instinct and his lips stretched in a tight smile. A challenge again, perhaps more promising than the motor-boat incident.

The Jaguar had to be somewhere in the large open car park on the hard packed sand, constructed for day trippers to Denmark. As he drove slowly towards it he saw Jessup walk away from the car park, making for the booking office. There were ten people standing in the queue. It would give him time to park the car. The deerstalker went well with his tweed suit. He certainly didn't look Scandinavian. Perhaps nineteen-thirtyish

BALTIC INCIDENT

English. The hat was functional, too. Derringer pulled the peak over his eyes and stepped out of the car.

Carol and Martina sat talking in the back seats of the Jaguar. Carol stopped in mid sentence. 'Just a minute. That man over there. I saw him last night outside the flat.' She frowned.

Martina followed her gaze then let out an excited exclamation 'It's the man who was supposed to be watching Heinrich. It's Derringer.!'

Carol sat up, fully alerted, 'And he's certainly following David.'

The queue at the kiosk had quickly dwindled and Jessup was the third in line. Derringer had paused at the exit of the car park, watching the queue.

Carol stepped out of the car to watch. Although she was some distance away, she could still recognize her husband at the head of the queue. Then the two men moved at the same moment. Jessup walked away from the kiosk, following the trickle of passengers round a corner and out of sight. Derringer walked quickly from behind the protecting cover of a car and started towards the ticket window.

'And what could he have been doing at midnight outside the flat?' said Carol.

Martina joined Carol outside the car and leaned her elbows on the roof. 'If he's following David, he's heading straight for Heinrich, too, and that could make things difficult for us. Do you think we should do something?'

'I think we should,' Carol said, thoughtfully. She looked at Martina, considering the possibility. Then she said 'If you're willing, I suggest we do it now.' Carol's face took on a grim smile that brought out lines of determination at the corners of her wide mouth. She looked across the car roof at the younger woman. 'Fancy a short boat trip?'

After a moment's incomprehension, Martina's lovely face reflected the mood and her large eyes twinkled. 'Why not? Why leave all the fun to the men?'

BALTIC INCIDENT
Chapter Seven

From the sea, the enormous pile of Kronberg castle was an impressive landmark. Its massive greyish brown walls rose directly from the waves and rocks of the Öresund, the green of its coppered roofs strongly reflecting the bright sun. Built in the sixteenth century, the large dormer windows marked its Dutch style. Four towers rose from different points in the castle walls. Three of them looked like the slender minarets of a mosque. The fourth was a great rounded structure resembling, at a distance, a fattened and straightened leaning tower of Pisa.

Jessup threaded his way through the crowds as he crossed the first moat towards the heavy arch that led to the inner grounds of the castle. Beyond the archway – broad enough to carry a row of houses – a second wide moat faced him, the walls of the central structure rising straight out of the still water on the far side. Ducks and swans were being fed by children. Every nationality seemed to be represented. Lean, sober-suited Japanese husbands gently shepherded their black haired and brightly dressed daughters. A coachload of middle-aged Americans, sporting large straw hats among the women and loosely hanging, multi-coloured shirts among the men, straggled along the way. A strong smell of Gaulloises cigarettes pervaded the air under the archway as a group of young Frenchmen jostled to look more closely at the Danish porcelain models of the castle on the over-full souvenir tables. A German couple moved to one side of the counter to study an old wall poster advertizing Derek Jacobi playing Hamlet in the castle grounds.

The crowd proved to be useful cover for Derringer. He stopped at the souvenir counters, for the dirt road along the side of the inner moat was broader and more open and he could be spotted more easily if Jessup should look round. He was convinced Jessup was on his way to meet Dorn. When Goddard, on the telephone, had told him Dorn was missing, he hadn't immediately connected that fact with the brief he'd received to keep Jessup under wraps. He knew now. There could be no other explanation for Jessup's sudden desire for sightseeing.

At the end of the moat, the hard sanded road turned sharply right, away from the ancient grassy breastworks facing the sea and the coast of Sweden, and entered a thirty foot-long tunnel that led directly into a central courtyard. Jessup seemed to know his way around. Derringer almost lost sight of him in the glare of the sunshine as he emerged from the tunnel. A hundred or more tourists chatted and strolled about, singly or in groups. One group of Dutch youths was playing with the drinking water fountain, a modern transformation of the old castle well, in the centre of the yard. Another had clustered at the far side near a door that led to the naval museum housed within the castle.

Just in time, Derringer saw Jessup enter an open doorway next to the museum entrance. Derringer crossed the courtyard and, with the air of a curious visitor and to all appearances casually, he looked inside. Slowly his eyes adjusted to the gloom of the royal chapel. Beyond the first age-old pew the aisle stretched away to his left towards the transept and altar. The chapel was empty and the silence inside was a marked contrast with the crowded courtyard. Jessup, it seemed, had been translated. Derringer stepped inside, automatically casting a swift look to left and right of the doorway, and closed the heavy oak door behind him. He began to walk towards the altar at the east end of the chapel. He saw, without registering it, the old Germanic and the more modern Danish inscriptions carved into the stone walls; he had eyes only for movement. Ridiculous though he knew the idea to be, he was alert to the possibility that Jessup just might be waiting to pounce on him from behind one of the low doors that closed the entrance to each pew.

He reached the dim transept. The only light came from low-powered, ornately shaded electric lightbulbs hanging on chains from the ceiling and dully reflected from the brass cross and seven-branched candelabra standing on the communion table. The subdued sounds of the holidaymakers outside only served to emphasize the silence of the sanctuary. Derringer began to think he'd been mistaken. Perhaps Jessup had not entered the chapel at all. He looked again at the altar. On each side of an elaborately woven Chi Rho fabric, remembered from his Greek Orthodox childhood as the first two letters in the Greek word for Christ, was a small round grid, a latticed hole of about an inch in diameter. Another memory from his innocent years; of the devout congregation, at least those near the front, straining their eyes to see if the priest was looking at them through the peephole; of his mother, shawled in black, warning him to behave in case the priest was watching them. He should have thought of it before. The vestry was behind the altar.

He moved silently to the side of the communion table. There was no door. Just a heavy velvet curtain covering the entrance to a short passage leading to the vestry. He stepped through into the passage. It should have been dark behind the altar. Instead, a slender thread of light shone on to his feet as he came carefully up to the partly open vestry door. Looking through the crack he could see nothing but the wooden panels of an opposite wall. But the voices were clear enough. Dorn's, then Jessup's. He took from his pocket the small P38K Walther and eased it into a handy position. He didn't expect to have to use it with Jessup, but Dorn was quite a different kettle of fish.

Jessup had entered the vestry less than five minutes earlier. The whitewashed, shabby room could hardly be called furnished. There was a wall-long wardrobe containing an assortment of clerical clothes, a sofa and an old table. Dorn had made the best of his third night's confinement. The deep shadows under his eyes from too many rough episodes were fainter. He had even managed to bathe, not without a certain agility, in the cracked handbasin. Only his tousled hair and less than white shirt remained to indicate the week's ordeal.

If Dorn was surprised to see Jessup, he hid it well. After only a moment's hesitation he had come towards him enfolding him in all his old warmth. 'You turn up in the most unusual places, old friend' he said, stretching out both hands to Jessup.

Jessup had been prepared for at least resentment, even anger, despite what Martina had told him. Instead, he was confronted by an apparently unchanged friend; he was certainly relieved at Dorn's normality. Under the circumstances he could have expected a much worse reception. Jessup had to concede Dorn had nerve. 'Frankly, Heinrich, I think that's my line. What's more, you have an abominable taste in furnishings.' He indicated the rough room with a sweep of his arm.

'Can't afford any decent help at today's prices, David.' He nodded towards the door, 'Haven't brought the cavalry, I hope'

Jessup shook his head. 'Of course not. They've got everything they need.' He began to feel the tension ebb from his tautened nerves. It had cost him something to walk unannounced through the vestry door. 'Take this, for starters. Carol's idea.' He handed Dorn the packet of sandwiches and the flask of hot coffee she had thoughtfully provided.

'A gem of a girl, that wife of yours.' Dorn opened the wrappings and began to munch hungrily at the bread as Jessup untopped the coffee. Dorn spoke through a mouthful of crust and ham, 'How in hell's name did you know I was here? Nobody's supposed to know about this place.'

'Nobody?' said Jessup. He couldn't help the smile that came.

Dorn stopped chewing. 'Absolutely correct, old man. Martina. Right? Bright girl. Only gave her a hint. Surprising what the ladies can recall under certain circumstances, isn't it? She alright?'

Jessup gave Dorn a keen look. If Goddard had shown signs of intelligence, Dorn must be a genius by comparison. 'Heinrich, this is plain crazy. You can't go on pretending nothing's happened. How long do you think you can keep running? You can't hide here forever.'

Dorn took the steaming coffee from Jessup. He did not reply immediately. He wiped a crumb from his drooping moustache, eyeing Jessup thoughtfully. Then he said, abruptly, 'Listen, I've had a lot of time to think about what you said yesterday. Maybe there's something in it after all. I mean staying in the West. The big question is, though, what could I offer? They'd want something pretty important in return, wouldn't they?'

The door burst open and Derringer stood four paces from them, his gun pointing at Dorn's belly.

Dorn gave Jessup a thunderous look. 'I see you didn't bring the cavalry, only the fifth column.'

Jessup was speechless for several seconds, trying to comprehend both the gun, so rudely thrust towards them, and the accusation put to him so uncharacteristically harsh by Dorn.

Derringer answered for him. 'None of his doing.' he said to Dorn, motioning to Jessup. 'I don't have to rely on amateurs like some people.' Derringer's big head, with its sandy hair protruding from beneath the incongruous hat, was jutting slightly forward, the gun in his outstretched hand.

'Is that correct? Dorn barked at Jessup. 'You didn't know you were being followed?'

Jessup finally found his voice. 'Absolutely not. I had no idea.' He wasn't at all sure what Derringer intended and he didn't like the gunplay one bit. Somehow the game had changed course while he blinked. It felt as if somebody had taken the ball from his feet and now he was no longer sure which goal to run for. For that matter, he wasn't even sure which team he was playing for. A smile flickered again to Dorn's face as he turned his attention to Derringer. 'You look ridiculous, Stanley. An old man playing with toy guns. You intend using it?'

'Not on him. He could still be useful.' Derringer nodded slightly towards Jessup. He knew his reflexes weren't as fast as they used to be. Long experience, the only safe substitute for fast reflex movement, made him keep the gun pointed at Dorn. 'But it would be no loss if my finger gave an old man's twitch when you're in line.' He jabbed the door shut with his right foot. 'The party's over, Heinrich. You've done what you came to do. According to your boss, Stavrinsky, "M" section is delighted with your work. Wish I could say the same for you, Jessup. Your boss doesn't seem so pleased. You've become a little too curious. Killed the cat, you know.'

'If you're referring to Goddard, he's not my boss.'

Derringer interjected 'Oh, you did know, didn't you, Heinrich, that Goddard was the guiding light for our friend here?'

Dorn turned to Jessup, his eyes narrowed. 'I guessed.' he said shortly. 'And it's of no importance.' He raised the plastic cup still in his hand. 'Mind if I finish my breakfast?'

Jessup had finally recovered from the first shock of having the wrong end of a gun face him. His expression changed. He would obviously have to get used to the bizarre incidents that seemed to be the lot of the undercover agent. He'd swallowed nearly everything that had happened until now. His mood changed to one of anger. He was determined not to be pushed around any more, like a blindfolded man in the dark. He said to Derringer 'Since you appear to know precisely what is going on, be good enough to explain what the hell you're doing here waving that thing around.' He deliberately looked away from Derringer, sat on the sofa and felt in his pockets for the tobacco pouch, perfectly aware that his movements might change Derringer's mind about pointing the gun at Dorn. He began to fill the bowl of his pipe with studied carefulness.

'Let's just say I have a watching brief. About twenty-four hours, to be more precise.' Derringer smiled broadly. Without taking his eyes from Dorn he took two paces further into the room and ledged himself comfortably on one end of the table. 'And if Goddard's not exactly your boss, you did tell him he could pull the strings.' Derringer gave a throaty chuckle. He was enjoying himself. He had the air of a completely heartless child, whose moral sense has yet to be developed, watching the fly whose wings he has just torn off stagger in hopeless circles. Only he hadn't the excuse of immaturity. 'I'm acting as your baby-sitter again, Dr Jessup. And now Dorn's here, I don't doubt I'd be doing somebody a service by keeping him here, too. Just for the duration.'

'You've flipped, old man.' Dorn's grin had disappeared. Derringer was attempting to play God when everyone knew he was an outsized lackey. 'You seem to forget I know your form. You're just a little man with a big mouth. What do you know that the world didn't know a week before?'

'Tiresome, tiresome, Heinrich. You think Moscow doesn't know about your weakness for the Western flelshpots? You think you've managed to hide your flirtation with the West and' Derringer paused, relishing the moment 'with that delicious filly, Martina?' The grin was wide; it looked like the mouth of a frog.

'None of your damn' business!' Dorn spat out the words.

Derringer's amusement increased as he realized he had succeeded in goading Dorn. 'Right, Heinrich. It's not my business. But how in heaven's name do you think Stavrinsky wouldn't find out? Silly boy. Absolutely against the rules to keep her in your house for days on end – or should I say endless nights? And really, Heinrich, to talk marriage with her as well! Quite reprehensible.'

'You bastard! You bugged my bedroom!'

'Correction, dear boy. It was the whole house. And done on the express orders of Stavrinsky. But don't let that detail concern you. You were, as our American friends would say, the fall guy from the beginning.'

BALTIC INCIDENT

Jessup spoke to Dorn, jabbing his pipe stem in the direction of Derringer, 'Why should Goddard feed him nonsense information like that?'

'Oh, it wasn't Goddard.' Derringer was warming to the baiting game. 'Sure, Goddard pays me to look after you, but the real jam on the bread comes from Stavrinsky's "M" committee over the water in Leningrad. And for your information, Jessup, Stavrinsky is Heinrich's personal puppeteer, his boss right here in Sweden.'

Dorn turned to Jessup with a sardonic grin produced for Derringer's benefit. 'Might have guessed it. He's never left Moscow's payroll. Working for both sides, as usual.'

Jessup didn't like the sound of that and wondered just how well Goddard knew Derringer. Was it credible that Goddard had told Derringer to keep him a virtual prisoner? And if so, for what purpose? Goddard could certainly not know that Dorn was here, too. Derringer had practically admitted that, anyway. It occurred to him then that the time spent in the castle was, in some obscure way, only aiding the Russian plan, which was why Derringer could afford to sit back and enjoy their discomfort, turning the screw with bits of information to torment them, and in the knowledge that whatever was said would have no significance in a few hours time. Apart from the complications involved by the fact that the women were waiting for them on the other side of the Sund, it now seemed imperative for Dorn to defect, carrying with him some key item of information to the Swedes, perhaps the whereabouts of this Stavrinsky. The imponderables flashed through his mind as he heard Derringer respond to Dorn.

'Of course I am. And they both know it. That's why I'm still useful and you're not.'

Dorn had leaned back against the wall after draining the cup and placing it on top of the wardrobe at his side. He had stuffed both hands deep into his pockets and seemed to be trying to dispel the tension that Derringer had created in the room within the last two minutes. 'Explain.' he said. 'You said yourself Stavrinsky was satisfied.'

'He is.' Derringer eased his position on the table. Dorn's relaxed attitude was infectious. 'Perhaps you overlooked the key word in the operation's code name. "Operation Searchlight" means just what it implies. You, of all people, ought to know. Wars are won and lost by intelligence – or the lack of it. "Searchlight" is an intelligence operation, not a military one. The Soviet Union has no intention of invading Sweden. At least not yet.' Derringer tapped his head with his left index finger, 'Information, lad, that's what's needed. Lots of it. Piddling about with submarines along the coast, playing with a load of sophisticated computer information – all that's important, but only up to a point. What really matters is, How does it work? What exactly do the Swedes do when faced with invasion? Precise numbers, timing, organization and the lack of it. What's the code system that will open up those ammunition dumps? How will the population react? The Russians had the final answer to all those problems: persuade the Swedes to lay it open of their own free-will. The pressure point was to get them so worried that they'd have to implement their "Execute" directive. I'm sure I don't have to tell you what that involves.

In short, get them to react to an invasion without Russia having to go to the trouble of invading. Neat, isn't it? You collected every bit of information as conscientiously as only a German can. Your job, Heinrich, was to make an invasion look convincing. You had to get caught with the genuine goods. All that marvellous information you collected had to be replaced in your possession. Stavrinsky himself saw to that. He even made sure Jessup would find the first lot of bait while you were out. Five times Stavrinsky had to use the guest key you gave him to get back into the house when you were out. The evidence had to be placed and replaced until Jessup found his moment to look for it. Couldn't have you getting suspicious if you stumbled over all the paperwork you thought was safely in Moscow, could he? It took a month for Stavrinsky to make sure of your erratic programme with Martina and Jessup.'

Derringer poked his gun in the air towards Dorn. 'You see, lad, you had the two qualities essential to the whole intelligence operation. You had the right background and the best training. And you had become expendable – even while you were still operating in West Berlin. "Contaminated" is the word they use, I think. Indeed, it was better to have you arrested. And there was Jessup, right on hand, to see that you were. Much more genuine that way. Only you were not supposed to escape.'

If Dorn was shocked at the knowledge that he'd been taken for a long ride, he did not show it. His big frame seemed to remain relaxed against the dirty white wall. But although he hid it well from Derringer, Jessup could almost feel the tension build up in him and in that moment Jessup knew Dorn was seeking the crack, the weakness, in Derringer's grip on them. It wouldn't be easy to find one if Derringer kept his distance.

The revelation that he, too, was part of a Russian plan against Sweden made his stomach turn over. Now he knew why he'd had reservations about Goddard. Obviously a handpicked man for a very dirty political manoeuvre. It was unbelievable that Britain should be aiding the Russians in a Machiavellian attempt to cheat Sweden of her most important military secrets. It was a laugh, a thundering good giggle, if it were not so bloody serious, that he and Heinrich had been well and truly conned. Jessup could see Derringer had relished enlightening them with that damning snippet. Whatever talents he'd had were clearly being reduced to a worn and cynical man's crude self-indulgence. There didn't seem to be a thing he or Dorn could do about it.

Derringer stood away from the table, the gun hardly wavering from Dorn's stomach. 'All that is necessary now is to keep you both out of the way for a few hours. Let's see, about twelve hours from now and the fun should begin. After that,' he spoke to Dorn, his sandy eyebrows twitching maliciously, 'you can resume your running for all I care, though I doubt you'd get far. Our friend Jessup can go home to bed. It'll be a little too late to talk to Säpo, and I'm not sure they'd want to listen again, anyway.'

'Why twelve hours?' Dorn asked the question naturally, but Jessup knew there was a coiled spring hiding behind Dorn's calm demeanor, waiting for the right moment.

'Didn't I tell you that?' Derringer raised the eyebrows another half inch in a mocking question-mark above his bulbous nose, a drinker's protuberance tinged permanently red. 'Your chief, Stavrinsky, is probably at Swedcom at this very moment. A few twiddles on the computer and the Swedish government will open their Pandora box.

Now let's get on with it. There'll be plenty of time to talk later. But first my arm's aching. Can't hold this thing forever. Jessup!' Derringer commanded, 'take a look in that wardrobe.'

BALTIC INCIDENT

Jessup turned to do so. There was no point in arguing. The old brown double doors creaked open to show a line of black gowns. The Danish Lutheran priests' garment was a cross between a cassock and a monk's habit, tied round the middle with a thin rope.

'Good. This place has its conveniences after all.' His voice went harsh as he spoke to Dorn. 'You know I'll use this, Heinrich,' he indicated the gun in his hand, 'try not to move a muscle in the wrong direction. Now, take the ropes off those gowns and tie Jessup's arms behind his back. I'll look after you myself.'

Dorn knew it would only anger Derringer if he did half a job. It was very necessary to keep him happy at this moment. Both instinct and training had led him, the night before when the crowds had gone and the castle had become quiet, to look for an alternative way out of the chapel. He had found nothing but the door opposite the chapel entrance, the one he'd discovered with Martina that gave access to the slim tower that pointed skywards like a beacon – and had probably been used as one in times past – high above the waters of the Öresund. Two hundred and thirty-four wedge-shaped stone steps, he had counted them, spiralled steeply upwards to the open balcony at the top of the tower.

It wasn't much of a chance, but if he managed to get into the dark tower without getting shot at least he'd have evened the odds by being out of the line of fire for a time. He'd have to play it by ear after that. He realized that part of the plan depended on the supposition that Derringer did not want to harm Jessup, since that could only pose more problems for him later.

For the moment, Dorn did exactly as he was bid. He took the cord from the vestments in the wardrobe and told Jessup to take off his jacket and roll up his shirt-sleeves. Fortunately, Jessup had left his overcoat in the

car. Derringer could not be fooled by the lack of elementary precautions, and he would certainly know that
you just don't tie a man's arms and wrists over any form
of clothing. Jessup's pipe slid out of the breast pocket as
Dorn placed the jacket on the sofa. Dorn chose a simple
seaman's simple figure of eight for Jessup's wrists. The
two loops of the knot would satisfy Derringer without
being too tight for Jessup.

Jessup turned his back to Dorn for the loops of the rope
to be drawn over his wrists and arms, but for the last
few moments his brain had been concerned with the
ten thousand dollar question. So he asked Derringer,
as Dorn worked behind his back, 'Why the devil did
the Russians want to bring the British into their operation?'

Derringer showed a childish delight in filling in the details. 'They didn't, old son. When Squawk – and that
means Goddard's boss, Gerald Dyson, by the way – received certain information from West German intelligence on Air Germanic, they followed the lead straight
to Heinrich. Most of Heinrich's spying activities are on
Dyson's Scandinavian file.' He relaxed a fraction more
and ledged again on the table top. 'No doubt there was
a beautiful diplomatic row about an apparent Russian
invasion. Then the Russians had to come up with the
truth about "Operation Searchlight" or be exposed.
Some influential hawk or other in British intelligence
had the brilliant idea of proposing cooperation instead.
After that, whatever "Searchlight" discovers will be
just as useful to the West as to the East. Knowing MI6
as I do, I don't doubt somebody, probably Dyson, persuaded the powers that be that Britain and her allies
could get more mileage out of the operation than if they
simply exposed the plan to the Swedes. Of course, that
will depend on the number and quality of the staff they

put into Sweden to monitor the Swedish reactions to "Execute". I guess the Russians thought they would do rather better than the British, since they have been establishing their network, run from the Gothenburg Consulate, for years. Got the better of the bargain, I should think.'

Jessup winced as Dorn pulled on his right shoulder from the wrist, and Derringer misinterpreted the look. 'Not very pleasant to think of good old England be-having like a second-rate ex-colony, is it?' Pleasant or not, the lines on Derringer's face creased in a mirthless smile.

Hell, he's right, Jessup thought. Betrayal of a friendly neutral ain't the first thing the great British public would think of. On the other hand it might just be con-sidered the art of the possible in the mind of an avari-cious grocer from Grantham.

Dorn straightened up from behind Jessup and stood to one side, facing Derringer. 'Satisfied?'

'Very rarely. Over here, Jessup.' Jessup felt the cord tighten and bite into his wrists as he tried to move his fingers.

It couldn't be described as a plan, the idea that formed in his mind just then. Jessup was simply aware of a cou-ple of basic facts. Dorn still had the free use of his hands while he, Jessup, would be momentarily between Dorn and Derringer. He had to admit it could be dangerous, too. But what chance had they, once Dorn's hands had also been reduced to immobility? He walked over to Derringer, looking deliberately more uncomfortable than he felt and with hesitating steps. He hoped Dorn had noticed.

Jessup turned his back for Derringer to check the bonds. Derringer sat, still confident, on the edge of the small table, his left leg on the floor for support, his right foot swinging a brown shoe carelessly to and fro. He raised his left hand to test the cord on Jessup's wrists. For a moment – all that Dorn needed – the gun wavered as Derringer pulled on Jessup's wrists. In that fraction of time Derringer was a dead man.

He was pointing the gun at Dorn from the right side of Jessup. The door to the tower was on their left. As Derringer tugged on the bonds, Jessup leaned swiftly and heavily backwards. It was more than enough. Derringer toppled. Dorn took the chance Jessup had offered and dived for the tower door. The bullet missed him by two feet. Derringer, off balance, half sprawled on his back across the table. It collapsed under him. With his full weight Jessup, helpless without the use of his hands, fell on top of Derringer and the wrecked table. In those seconds, Dorn had wrenched open the door and was already four steps into the darkness beyond.

Shouting curses that would have dismayed a Peruvian parrot, Derringer heaved Jessup aside and rolled free of the splintered wood. Jessup struggled to a sitting position, hearing the receding sounds of Dorn's footsteps scratching on the stone steps. He knew that, having made the break, Dorn's next move would be to try and put Derringer out of action. That would be trickier.

Derringer knew it, too. He wasn't looking pleased as he stood over Jessup, rubbing the back of his leg where it had been caught by the tabletop. 'On your feet, Jessup.' None too gently, Derringer put his left hand under Jessup's right armpit and dragged him up. Jessup's feet scrabbled for a foothold on the floor. Derringer thrust his blotched face towards Jessup's, snarling like a lioness whose prey had been snatched by a desperate jackal. 'We follow. You first. If I even suspect you of breathing too hard my next bullet will mash up your kneecap. He's up in the tower, and if my guess is right there's only one other way down. Now move.' He poked Jessup hard in the ribs with the short muzzle of the gun, just to emphasize the point.

Jessup's mouth twisted open crookedly as he gasped with the sharp pain. The idea that he was caught up in some wild dream had first flashed across his mind during his clandestine visit to Dorn's cellar. It had come to him in the Rødvig house. Then again, but with more terrifying reality, as he struggled in the icy water off the Swedish coast. But no nightmare lasted as long as this. In the worst of them, as he dropped on the end of a spider's thread away from the moon, swinging like a pendulum and knowing the thread must break and that he'd fall for a long time before he crashed sickeningly to the earth's surface; in the worst of them he knew he'd always been able to shake himself awake. But this had gone on too long.

He began to climb the tower steps gingerly, lightly touching the dank walls with his right shoulder to keep a better balance. At each complete turn of the spiral, the arrow slits in the outer walls allowed sufficient light for a dim sighting of the grey stone beneath his feet. Every few steps Derringer prodded him painfully in the small of the back with the gun.

It had taken Dorn the best part of five minutes to reach the open air of the guard walk, the balcony that girded the top of the tower. Two hundred and thirty four steep and twisted steps, taken with hardly a pause, would wind a man in the best physical condition. Dorn was hardly that after the past week's strain. With the heightened tension of the past half hour, adrenalin pumping fast and easily, he barely noticed his labouring chest, nor the bruises on his shins and the torn skin of his knuckles, caused as he stumbled and fell upwards in the semi-darkness. He leaned heavily on the wall next to the doorless opening, panting and blinking in the strong light of day.

After a moment, he let out his breath in a disgusted snort. He hadn't fooled Derringer. Not for more than a second. Derringer must know there was no other way from the tower. He stepped over to the waist-high parapet. It was a long way down. There was more than one way of killing a man; and some ways were less incriminating than a bullet. Sightseers crowded into the courtyard below him, most of them headed for the naval museum at twenty kronor a ticket. Beyond the courtyard and the tunnelled entrance of the outer gate, others were turning towards the second wall of defence from the seaside. The sharp incline of the grassy slope to the breastworks was flattened by his bird's eye perspective. Some of those in the courtyard looked up at him curiously. A few children waved. He hardly noticed them. He turned away and walked halfway round the tower facing east. Four miles across the water lay Sweden. Not to be invaded, but to be raped of its vital secrets nevertheless. He could just distinguish the green-topped two-tiered square clock tower of Helsinborg Rådhus. It looked peaceful in the sunshine across the water.

A few minutes more and Derringer would be here, presumably with Jessup. Dorn had won a breathing space, a few moments in which to think. But it was no more than that. The balcony round the grey tower was devoid of even a large stone that might be used as a weapon. He looked up at the remaining fifteen feet of the copper-topped tower and saw what he had missed in the darkness the night before. Immediately under the metal plating there was the outline of a two feet square embrasure. Wooden slats, painted grey to match the colour of the stone, covered what could only be an aperture. It was obviously the highest lookout point on the seaward side of the castle. He checked quickly to find there were two other similarly boarded openings, spaced regularly around the tower. No doubt there was a wooden floor built into the hollow space and the slats were needed to keep the rain from rotting it.

He realized at once that the lookout point at the top of the tower must have been served by wooden steps that had long since rotted away. He looked closely at the rounded wall below the aperture. There were no signs of ancient fixtures where the wood may have been attached to the stone. If it had been a semi-permanent stairway on the outside of the tower it would surely not be vertical, it would wind in a half spiral beginning well to one side of the vertical. He stepped quickly back to the tower entrance. There, to the right of the opening and a foot from the ground, he saw that the top of the first grey black of stone projected from the other blocks by about three inches. Obviously built that way to support the architect's wooden ladder leading to the top of the tower. Two feet up and further to the right there was another block, the top edge of which jutted outwards by about the same amount. He followed the line of the projecting stone surfaces with his eye. The ledges rose like widely spaced, narrow steps until the curve of the tower took them from his view. It was not his idea of a safe climb, but it was the only weapon he had. That and the strength to try.

Three arduous steps later, toes thrust on the minute ledge and into the deep mortarless gap where the wooden supports had fitted, hands and arms flung wide and flat against the near vertical wall, Dorn had moved round and out of sight of the tower entrance.

Jessup was breathing hard as he reached full daylight at the top of the winding steps. It would have been bad enough with free hands; it was sheer punishment with them tied behind his back. But it was nothing to Derringer's distress after the first seventy steps. The older man had gasped out the order to stop in the light of an aperture. Jessup had sat on a step facing him. The brutal hardness was still in his manner and the gun still menaced in his hand, but his face was tomato crimson from the strain; beads of sweat were fusing to form rivulets running into the corners of his eyes. His chest heaved with great effort under the tweed jacket; the deerstalker lay with the wreckage of the table and Derringer, without it, looked more like the ageing peasant Jessup had found in Dorn's kitchen the evening after the boat incident. After that pause they had climbed more slowly, stopping often for Derringer to wipe the sweat from his face. Now, in the full light, and as he drooped to catch his breath, Jessup knew that Derringer was recovering like a wounded animal and, like a wounded animal, was twice as deadly. Derringer must know quite well that Dorn couldn't afford to play cat and mouse in the open. One sighting was all Derringer needed, and Dorn would have to choose between submission and oblivion. It seemed Derringer didn't care which.

When Dorn had looked over the parapet to the crowds below, he had had neither time nor inclination to distinguish individual faces from the dozen or so who had noticed him. Exiting the tunnel into the courtyard, Martina had caught a brief but positive glimpse of Dorn as he raised his head to look beyond the courtyard to the outer ramparts. She turned excitedly to Carol, pointing to the tower. 'It's Heinrich! Look, up there!' But Carol had seen only the movement of his hand as he'd moved inwards again.

BALTIC INCIDENT

Half an hour after Derringer had followed Jessup on the ferry, Carol and Martina were beginning the twenty minute trip on the next boat.

The two women hurried across the courtyard and entered the chapel. An elderly man, dressed in a light grey suit, kneeled in a back pew, his head bowed low, a hand to his forehead. At the vestry door Martina, leading the way, stopped to listen. She heard only the chatter and laughter of a gay holiday crowd, dulled by distance and the thick ancient walls. The black iron knob turned easily. They stepped quietly into the vestry. They saw the splintered table first.

'Isn't that the hat the old man was wearing?' Martina was looking at Derringer's deerstalker in the wreckage. 'Got to be. Nobody's worn a hat like that since Sherlock Holmes. There's no question about it, is there? He was definitely following David.'

'And Heinrich is trying to keep out of his way. That's why he was up there on the balcony.' said Martina.

They took two more steps into the room. Carol caught her breath as she recognized Jessup's green jacket on the sofa. She picked it up to take a closer look.

Martina came to her side and spotted Jessup's pipe caught in a fold of the settee. She handed it to Carol. 'David's, too, isn't it?' She knew it was. She'd seen him fiddle with it often enough whenever they'd met. Its bowl was roughly worn down on one side from Jessup's habit of knocking out the tobacco ash on a hard surface.

Carol's oval face turned a shade paler. 'He'd never leave this behind.' she said, taking the pipe from Martina. 'I think something unpleasant has happened, right here.'

'And nobody's left, yet.' Martina observed, indicating the coat Carol was holding, and the hat on the floor.

'Of course. The tower!' Carol looked across to the open door and the steps leading upwards. 'And what's that broken table suggest to you? Come on. I've got a feeling we could be useful. They didn't go all the way up there just for a picnic.' She used the schoolteacher voice Jessup had come to associate with an agitation that would lead to an explosion of her temperament.

Martina soon discovered her fashionable high-heeled shoes had not been designed for climbing steep and uneven stone steps in the dark. Carol's were more serviceably wedge-shaped, but it was still easier to climb without them. They finished the ascent in a breathless silence, carrying their shoes.

It was as well they did. Turning the final bend in the tower exit, Carol stopped suddenly. Derringer was less than three yards in front of her, leaning forward on the top two steps, facing the outside. There was a gun in his right hand. Beyond him she could see her husband, crouched on one knee, hands bound behind him. The sounds from the crowds below were clearer now. She realized the noise from that quarter could be heard more plainly by the two men and had covered their own rustling movements. With an effort she prevented herself from calling out. Instead, she crouched low on the cold stone, turned her head to Martina three steps below, and placed her finger on her lips. Martina read the signal and froze. Carol backed carefully down to Martina and stood beside her.

'Not a sound.' Carol warned in a low whisper. 'He's got David tied up and covered with a gun.'

They stood in the gloom, their shoes held by their sides, one brown and one blue pair of eyes on the brighter curve of the wall ahead, uncertain of their next move.

It was Derringer who gave them the lead. His voice sounded strangely loud as he spoke to Jessup. 'Right.

BALTIC INCIDENT

Out you go. Slowly. Turn left first.' Derringer raised his voice. 'I think you ought to know, Heinrich, next time you try anything our professor here will take the first bullet in his leg.' The two men rose and stepped on to the balcony.

The younger woman gripped Carol's arm tightly. 'We can't cope with a gun.' she said, dismay in her voice.

'Absolutely right. Not entirely a woman's style, is it? But there's always the female weapon.'

'What do you mean?'

'Some men don't expect a woman to act sensibly in a crisis. I'm making a bet that that character, Derringer, is as antediluvian as you can get where women are concerned. Listen, can you act the helpless blonde?'

'I don't have to do much acting, do I? That's exactly what I am.'

'Right. That balcony runs right round the tower, doesn't it?' Martina nodded.

'Those two have just gone to the left. You take the other way round. It'll take about one minute and you'll be facing David and the gentleman with the pistol. But put your shoes on half way round and call out for Heinrich. They've got to be expecting you for a split second. Make it noisy, it wouldn't be nice to get shot by accident. Can you do it?'

'I've a feeling you're giving me the easy role. What do you do?'

Carol lifted her shoes in answer. 'If I'm lucky, I'll give him a headache from behind with one of these. It's not much, but can you think of anything better?'

Dorn had almost reached the shuttered lookout embrasure when he heard Derringer call out. His fingers were crooked inside the crack under the wood, the toes of his now badly scratched shoes thrust into the highest stone gap where the ancient ladder's support had once been fixed, twelve feet above the balcony. He felt like a fly on the wall about to be swatted. He twisted his head and looked down to his left side. Jessup appeared at that moment around the curve of the wall. Derringer was right behind him. Jessup looked up. He knew Dorn had done his best and had failed. Derringer wouldn't shoot unless he had to, and there seemed no need for that now. Dorn would be kept, like himself, out of action until "Operation Searchlight" was well under way, then, unlike himself, would doubtless spend years in prison, unless he got political asylum and had something to offer in exchange. What a waste.

He threw a wry grin upwards. 'I've heard of people going up the wall, Heinrich, I've just never seen it done.'

Derringer stepped away from Jessup and raised the angle of the gun. 'Walk's over, youngster. Down you come. Can't stay out here all night.'

Dorn gave a grunt. There wasn't much else he could do. His toenails weren't half as effective as a climber's spikes, they tore off more easily.

As gaily as a child at play, Martina called loudly, right on cue and still out of Jessup's and Derringer's sight. 'Heini! Heinrich! You up here?' What she lacked in invention she achieved by surprise.

If Hamlet's ghost itself had appeared, Derringer could not have been more taken aback. Martina seemed to walk straight out of the blue sky behind her. Golden hair cascading down to below shoulder level, red dress swinging in a breeze that could not have been felt at ground level, Martina was the epitome of a beautiful damsel in distress. She looked disarmingly innocent.

'Martina!' Jessup articulated what the others felt. 'What the hell are you doing here?'

Dorn had not seen her. His spider-like stance, right cheek pressed against the stone, did not allow him to turn his head with facility. But he'd heard her call out, and had seen the expressions on the faces of the two men. For all three, the moment lasted no longer than the intake of a breath.

As Martina confronted Derringer, she, too, could not fail to see Dorn, spreadeagled on the wall, the soles of his shoes six feet above her head. 'Heinrich!' Her astonishment was genuine.

Carol timed her entrance well. With Derringer's attention fixed on Martina, she sprang from behind, barefooted, towards him. The toe of a shoe was held firmly, raised above her head ready to bring the wooden heel hard on to his skull. Only Dorn, unable to turn his head, saw Carol begin to cross the three yard gap. Then, in an instant, he realized she was not going to make it. He watched the old man move. Derringer's instinct served him well. He could not have seen her; he must have felt the hostile presence. He turned, swift as a bull tormented by the toreador, and fired.

Chapter Eight

Blood sprang from a two inch slit in the skin above Carol's left cheekbone. The shock of being hit, the loud crack of the discharge stunned her senses and she didn't leave the ground for the final leap towards Derringer. She spun in a semicircle, losing height as her legs refused to move with her body, and crumpled into an untidy heap against the hard stone of the parapet.

Derringer did not see her fall. On the instant he turned to fire, Dorn pushed himself off the wall in a twisting movement and dropped heavily. His feet struck first, just above Derringer's knees. Derringer's gun arm, swinging in an arc back from Carol, did not complete its course. Dorn's right hand, palm-edge down, smashed on to Derringer's wrist and the gun flew against the wall of the tower and clattered to the ground. Derringer staggered backwards from the force of Dorn's body and Dorn went down on his knees from the impetus of his leap. There was no time to get to his feet, for Derringer, although winded by his fall, began to roll like a fallen tin-can in the wind, towards the gun. Dorn flung out his powerful arms and grasped the older man's legs in the best rugger tradition. For a moment it seemed that Derringer was finished.

Jessup had turned in time to see the effect of Dorn's jump. He could do nothing with his hands, but he knew the gun was the key to the argument. He took a step towards it, intending to kick it either out of the way or towards Dorn. Derringer surprised them both. His legs pinned firmly by Dorn served as an anchor, and he was able to use Dorn's weight as a counter balance. He jackknifed upwards, the fingers of both hands intertwined above his head as if practising ballerina floor exercises. The thick flesh and bone came crashing on to Dorn's neck. Dorn's shoulder muscles went limp and he gasped with pain. His hands released their grip and Derringer was instantly on his feet.

Jessup closed on the gun but it was too late to kick it away with Derringer now free of Dorn's tackle. Nor could he be certain Dorn was in a position to use it if he kicked it towards him. He was conscious only that if Derringer laid hands on the gun again they'd be back where they started, with the additional knowledge that Derringer wouldn't be likely to make the same mistake twice. It was no time to hesitate and no time for half measures. He didn't just lash out at Derringer, now half-crouched and stretching out for the weapon. He threw his whole body into the kick; leaned forward on the ball of his left foot, twisted his right hip in a swing that tautened the thick muscles into a corded spring, straightened the knee at the last moment, and made contact with Derringer's jawbone, just forward of the windpipe. The effect of the heavy English brogue, aimed with such force and at that point, was as spectacular as it was disastrous. Derringer's big head whipped back on to the cushions of fat that formed at the base of his skull. The left side of the jawbone fractured; pointed splinters were thrust upwards and outwards into the cartilage of the ear cavities, the jagged end of the main bone pierced the cheek from the inside. The sound was of a porcelain plate being crushed beneath a steamroller. The weight of the head, driven by the blow, carried Derringer's body staggering upwards and backwards to the parapet. He flung up his hands as if to ease the agony in his face; the top edge of the parapet caught him in the small of the back, and he threw his arms involuntarily towards the sky, fingers clawing at the air as he toppled into oblivion with what should have been a shriek, but came out of his mutilated face as a horribly loud gurgle.

Jessup limped over to Carol, feeling the pain of the kick still in his foot. Her face was streaked with blood and she was in a state of shock. But the bleeding, from an open wound where the bullet had scored her skin, had stopped. He kneeled awkwardly beside her.

'Sorry, David', she said. 'I seem to have missed him. What happened?' The action between the three men had taken only seconds and she had hardly been aware of the fight.

'It's alright, darling,' Jessup spoke soothingly. 'It's over. That was a brave thing you did.' 'Tried to shoe him away,' she quipped nervously. 'Didn't work, though, did it?' She looked up at him with a smile twisted to the uninjured side of her face.

'It certainly did, my love. Heinrich was able to jump him with your little diversion. He's dead. Went over the wall. I'm sorry about that, but I had to kick him or he'd have got the gun. I couldn't use my hands.'

For the first time since she had been dazed by the shot, Carol became aware that Jessup still had his hands bound behind him. She struggled to her feet. 'Oh, my pet! I've got scissors in my handback. It's over there by the stairway.'

Dorn had got to his feet, rubbing the back of his neck, and Martina had rushed over to him, relieved to see him comparatively unharmed. He gave her a hug then led her by the hand to the parapet.

Carol had made quick work of the thin rope with the scissors and she and Jessup joined the others at the parapet. They could see the body on the rocks far below, crumpled and twisted like a multi-jointed marionette whose strings had been dropped by a clumsy manipulator.

BALTIC INCIDENT

The stooped, grey-haired dockside cleaner leaned on his shovel with his back to the wall. He watched the dozen or so passengers as they shuffled past him towards the gate of the Helsingborg ferry that had just been opened for them. As usual, they looked straight through him if they happened to turn in his direction. He was a non-person to them, taken as much for granted as the asphalt on which they walked, and of much less importance than the boat they were about to board for the short trip to Denmark. There were the usual types. Two or three middle-grade, grey suited commuter office workers returning home early; a group of noisy teenagers anticipating the joys of an evening in Denmark's less inhibited social life, and a number of silent old-aged pensioners with special low fare tickets who had crossed to buy the less expensive food in Helsingør's shops.

It was almost routine for someone to be sent to look over the embarking passengers. But more often the plain clothed security officers were told to look for their drug smuggler coming into Sweden rather than leaving it. Sergeant Dick Helge saw absolutely nothing of interest in this group. No tall, moustached German remotely resembling the man who'd been described to him. He crossed one dirty boot over the other and glanced towards the boat. It was refreshing, after three hours of boredom, to watch the elaborate old-fashioned courtesy with which the attractive blonde assisted the long-robed priest from the ferry. Even a priest, thought Helge with justifiable if lascivious envy, was a man.

Jessup had felt as ill as a raw recruit before his first battle the moment they'd set foot on the ferry back to Helsinborg in Sweden. It wasn't seasickness. He knew it was nervous reaction to the violence, the sheer brutality, of Derringer's death. It was difficult to cope with the knowledge that he had been directly responsible for the killing of another human being. Carol leaned forward with him, an arm stretched reassuringly round his shoulders.

Dorn, sitting on the other side, said quietly, 'Pull yourself together, David. It's rough but we had no choice.'

'And he would have killed Carol', Martina added pointedly. 'Anybody in your position would have done the same.'

Jessup turned his head, first to Carol, then to the others. A wan smile reached his eyes. 'I'll be alright. Just a touch of shock.' He leaned back on the bench of the boat's upper deck, the smile broadening as he looked at Dorn's garb.

Dorn was covered from neck to ankle in the black robes of a monk. It had been Martina who had suggested they use one of the priest's garments from the vestry, and Carol had produced her small sharp scissors to cut off all but the barest outline of his moustache, together with much of his thick dark hair. They could do nothing about the stubble on his chin. He'd have to become a priest of the contemplative kind and keep his head bent, cowl tightly about his neck. Besides being the perfect disguise, it had the additional virtue of hiding all signs of Derringer's gun Dorn had picked up and stuck into his waistband as they left the tower.

They were lucky Derringer had fallen on the rocks awash with the waters of the Öresund rather than into the crowded courtyard. But it wouldn't be long before somebody from a passing boat, or even an adventurous child clambering about behind the castle, spotted it.

Dorn seemed to need no more persuasion about whether to defect or not, it had been what he could offer to the

BALTIC INCIDENT

West that mattered. With the question posed, Dorn had come up with the answer. It was the black bag that Jessup had accidentally kicked over in Dorn's Ljunghusen house, Dorn told them. That was the key to Stavrinsky's operation. Dorn had filled them in on the Russian agent's role as controller of 'Operation Searchlight', and had explained how he himself, through Air Germanic, had provided the computer sales firm, Swedcom, with the sophisticated equipment needed to link together the master military computer system at Karlskoga with its duplicate in the warehouse at Swedcom, on Lake Vänern. The American firm that had developed and made the new Super Atlas machines had had no problem in obtaining government permission to sell it to the South African company, under contract to the South African government. With the right amount of persuasion, payable in Rand gold, the equipment had been smoothly handed over to Air Germanic on production of a bogus West German certificate from Bonn. The shipment had gone through Frankfurt airport and on to Sweden without even being checked. All that had been needed there was for Air Germanic to produce a new set of documents showing a revised delivery address.

That had been two years ago. It meant that the Russians had had plenty of time to prepare the deception Derringer had told them about.

On the twenty-minute crossing from Denmark to Sweden, Dorn had gone into more detail. He knew, Stavrinsky hadn't had to tell him, that the briefcase Stavrinsky had brought with him from the trawler had been sealed in Leningrad. What Stavrinsky had told him, and for obvious reasons, was that only he, Stavrinsky, could open it without disturbing the electrically controlled detonator that would trigger off the four pounds of plastic explosive packed into the lid. The only reason

Dorn had had the case in his possession that evening when Jessup had accidentally knocked it over was because Stavrinsky had been unexpectedly called to the Gothenburg consulate with only an hour's notice. Since Stavrinsky could not risk taking the case on the 'plane from Malmö, he had left it overnight with Dorn.

Dorn didn't doubt Derringer's opinion that Stavrinsky would be on his way to Swedcom as soon as he was satisfied that the Swedes had begun to act on the invasion information Dorn had himself provided.

They had been in mid-channel. On a headland behind them, the weathered roofs of Kronborg castle shone in the sunshine like the sapphire on one of the sea-blue crested tapis de veleurs of a Cartier's display table. Jessup, standing at the rail to catch the fresh breeze, turned from the receding view with a shudder, to face the others on the bench. There was no one within earshot. 'So we have to try Swedcom.' he said. 'If that's where Stavrinsky is and the briefcase does contain the key to the operation, as Heinrich thinks, then we have no choice. But the ladies have had sufficient excitement for one day. I suggest they return to Malmö by train while we go on to Swedcom by car.'

Carol didn't say anything about the pompous reference to themselves. She had the instinct of the perfect wife and kept the intimate comments for their privacy. Nevertheless, she stubbornly refused to be left out and was backed firmly by Martina. She pointed out, reasonably, that if it hadn't been for them, he and Dorn would still be stuck in the tower with Derringer.

Dorn was silent for a moment, then said, gently 'David, I think it's time for you, too, to retreat. You've done more than enough. Remember, although Stavrinsky knows by now that I'm no longer in the hands of Säpo, he has no reason to think of me as an enemy. Technically, he's still my boss. Hell, he'd even expect me to reach him, if I could do it without endangering his cover. The consulate would get me out of the country later. That would be normal procedure. So you see, alone, I could get to Stavrinsky and play it by ear after that.' Dorn's plan had seemed convincing.

Dorn went on. 'The head of Swedcom, a man called Görman, knows nothing of the operation's details. He's been bought. As far as he's concerned I'm simply a businessman doing a deal with the Russians on the side, like him. He'll certainly know nothing of my arrest. All I have to do is telephone him as usual. Play it smooth, as if nothing had changed.' Dorn stopped, and looked from one to the other for confirmation of his plan.

But Jessup had been thinking of the loose ends. Was he growing cynical? or just learning how to be careful? Whatever it was he felt uncomfortable at the thought that he should just fade out and leave Dorn with the final load. The wind had thoroughly roughed his thick hair, and he felt it beginning to seep through his jacket. He moved from the rail and stood looking down at the others.

'It's good, Heinrich. Very good. But what happens if you fail? Maybe you're not supposed to know it, but sure as hell Stavrinsky won't forget you've been used and discarded by Moscow. He wouldn't let you out of his sight until he could either get you to the consulate or arrange for Säpo to arrest you again. I propose a compromise, Heinrich. We stick to the plan you've just suggested, but with one change of detail. We come along as your back-up team. Up to Swedcom. You do what you can inside; we'll keep out of trouble on the outside. What do you say?'

Carol and Martina enthusiastically approved and Dorn, insisting that they should keep the bargain and stick to the car, had accepted the compromise.

They had disembarked at Helsinborg as two separate couples. The Jessups had made sure other passengers divided them from Martina who had taken on the role of assistant to the rather doddery monk beside her. Like everyone else, they, too, looked through the dock-side cleaner as he leaned carelessly on his shovel.

The four had walked briskly to the beach car-park and, making sure they had not been identified, got into the car with Jessup in the driving seat. Ten minutes later, and on the other side of the town, Dorn had struggled out of the monk's habit and made his telephone arrangements with Görman at Swedcom. Now they were on their way northwards and Jessup didn't have to be reminded that midnight was the deadline.

--- --- --- --- --- ---

The Prime Minister began soberly. 'Gentlemen. I have to tell you that Warsaw Pact sea and airborne forces are within a few hours' sailing time to longitude 13º 30" East.' The heads of the military and security departments were again assembled in the comfortable conference room at Karlskoga headquarters. The atmosphere among the uniformed men was electric and tense. If the highly accurate and atomically controlled clock, mounted in the wall behind the first minister, had suddenly ticked, at least half a dozen of those toughened servicemen would have jumped in their seats.

'We have again been in contact with Moscow. The answer is the same; the Warsaw Pact movements are completely normal springtime exercises.'

Field Marshall Stig Holmberg shuffled his feet with some impatience. The action that had to be taken had already been decided by the inner cabal, of which he was a member, and now he felt they were losing time.

The Prime Minister was saying 'I have had another meeting with the Soviet Ambassador, and again he has assured me that no belligerent plans against Sweden have ever existed. He also again denied all knowledge of the spy Heinrich Dorn and the detailed information for invasion Dorn has collected.' The Prime Minister stopped again, the habit of dramatic presentation had not left him, even in a moment of extreme crisis. He looked deliberately at each officer in turn. Nobody shuffled now. They knew they were being appealed to, personally and individually.

Then he made his final pronouncement, 'Gentlemen. We cannot ignore the evidence. We must prepare now. "Red Alert" will be put into operation in one hour's time.'

– – – – – – – – – – – – – –

Known as area 'D.T.K.' – DefenceTraining Karlsborg – the forested northwest section of Lake Vättern, centring on the town of Karlsborg, contained Sweden's most closely guarded tract of land. For Karlsborg, on the edge of the lake, was the focus of the country's highly secret army, navy and air force testing region, and a major centre for the deployment of the largest concentration of troops in Sweden. All but the southern third of the lake was swept, from time to time, by gunfire or missiles of the most sophisticated kind in conventional warfare. Local fishermen were issued with transceivers so that they could be called back from their fishing grounds at a moment's notice. There were secret arms dumps in the area. From the height of a few hundred feet, great swathes of nakedness could be seen where trees had been cut from the thick forests. They looked like six-laned motorways beginning from nowhere and ending in a blank wall of trees. They were roads, built not so much for aircraft with minute take-off capability, as for the gigantic ammunition and weapons carriers that would be needed in time of war. Never used to capacity in peacetime, they took a battalion of men every week to keep them clear of windswept rubbish, fallen trees, undergrowth and other debris from the living vegetation by which they were surrounded.

Lieutenant Lars Dahl, sitting atop his turretless tank, was twenty-four years of age and not a little afraid. The battalion had gone through the motions of Red Alert many times, but only in training sessions. He knew this wasn't just another exercise. On all the other occasions there had always been an hour or two's tip off from the Commanding Officer, well aware of the problems in the armoured section of the field forces. There'd always been time to get the crews sobered up. This time, Dahl had had to haul his radio-operator – who doubled as a rear driver – from a heavy drinking party. To make matters worse, the forty-ton Mark 2 version of the 103-type tank had lost its driver and gun-layer to the recent drastic military spending cuts. That meant he'd have to drive, operate the 10.5 centimetre canon as well as command the tank's tactical movements. He'd done his best to impress upon the radio operator that in Red Alert conditions only live ammunition would be used. The yellow seals from the ultra modern lightweight ammunition boxes had been broken and the dummies hurriedly thrown out, according to instructions, so that they couldn't be fed by mistake to the guns. Through the faded light of the forest, made misty by concentrated tank exhaust fumes, he watched the base armourers picking up the discarded used and unused boxes of blank machine-gun cartridges. Dahl tightened the strap of his helmet under his chin and waited for the voice of Red Leader to crackle into the earphone.

- - - - - - - - - - - - - - -

Goddard, alone in Svensson's flat, crunched into a Swedish crispbread with butter, layered with rich tasting paté, and topped with three slices of fresh cucumber. In the time Svensson had left Lund to drive to Stavrinsky in Gothenburg Goddard had become something of an expert on the great variety of smörgås-type knäckerbröd delicacies. Fastidiously, he brushed away a crumb with an elegant gesture from his little finger. The day had been hectic with calls to and from Stoke Poges. Dyson had absolutely insisted on keeping a close track on the whereabouts of the star witness contributed by the British to 'Operation Searchlight'. He had forced his ice-cold sarcasm to bite through the telephone wires when he'd learned of Jessup's escapade with Dorn in the Baltic. Dyson had been somewhat mollified to hear that Goddard had anticipated his thinking and got Derringer to stay on Jessup's tail for the following twenty-four hours.

He glanced at his watch, then turned on the television to catch the six o'clock news. His spoken Swedish was practically non-existent, but a concentrated course in the Scandinavian language, in London, had enabled him to understand something of what was said when it was clearly enunciated. It helped when, as on the news, subscript was also shown for the benefit of the deaf.

But he believed neither his eyes nor ears when a still picture of Derringer was flashed on the screen and the newscaster said the death-fall of the university professor was presumed to be accidental. It was as though Goddard had been stumped by an alert wicket-keeper, an inch from the crease, without his having begun a run. For fully three minutes he sat motionless, ob-

CHARLES SMART

livious to both sound and sight of what issued from
the box in front of him. He sat back in the easy chair
and pushed a hand through his fair hair, crunching
on the forgotten Knäckerbröd without tasting it. His
pale brow puckered into the resemblance of a frown.
With Dyson temporarily off his back and Jessup being looked after by Derringer, Goddard had allowed
himself to relax, knowing that despite Dorn's escape
the Swedes would have to act on the information they
had. But Jessup had been the catalyst. With his disappearance 'Operation Searchlight' could be jeopardized.
There just had to be a link between Dorn's escape and
Derringer's death. And Jessup was somehow involved.
It had to be that way because the only reason Derringer
had for being in such a damned strange place was that
he had followed Jessup to it. Yet, since the unaccount-
able 'accident' could not be attributed to Jessup – there
was no way Goddard could be wrong about him – then
Dorn had to be involved, too. After all, Dorn did at least
know Derringer's track record.
The operation was beginning to look decidedly ragged
at the edges, and Jessup was somewhere near the middle of this unfortunate incident. Jessup had better be
found, and quickly.

Boris Stavrinsky slipped the plastic disk into the decod-
ing machine and tapped out a string of requests on the
computer keyboard. He nodded Viktor Karjagin's attention to the screen in front of them.
'Operation Searchlight' had to have a political adviser
to whom the field commander must report. It was part
of the system, whether the operation was social or military or political, at home or abroad. On the small col-
lective farm on the other side of the Urals, the political
adviser could be a field hand, picked for his astuteness

and enthusiasm in party politics; in East Germany it could be a first lieutenant advising a general. But whatever his rank, the political adviser was the guardian of the sacred doctrine. To the faithful, he was regarded as the custodian of the Truth, to be deferred to in a manner befitting representatives of the politbureau in Moscow. To those for whom professionalism for the job in hand was more important than politics, advisers were a damned nuisance. Not just because they had to be consulted every time a new step was taken, but because more often than not the political power invested in them went straight to their heads, and they felt it necessary to question every technical detail as if they were themselves experts. A professor of politics who questions the surgeon is not calculated to make the next heart transplant any easier.

Karjagin was Stavrinsky's political adviser and much more. He was a diplomat and he was clever. Heavily built and slightly round shouldered his head appeared to thrust forward, not in self assertion but with what appeared to be an intense and even jovial interest in what the other person was saying. He had done his job well in London before the British government could find an excuse to get rid of him in 1971. He was, after all, one of the more important members of the KGB.

Industrial espionage in Sweden was a much more fruitful operation and, since early in 1984, Karjagin had been the bosom pal of a number of Swedish industrial chiefs and, not so obviously, the drinking partner of at least two faceless cabinet ministers. But his main task in the last six months had been to keep a close watch on 'Operation Searchlight'. He had himself vetted the information-collecting groups that were now stationed in many different parts of the country and ready to monitor the Swedish military and service units' movements that would be brought about by the Swedish government's decision 'Execute'. He was fully aware that the information gained would be the biggest bonanza for Moscow intelligence, ever. It was in the nature of all great power intelligence systems that all-important items of information should be fragmented. No single person could know everything. Not even the infamous Hoover of the United States Federal Bureau of Information had managed that. Which was why Karjagin himself, with all his charm and intelligence, could expect no more than portions of secret information on the Swedish defence system from his Swedish contacts. 'Operation Searchlight' was intended to break this Gordian knot at a stroke.

The program Karjagin was looking at was a duplicate of that in the Swedish military headquarters at Karlskoga, and in the Swedcom warehouse on Lake Vänern. It had been finally approved and coded by Moscow and brought to Sweden by Stavrinsky. It had been tested many times, the last, some weeks earlier, when a computer-directed radar net on the east coast of Sweden had tracked two wholly fictional Russian Tupolev Fiddler rocket-firing fighter planes flying at one and a half times the speed of sound from the Baltic Sea in towards Stockholm. Swedish protests that their airspace was again being violated were simply denied by Moscow. The throaty Russian chuckle had echoed through the gloomy corridors of the Kremlin at the thought that, for once, no Russian plane had been within five hundred miles of the Swedish east coast. Of course, the Swedish tracking devices had sent no such signals. Only the Swedish computers, fed by the control keys at the Gothenburg Consulate, had falsely shown the mythical planes to be flying twenty miles inland before turning back to the Baltic Sea.

BALTIC INCIDENT

The graphs and figures now being finally checked by Karjagin were far more elaborate. The disk program being reproduced on the large screen was the decoy plan central to 'Operation Searchlight'. In diagrammatic form, Warsaw Pact forces were shown moving westwards across longitude 13º30" East, and heading for the south west coast of Sweden. Ten major warships and fifty supporting vessels were shown to be within twenty miles of the Swedish coast. Figures showed fifty-five naval hovercraft, capable of landing fifteen thousand troops with equipment, approaching at a speed of thirty knots. A thousand rocket-firing fighter-bombers circled above the fleet.

Stavrinsky hardly needed to explain that military planners in Karlskoga could interpret the figures in only one way. A dawn landing in force by hovercraft-carried troops could swamp the whole area known as Näset – the Nose – of Sweden, right up to the ship canal that divided the Nose from the mainland, some six miles north of Falsterbo lighthouse. No Swedish counter forces existed in the area, and only the order for Execute, issued from the Karlskoga headquarters, could save the whole of Sweden, south of the Göta canal, from being overrun within twenty-four hours. It was a compelling picture and Karjagin was impressed with the final and authorised version.

'I understand you helped to produce this strategy? You are to be congratulated, comrade Stavrinsky.' The Consul General beamed at the colonel and there was a twinkle in his eyes. 'But since we don't intend any such invasion, how do we cancel this program?'

Stavrinsky was well aware of Karjagin's reputation for thoroughness, and he knew that Karjagin already had the answers to most of the questions. 'We use the code.' He turned to the scuffed black leather briefcase and took out a second bulletproof box. 'As you can see, comrade,' he said, opening the box with his fingers, 'this part of the operation requires only the correct series of numbers to be fed to the computer.' He fingered the keys again and the screen went blank except for the local identification number glowing in the top left-hand corner. 'If we had called up the Karlskoga computer first, this screen would show us what they are looking at right now. In other words, when this code is keyed over the false program, the false program will not be received. Their computer will no longer be controlled by us and will function normally. They will once again be able to receive the data conveyed to them by their radar and other detection devices. The Warsaw Pact 'Exercise' signal will be received in the normal way, from the fleet, from Peenemunde and from Moscow.'

'By then it'll be too late for them to call off "Execute",' finished Karjagin.

'Even if they do rescind the "Execute" order it would take many hours to restore normality. Their troops would be already in the air and on the way south, for example. Sealed orders would have been opened; secret codes would already be in use.' Stavrinsky allowed himself to smile with his adviser. 'And our monitoring groups would have already collected about ninety per cent of that intelligence.'

'Those monitoring posts,' Karjagin said, 'are they all deployed?'

Stavrinsky knew Karjagin was referring to the many groups scattered around Sweden, both in the countryside and, as paid informers, inside the defence system itself. Stavrinsky had checked them all by radio within the past two hours. 'They are, comrade Karjagin.' He knew the next question and answered before it was asked. 'And they know nothing of "Operation Searchlight". They'll be very surprised at the volume of tracking and recording to be done, but they have the equipment to cope with that.'

'Good. And the schedule for this?'

'At this moment, Swedish aircraft are tracking Warsaw Pact movements.' Stavrinsky looked at his wristwatch. 'There are some seven hours sailing before the fleet is due to arrive at longitude 13°30". We shall infiltrate their system at about eleven o'clock tonight. That will give an hour or so of precise synchronization with what is really happening out there in the Baltic, although in fact they will be taking their readings from our master computer at Swedcom. From about midnight local time, when the fleet actually swings southwards towards Peenemunde, away from Sweden, the computers in Karlskoga will show the fictitious movement of the fleet continuing westwards. That will be the program we have just been looking at. With the information we have already fed them from Heinrich Dorn the Swedes will be expecting to see this anyway. Any time after that, when they decide the "Exercise" signal is not coming through from the fleet, we think they'll order "Execute". That will be about midnight.' He smiled at Karjagin. 'That's when our units will begin recording their reactions. We'll keep the program running for up to twelve hours if possible.'

'Yes, well, in that period, they should have got to know the true location of our fleet from other sources,' said Karjagin.

'And by then we'll have got all the information we could wish for.' Stavrinsky concluded.

Karjagin was silent for a moment, looking down at the screen. 'You have the pre-operational diversion prepared?'

'Everything in readiness, comrade Consul. It has been arranged for this evening.'

Karjagin grunted his approval. He thought for a moment then said, 'You've made quite sure the operator can't be traced back to us?'

Stavrinsky lost his good humour for a moment. Karjagin had sounded like the petty advisers he'd known in the Ukraine years before. The man was under pressure, Stavrinsky suddenly realized that although 'Operation Searchlight' was his immediate priority, Karjagin held, in one of the few – certainly the most important – remaining buffer countries in Europe, the strings of a most complex secret organization. He ignored the breach of etiquette that had made Karjagin sound as though Stavrinsky might have slipped up. He knew the Consul would not want the details spelled out, nevertheless, it would be wise to place emphasis on the words. He said, 'Comrade Consul, the contact at Hjälta will be traceable to no one. And your operation at the Swedcom location has already been isolated from the consulate here and from the embassy in Stockholm? My instructions on that score were given to Feldt two weeks ago. There must be no obvious connection between "Operation Searchlight" and our normal diplomatic and political activities.'

'Watertight, comrade. I shall double check when I arrive at Swedcom. Any initial post operation investigation will show that the owner of Swedcom, Olle Görman, is fully responsible. The documentation will prove his motivation for bigger profits and will expose his participation on illegal arms contracts with Czechoslovakia.'

'I take it that the independent generators at Swedcom are in readiness?'

'As power-tight as you are in the Consulate.'

BALTIC INCIDENT

Karjagin idly tapped his fingers on the computer top. His smile turned to a slight frown. 'Our agent, Heinrich Dorn, I suppose I should call him our "ex-agent" now, can his escape from the Swedish security police have an adverse effect on the operation? Is he in any position to harm us?'

Stavrinsky knew what was in the Consul's mind. Dorn should have been quietly eliminated in the eyes of field operators. They both knew that Moscow's decision that he should be instructed to give himself up was sheer politics. Dorn was a German. Moscow had judged it unwise to go to extreme lengths with their front line allies. It had been the only snag in an otherwise perfect operation. They had not banked on Dorn's escape from Säpo. It should not have happened. The other alternative had been impossible, too. With straightforward discovery, a spy could ordinarily have been sent back home. Dorn was a special case, for the Russians had themselves supplied the evidence that had betrayed him. Even that would not have been insurmountable, but in Dorn's case the British and, indirectly the Americans, had also been involved. They knew what the details were, and that could prove more embarrassing. It was logical, Stavrinsky had to admit, for Moscow to order that he should give himself up in order to maintain the semblance of genuineness demanded by 'Operation Searchlight'. It was logical, Moscow was always that. But it wasn't very safe for the operation.

Stavrinsky said, carefully, 'There's nothing he can do. If he's not already back in the hands of the Swedish security, he'll probably use normal procedures and contact me as soon as he can. Then I'll give him the sad news.'

Karjagin looked harder at Stavrinsky from beneath long, sandy-grey eyebrows. He hesitated for fully thirty seconds, his head thrust slightly forward, as though measuring the depth of Stavrinsky's character. Then he said, weighing his words with minute attention to detail, 'Moscow does not make mistakes; but the "M" section committee is so pleased when we read discreetly between the lines.'

For the shadow of a moment Stavrinsky's heavily contoured face showed a question mark. Then he knew that the senior KGB officer was presenting him with a serious, professional option. A challenge that, if accepted and executed with the necessary finesse, could only enhance his prestige with the Kremlin's external security committee. If not accepted, would place him firmly in the category of the mediocre. He recognized the game and the stakes: Dorn would be dealt with quietly and without fuss. Stavrinsky gave a single, slow nod of the head.

A genial smile broke over Karjagin's face. 'You have time for a drink before you leave?'

Pekka Hainnu was meticulous to a fault when it came to his work at the Hjälta power plant. Even when it concerned the rather irregular sealed boxes he'd been fitting for the Stockholm research company. He could have sworn, though, that he'd pulled out the small telescopic aerial from the casing of the measuring instrument. But the telephone caller had been politely adamant that he should at least check it, since no signals were getting through. Still more strangely, they had specified he should make sure the aerial was extended at precisely seven o'clock that evening. They knew he was on the evening shift, but the timing still seemed a little strict. There again, who was he to complain, with the sort of money they were paying?

A comfortable, soft humming of machinery greeted him as he stepped into the large, brightly transformer building. Water from a hundred waterfalls had contributed to the production, in this plant alone, of thousands of megawatts per hour to be distributed throughout the country. Structured on raised concrete platforms and protected by aluminium casings, six giant four hundred kilovolt leads fed their power to the national grid. They were Hainnu's chief playtoys, as his wife called them. In a way, that was true. He had never lost his enthusiasm for electrical gadgets ever since, at the age of ten, he'd been given the small 'do it yourself' dynamo kit that seemed to drive his miniature windmills and light up his sister's doll's house with an invisible, magic energy.

But tonight he didn't give the transformers a second look. It was three minutes to seven and his first concern was to satisfy the generous computer firm that was to make him a rich man. He made his way to the contact breaker attached to number one transformer. Almost two yards long, the solid-looking metal pole regulated the power fed to the transformers. Hainnu unlocked the protective casing at one end of the arm. There'd been no mistake. The little black box he had taped so carefully to the head of the metal bar showed the projecting antenna. Just to make sure, he held the box tightly with one hand and with finger and thumb depressed the aerial into its socket.

It was precisely seven o'clock when Pekka Hainnu died.

The retina of his eyes that might have recorded the event would not have had the time to transfer the image or the sensation of the explosion to the brain before they were vaporised. The bloody mass that had been the top part of the Finn's torso was flung violently, in its several parts, against walls, floor and ceiling. The contact breaker arm disintegrated. Pieces of metal flew like shrapnel across the expanse of the room, cutting through machinery and cables indiscriminately and embedding themselves into walls.

Recording devices in the central control room showed an enormous surge of power and, within forty-five seconds, some seven and a half million people were without electricity. Half a mile away, on the perimeter road of the Hjälta plant, a small unmarked van retracted its two radio aerials and pulled smoothly away from the curb.

The destruction of the contact breaker arm was the cause of a chain reaction. Unregulated and massively excessive power now flowed to the six transformers for the space of ten seconds before their individual safety cutout devices automatically uncoupled them from Sweden's electricity supply. In the following fifteen seconds the country's twelve nuclear power stations reached overloading point and in quick succession they, too, were forced out of the national grid by their security controls. Within minutes, the normal life of a large, modern state, together with that of one and a half million inhabitants in the Copenhagen area of Denmark, also dependent on power from Sweden, was reduced to an erratic and makeshift chaotic existence.

Peter Svensson pushed his supercharged mini 'S' Cooper engine to the limit. At one hundred miles an hour he eased off the accelerator, deciding he'd keep a balance between watching for following police cars on the dual carriageway behind him and the urgency of the job in hand.

It was, after all, unlikely that Jessup would head north towards Gothenburg. Much more likely he'd been on a weekly shopping trip and was now on his way back to the Malmö area. Still, Goddard had sounded pretty anxious, as anxious as any cold English bastard could be, that was, and insisted he keep a sharp lookout for the Jaguar. Somewhere between them, Goddard driving north from Lund and himself southwards from Gothenburg, they should pick Jessup up easily enough. It wouldn't be difficult to spot a sleek classic Jaguar among the stolidly built Volvos and Saabs.

Thirty miles south of Gothenburg the red bleeper box on the seat beside him, the CIA's twin to the one in Derringer's car, gave a couple of well-spaced signals. Extreme limit, about five miles ahead on flat countryside. Svensson smiled to himself. Just as he thought, Jessup was on his way home. If he pushed it, he'd be in visual before they got to Lund.

The sounds from the box interrupted his thoughts. The bleeps were closer together. He glanced at it in mild surprise. The Jaguar must be travelling very slowly since, within a matter of moments, he'd gained on his prey by something like a mile. Then the bleeps came faster still. He switched tracks in his thinking. He wasn't overtaking at all. The Jaguar was coming towards him and the two vehicles were approaching one another head on at a combined speed of about one hundred and eighty miles an hour.

To his left, the dual carriageway was divided by a wide ditch and, although the red mini's performance was good, it hadn't been provided with wings. Then the Jaguar was in sight. On the fast lane, flying past slower vehicles, its speed registered by the high pitched and almost continuous buzzing of the box beside him. The two cars passed each other with a mere five yards of grassy hollow separating them. Only then was the force of Goddard's anxiety transmitted to Svensson. For, since the Jaguar was made for British roads, it was the front passenger seat that was nearest to Svensson.

With a small shock of disbelief he recognized the figure of the East German spy and, beyond him, Jessup at the steering wheel.

If he lost Jessup now, knowing full well that Dorn, too, was with him, it wouldn't be Goddard he'd have to answer to. It would be his own crotchety CIA boss and the near certainty of an untimely end with the organization. Svensson slowed down. There wasn't much point in racing on the wrong circuit. The signals from the transmitter attached to the Jaguar were rapidly weakening. He could see no bridge indicating a motorway exit and no apparent shallowing of the central ditch. Then came the signs for road works, threatening to waste more time, and he groaned aloud. Four flashing orange lights showed the spot where a yellow coloured motorway vehicle straddled the dividing hollow. Svensson slowed even more, a bizarre idea forming in his mind. A characteristic creative ability not always appreciated by his long-suffering tutors in Seattle. From a hundred yards away he could see the extra long fork-lift, fixed to the front end of the motorized contraption, dipping deep into the ditch to clear the winter's detritus. Timing had to be faultless and he checked in the mirror to make sure there was no traffic behind at a problematic distance. Twenty-five yards from the yellow vehicle, now stationary as its vertical piston forced the wickedly long prongs deep into the ditch, Svensson swung into the slow lane on his right. When the prongs of the fork were again raised to road level they would provide a perfect cattle-grid-like crossing from south to northbound carriageway. Almost side by side with the yellow digger, and praying that the fork would bring up nothing bigger than dead leaves, Svensson pushed down on the accelerator and swung the mini violently to the left at nearly thirty miles an hour in a right-angled turn that took two wheels momentarily off the road, and two millimetres of tread off the other two wheels.

If the fork lift driver saw the red blur across his vision his reactions would have been far too slow to do anything about it. The car, lifted at the rear and by the rising fork, bounced across the makeshift platform scattering leaves and old tin cans in all directions. Again Svensson tugged at the wheel, turning the car left into the fast lane, in time to avoid colliding with slow lane traffic. The driver of the Saab, in the fast lane, thought he had a clear stretch of road. Then he made a double take at the yellow ditch cleaner and was horrified to see the red mini appear, like a fairground bumping car run amok, fifty feet in front of him. With reflexes operated more by panic than good sense, the Saab driver pulled to the left in an attempt to avoid a car in the slow lane. Beyond the ditch cleaner the Saab entered the narrow ravine at seventy miles an hour, trying to bury its nose into the far wall at a forty-five degree angle. The car cartwheeled across the southbound carriageway before landing on its four wheels, a twisted wreck with a foreshortened front end.

Like the driver of the Saab, Svensson was oblivious to the chaos he had caused. Accelerating fast, back towards Gothenburg in pursuit of the Jaguar, his first priority was to call Goddard on the car telephone. This time he could reasonably expect at least one expletive from the MI6 agent when that gentleman heard that Dorn, too, was with Jessup. But once again Svensson was baffled at the Englishman's coolness. The unimpassioned, metallic voice from Goddard's own mobile telephone returned merely a brief explanatory comment and a controlled instruction.

'They're on their way to Swedcom. Be glad if you would maintain close contact.'

'How the hell am I supposed to catch that Jaguar? You got a helicopter or something?'

'You don't have to catch it.' returned the maddeningly calm voice. 'Repeat, don't stop it. Just report when they arrive.'

How in God's name did the toffee-nosed Brit know they'd be heading for Swedcom! Svensson banged the phone back in its holder, making sure it was in place before loudly casting doubt on Goddard's paternal pedigree. Then he switched off the bleeper. If Goddard was so goddam sure about their destination the he didn't have to put up with that racket. He turned up the volume on a Danish programme and started to sing with the 'Police' playing reggae.

- - - - - - - - - - - - - - - -

There should have been a long line of sodium lighting along the main road into Gothenburg. Instead, Jessup, Dorn and the two women were greeted with lines of shadowy sentinels on both sides of the road. The only visible lights were those of other road vehicles. In the distance through the dying daylight the city was strangely silhouetted. At the first major crossroads leading to the town centre, they realized something was wrong. At the last moment Jessup noticed the traffic lights were not working. He had to stand on the large pad of the Jaguar's footbrake to avoid collision as other cars crossed at speeds far in excess of caution.

Deserted trams had stopped, and nobody seemed interested in getting on or off them. There were just too many people on the streets. Some hurrying, some hesitating at curbsides, others gathering in groups outside unlighted shops. From the enclosed comfort of the Jaguar Mary voiced a feeling they all had.

BALTIC INCIDENT

'Like something from a Hitchcock film. It's uncanny. What's going on?'

They were nearing the centre of the town. The daylight had all but gone. Crowds thickened on the pavements. A number of people, trying to cross the road, wandered into the headlights of cars, regardless of the crazy driving. With no traffic and pedestrian crossing lights, crossing a busy road was a hazard town-dwellers had quite forgotten how to cope with. Candles and storm lanterns appeared in shop windows, one of two people had torches.

Jessup pulled to the side of the road and stopped the car. He opened the nearside window. Until this moment all sound of the city life had been disguised by the muffled roar of the powerful motor. The clamour that assaulted their ears now came as a shock, for it was not just that of the city's overloaded streets and pavements. Everywhere there was the tumult of frenzied hurrying and shouting, a bedlam of disorganized humanity such as one might imagine of a terrifying dream. Four yards away, two men fought for the receiver in a yellow telephone kiosk; behind them, a dozen more pushed and elbowed one another in efforts to reach the booth. From half a dozen shops in the immediate area came the insistent, ear-piercing wail of alarm bells. Car drivers frenetically flashed their headlights and blew their horns, trying to force their way past major road crossings.

Carol, from the seat behind Jessup, called out, 'My God, look at that!'

Not five paces from where she sat, nearest the curb, two young men snatched at watches and jewelry from a smashed shop window, while people rushed heedlessly past.

'They're all mad,' Martina breathed aloud. 'What's happening?'

'Whatever it is,' said Jessup as he opened the car door, 'I wish we hadn't had to go through the town to get to the main road north. And now we can't even see the damned road directions. Hand me the torch, Heinrich. It's in the glove compartment in front of you. Better if you stayed with the ladies, old friend.'

Dorn had sat without comment as the others looked in amazement at the chaos around them. Now he placed a hand on Jessup's arm. 'You don't have to go out there.' Carol looked at him, saying nothing, and Martina watched his face in profile, aware of an awful tension knotting her stomach.

Jessup turned to him, pulling the door shut again. 'Did you have something to do with this?' he asked sharply. 'Not directly.' Dorn turned so that he could see the women as well. 'It's part of the Russian plan in "Operation Searchlight". I didn't want to disturb you unnecessarily. We might have been in time to stop it.'

'So what's going on?' Jessup asked quietly. He was trying hard to believe Dorn hadn't taken him in for a second time. He'd already railed on himself for placing Carol in physical danger at the castle.

Dorn was aware of the implications in Jessup's question. 'David, you have to trust me.' He gestured to the confusion in the streets. 'They're not mad. It's a very normal – and planned – reaction. This is happening all over the country. A pre-operational diversion. Railways stopped. Telephone lines overloaded. Thousands of elevators stuck at mid-floor levels. Alarm bells set off automatically. Fires will soon break out from overheated alarm systems, and there won't be a sufficient number of engines to cope with fighting them. Can you imagine how many people are trapped in Stockholm's underground at this moment? Sure, there are many back-up systems, in hospitals and for the military and

BALTIC INCIDENT

other priority institutions. But apart from accidents, if only a handful of key personnel are stopped or delayed in getting to their posts Stavrinsky's plan would still be a success.'

The others looked at him with horror as he unfolded the details.

'It's just a preliminary stage in the operation,' Dorn ended lamely.

To Jessup, Dorn's manner had the ring of sincerity. In any case, he reflected, there were only two choices. They could turn him over to the police directly. And Jessup knew that that alone would not prevent Sweden from going ahead with the programme Derringer had called 'Execute'. Dorn was right. He had to be trusted. Jessup felt easier with the thought that things could not be worse anyway. He opened the car door again and stepped out.

Dorn looked over his shoulder at Martina with such deep tenderness, his brown eyes very dark in the big handsome face, that Carol had to turn away in a moment of surprise and embarrassment.

'My dear, I'm so sorry to have got you involved in this. Things could have been different.'

Martina's face glowed with softness in the dim reflections of light as she squeezed his shoulder in response. 'We'll get through, somehow. Don't worry.' She leaned forward and kissed him on the cheek, tears welling up in her widened blue eyes.

Jessup was away for less than three minutes. When he returned he looked like a tramp. His tie was awry at the neck; there was a bright red bruise on his cheekbone where some frantic woman, forcing a way through the crowd, had swung her handbag at him. A jacket pocket flapped open on threads where a pickpocket had tried his luck. He brushed off Carol's expression of concern.

CHARLES SMART

'Let's move. It's sheer hell out there.'

It was easier said than done. The traffic was thicker than ever and nobody was being polite. 'If this is a preliminary diversion,' he shouted above the roaring engine, 'we sure as hell ought to reach Swedcom before the real thing begins.'

He finally forced his way into the unending stream of headlights on his left. None of them in the Jaguar had had any reason to take special notice of the red mini 'S' Cooper thrusting its way aggressively through the traffic a few minutes earlier.

BALTIC INCIDENT
Chapter Nine

The 'Blue Belt' of Sweden, the Gőta canal, snaked for thirty-five miles between Europe's third and fifth largest lakes, Vänern and Vättern. After its external frontiers, the canal zone ranked number one in the country's defence system, since it was a natural barrier against attack from either north or south.

Lars Dahl's fears about being on his first 'live' mission had receded with the need to concentrate on following the calmly spoken instructions of Red Leader. The six tanks of the closely knit unit had threaded an unfamiliar route through the forest, their treads often sliding uncontrollably on the yielding thickness of a slippery, pine-needle floor. The silence of the woods was shattered by the constant roar of their engines. Several times Dahl had had to use the horizontal chain saw fitted to the front of all the Mark 2 tanks recently adapted for fighting in the thick central forests. The wickedly sharp, three-inch long teeth of the tree-cutting blades could be projected two yards in front of the vehicle, making queen Boadicea's scythed chariots look comparatively inoffensive. The money-conscious defence ministry had not given a thought to the undermanned tank commander, already doubling as driver and canon controller, who had to operate it.

Now, after an hour of negotiating forest trails, Dahl received the order that sent him on a lone reconnaissance to the south western opening of the canal itself. At this point a series of six locks carried the canal water from Lake Vänern, the more westerly of the two lakes, to a height of two hundred and eighty feet above sea level. In the event of an invasion it was vital to keep the locks intact, and in every Red Alert practice it was normal procedure for one member of the unit to scout the southern bank. Dahl should have been relieved, because the objective was to observe and report, not to expose the tank to possible attack. But the nervous tick above his youthful eyebrow began to throb again.

Two or three minutes more and Svensson would be through the small village of Sjötorp, just beyond which lay the big house and warehouse of Swedcom. Three miles back he'd turned off the E3 direct road to Stockholm and on to this narrow lakeside road. It sloped steeply towards the lake, a gash of asphalt cutting through the dark pine forests. He didn't expect to see street lighting after leaving Gothenburg and passing through three other darkened towns. He knew the main moves of 'Operation Searchlight' and guessed that the blackout was part of Stavrinsky's plan. At last he was to see some action, something more immediately rewarding than writing dreary reports on foreign students and visiting East German lecturers. He even felt a twinge of excitement after all the legwork he'd put into this special assignment, despite being attached to that toffee-nosed Englishman for the past six months. He hummed in tune with the light music from the Danish radio station.

Svensson was a little slow in recognizing the powerful red and blue lamps flashing across the middle of the road half a mile ahead. They certainly weren't village lights. Damn, Svensson said softly to himself. Another delay. Jessup and Dorn must have arrived at Swedcom by now and, whatever their intentions, it was his job to stick to them and report on their movements.

It wasn't a police check and there was no accident. Before he turned them off, Svensson's headlights had illuminated the drab green of soldiers' uniforms, slung

BALTIC INCIDENT

guns and metal helmets. Beyond them he could see the outlines of personnel carriers. And if he was not very much mistaken, there was something suspiciously like a heavy machine gun emplacement just inside the tree line. It seemed the land of his forefathers really was prepared to fight for its liberty. There was no ceremony and no time wasted. An officer brusquely asked to see his identity card. Then, in good English, told him to stick to the main road, drive slowly through the village and wait at the canal crossing. In reply to Svensson's question, the soldier merely said there were routine military exercises in the area.

Svensson didn't know whether or not to admire Stavrinsky and the Russians in general, for they must already be picking up useful intelligence. The Swedes had certainly reacted fast to the information produced by the East German agent. But the last thing Svensson wanted was another delay. Although the village centre consisted of only a short line of houses and scattered shops, there were already a dozen cars waiting to cross the canal bridge. The bridge itself was raised. A dotted line of small red lights powered, Svensson presumed, by an emergency generator, outlined the bulk of the roadway as it reared towards the darkened sky, hinged to the nearside bank. Perhaps a ship was passing. Perhaps it was a safety measure to prevent vehicles and pedestrians from crossing before they were security checked again. Whatever the reason, it was an impassable barrier to Svensson. If there was one thing he hated – or was it loved? – it was impassable barriers.

Even before he'd caught up with the last car in the queue, Svensson had decided on the detour. With every appearance that he knew his way around, for the benefit of watchful police, he turned right, without haste, at the village crossroads. Almost immediately he

183

was again among the trees and driving up a steep hill. There just had to be another road across the canal. He put his foot hard on the accelerator and shot up the narrow road towards the first bend.

Maybe, if the control officer had been a little more explicit, and maybe, if the car radio had not been on such a high volume, Svensson would still have lived to cross the next bridge, two miles ahead. But it was doubtful. Concentrated development of latent individual initiative had been an essential ingredient of his Seattle course. Any CIA aspirant would have been quietly dropped from the active service programme had he hesitated to exploit the quickest and most ruthless approach to an objective.

Rounding the bend at forty miles an hour, Svensson hit the first full grown tree lying across the road's width before his foot could leave the accelerator. At that speed, the mini Cooper should have stuck its nose into the soft pinewood bark and raised its tail end at the beginning of a cartwheel action. In which case Svensson might have walked away with no more than multiple injuries. It was the second tree, crashing on to the roof of the car and sliding off behind it, that prevented the cartwheel effect. For several seconds Svensson remained alive in the wreck of the mini, trapped between the two trees. His safety belt had stopped him from being flung through the shattered windscreen, but the sudden halt had twisted his body so that the right shoulder blade and collarbone had splintered against the dashboard. Crumpled and shocked and in no pain whatsoever, Svensson fumbled instinctively and uselessly to release the belt with his left hand.

From the driving window to the right of the canon's breech inside the tank, Lars Dahl had not been able to see the lights of Sjötorp village that should have been directly ahead and below him through the forest. He had tried three different directions as he steered the powerful war machine between the trees and down the steep slope. But those village lights that were supposed to be part of his navigation system simply didn't appear. Neither could he see the forward-thrusting chain saw jutting from the front of the tank like the jaws of an evil monster.

Only when the tank slithered heavily towards the two trees on the firebreak road did Dahl realize he was hopelessly lost. By then it was too late. The tree on his right front had been sliced down and across the road below him a second before the car shot out of the bend. As in a slow motion drama, he watched the second tree crumple the car roof. He jammed his foot on the break pedal. The tracks of the forty-ton tank stopped in obedience, making no difference whatever to the forward rush of the heavy metal down the steep bed of wet pine needles. Dahl's reactions were fast, and with a roar of the revving two hundred and fifty horsepower engine, he thrust the mighty machine into reverse gear. For that as well he was a week too late. Nothing Dahl could do was able to stop the monster's downward plunge. The gnashing fangs of the tank's chain-saw bit through the metal of the car door at seat level like a blowtorch through powdered snow. Svensson died instantly as the metal teeth chewed their way through the flesh and bones of his upper thighs. A moment later, even the traces of that dreadful mutilation were obliterated. For the left track of the tank, in furious reverse, reduced the mangled remains of the mini to a mush of flesh and metal, spreading it like a rumpled red blanket on the road behind the tank.

CHARLES SMART

Olle Görman was of average height with a fork-shaped receding hairline. Neatly grey-suited and wearing rimless spectacles, he could have been the respected local bank manager. But the furtive look that sometimes came to his eyes belied the impression. Görman was, in fact, a sententious character with a gift for hiding an extreme form of dogmatism under a cloak of very false humility. The humbug was readily overlooked by business associates who happened to know he had inherited a large family fortune – which he preferred not to share with a wife – and a certain amount of primitive business acumen to help him maintain it. His modest distinction, as he often told acquaintances, was that he was merely a poor survivor in increasingly depressing economic times. Just how well he survived could be judged by the value of his enormous collection of old paintings and antiques housed in the large modern villa he had built for himself on a rocky promontory overlooking Lake Vänern. Not even the closest crony knew of the ambition he'd nurtured for the past ten years to build an even bigger and grander house on a far more expensive plot of ground in the sunshine of Santa Monica. For that he needed a lot more hard cash. Which was why it had been necessary to arrange for his private Swedcom company to acquire certain foreign contracts.

Görman stood in the large candle-lit living room with his back to the enormous square-shaped stone fireplace, hands clasped behind his back to feel the comfortable warmth from the glowing logs. Above the fireplace a large gilt-framed portrait of his great-grandfather, the creator of the family fortune, frowned darkly into some middle distance. There was a slightly cynical smile on Görman's thin features as he faced the seated Stavrinsky. He said, in German, 'I don't know, and I don't wish to be told, the precise nature of your activities, Hr.Müller,

but did you have to include this damn charade power cut?'
Stavrinsky knew that Görman was not in the slightest put out by the event and his craggy face beamed back good naturedly. 'Unfortunately, it was necessary. There are very few countries where our electronic equipment could be tested so thoroughly and so widely. Besides, I believe you're satisfied with the price?'
A candle flickered reflectively in Görman's thick lenses as he inclined his head in agreement to the man he knew only as Karl Müller, principal of the Dresden components firm. Two hours earlier he had telephoned his Zurich manager at the Union Bank of Switzerland to confirm that payment had been made by Müller.
On three occasions since landing on the coast, Stavrinsky had had to talk with this avaricious weasel and had come to dislike intensely his sharp-nosed money conscious manner and the servility with which he over-garnished his greed. It was time to be done with Görman. At least for the moment, for he was well aware that, with the high-placed contacts Görman had been able to make with the chiefs of Datasaab and Asea – Swedish companies of the highest national and international distinction – in order to gain admittance to the sensitive Karlskoga equipment, Görman would undoubtedly now have access to Stanford University and MIT computer codes. With careful planning Stavrinsky could avoid that intrigue, assuming 'M' section was to be given some hand in the matter, by pleading detailed technical ignorance.
'Good.' he said to the Swedcom head. 'Now I think it is time to feed the computers.' Stavrinsky lingered as though it was an afterthought. In fact he'd not stopped thinking about it ever since Görman had told him Dorn was on his way to Swedcom. 'By the way, when Hr.

Dorn arrives he may want to see me, too. Please show him into the operations room. And' Stavrinsky hesitated, he did not quite tap the side of his nose but he gave Görman the sort of knowing smile he was undoubtedly familiar with 'please remember to turn a blind eye to whatever you may see or hear tonight. I believe that is part of our agreement?' He picked up his black briefcase and rose from the soft leather armchair.

Görman hurried to see him to the door. 'I'm sure you will find everything in order, Hr. Müller,' he said, bowing Stavrinsky through it.

Stavrinsky knew everything was in order. The four men discreetly patrolling the yard outside the warehouse might have looked casual to the unobservant. They were, in fact, highly trained gunmen assigned to Stavrinsky from the pool of specialists kept in readiness at the Leningrad base quarters. They had been on station long before his helicopter had landed on the lawn in front of the house.

The warehouse lay in its own grounds fifty yards from the villa and could be reached by a covered path joining the two buildings. Görman led the way to the side door of the house through the kitchen.

- - - - - - - - - - - - - - - -

There was a two hundred mile stretch of narrow road on the R6 between Helsinborg and Gothenburg. It was mainly flat and monotonous countryside, coming close to the sea only occasionally. During the first hour of the drive, Dorn had told them something of his part in 'Operation Searchlight' and nothing could stop Martina from asking him about his life in East Germany. They still had no final answer to the question of what precisely Dorn might be able to do, once they arrived at Swedcom. But Jessup had recognized a certain vagueness on some points in Dorn's explanation. He couldn't put his finger on it. After a while they fell silent and now Jessup was trying to concentrate on the road ahead.

His thoughts kept wandering. He supposed that some innate sense of fair play rather than an excess of patriotic courage and sensibility had made him decide to do what Goddard had asked on that first occasion in Derringer's room. And he'd had to admit to a burning curiosity about Goddard's cloak and dagger approach. No thought that he might be placed in a position of personal danger had seriously crossed his mind. Yet, in all fairness – that word again, he was too bloody English – what he'd done specifically under Goddard's directions had brought him no risk. Strange he'd not realized that earlier. The near drowning in the west Baltic could be indirectly attributed to his own desire to reinforce the evidence of Dorn's activities he'd already found. The fracas at Elsinore was a direct result of his offer of help to Martina, urged, it was true, by a curiosity to see the end of the business. Even on this caper to Swedcom Dorn had not asked for Jessup's aid. He had been prepared to go it alone. Indeed, had tried to insist. There was something in the equation that didn't fit.

He turned to look at Dorn. 'Do you think it's safe to walk in at the front door? If Goddard knows about your escape from Säpo, perhaps Görman does, too.'

'Don't worry. I'll think of something. And as a last resort, Derringer's little toy here will come in useful.'

Too glib, Jessup thought. He wasn't happy about the reference to the gun, or the tone of Dorn's response. How could he pass it off so lightly? 'Operation Searchlight' must be one of the most sensitive little jobs the Russians had worked on for ages. How the hell would a single handgun help if Swedcom were crawling with armed KGB men? Jessup slowed the car. They were about to enter the small town of Mariestad, some miles

south of Swedcom. It was in darkness, as had been the
villages and other towns they had passed through. The
power cut was obviously a major one. He stopped the
car at the side of the road and hauled on the handbrake.
He felt the questioning eyes of the others. Before they
could ask, he spoke to Dorn again.

'Heinrich, I still think there's something funny in all
this. I'm just an ordinary guy. Not too difficult to fool,
really. But I thought we had an understanding?' Jessup could feel the tension from Carol and Martina. 'Are
you levelling with me, Heinrich? This trip to Swedcom
isn't just a picnic. If there's the slightest possibility of
danger, at least I'd like to keep Carol and Martina out
of it. They could catch a train home from here. What
do you say?'

Dorn said quietly, 'I'd say that would be very sensible.
I suggested it an hour ago. As a matter of fact, perhaps
you should go with them.' He turned in the passenger
seat to look fully at Jessup. 'You don't trust me?'
Jessup relented a fraction. It was a late stage in the
game but he'd learned to be cautious. 'Let's just say I'm
nervous. Sure, I'm going to see this through. But I am
concerned for the ladies.'

'David', Carol spoke with a mixture of tenderness and
stubbornness, 'If you think I'd be happy to go back,
not knowing what's happening to you, you're wrong.
Please don't ask. I'm coming with you.'

'Me, too, Heinrich. You can't get rid of me that easily.'
Martina made some effort to be lighthearted. 'And I'm
sure you haven't changed your mind about stopping
this crazy plan of the Russians.'

Her comment didn't quite fit the mood; hung in the air
for a moment longer than was comfortable. Dorn said,
'My dear, whatever doubts David has about me, he's
right about one thing. I don't want to sound chauvinis-

tic, but this is not the right place for women.' He looked at Jessup again, 'Nor for amateurs, David. If you have the slightest doubt about me, you ought to turn me in at the next police station.'

Jessup knew it was a direct challenge. He also knew there was nothing he could do about it. If he changed course now and handed Dorn over – assuming Dorn didn't argue about that – the Russian plan would be activated before anyone of any importance was willing to make the necessary investigation. It would come to the same thing if Dorn was playing fast and loose. If, on the other hand, Dorn really meant to try and thwart the Russian plan, then there was the faintest chance he might succeed and, perhaps, a better chance if he remained with Dorn for backup help. 'So be it,' he said and, with his foot hard on the brake pedal, thrust the automatic gear decisively into the number two position.

Half an hour later, driving in a silence that was not altogether uncomfortable with decisions having been made, they were on the minor lakeside road. They had no trouble at Sjötorp; the army was there to ensure the smooth flow of increased military traffic, not to inspect civilians. Dorn, wearing the jacket bought by Jessup in Helsinborg, was not given a second look.

Jessup turned into a deserted stretch of the road on the other side of the village and the car headlights picked out the discreet Swedcom sign as they cruised past the warehouse drive. The chinks of light that could be seen coming from two shuttered windows told them that Görman had installed independent power sources. They saw no other sign of life. Beyond the warehouse, Görman's home showed only as an irregular block of blackness among the trees. Obviously Görman had not extended the power lines to the villa. Jessup parked the

Jaguar well into the trees at the side of the road, immediately before the house driveway.

Dorn said, 'I shall walk to the front door, see Görman, and ask for Stavrinsky as though nothing had changed. Casual is the way, I think.'

'The rest of you are the back-up team. If I don't give some sign of life within twenty minutes, you can assume it's not going well. Drive like hell to the nearest telephone. It'll be time for the police whether we like it or not. Agreed?'

He took Derringer's gun from his waistband and held it out to Jessup. 'I'd bulge in strange places carrying this. Take it, and don't look so worried. You won't have to use it.'

Jessup looked down at the weapon distastefully. He thought he'd heard all the most common famous last words and he didn't like the idea of making Dorn eat them one bit. But he took the gun without a word. The metal was heavy and cold in his hand.

'By the way,' Dorn added, grinning, 'that's the safety catch you've got your thumb on.'

'Thanks for the tip,' Jessup answered dourly.

Dorn turned in his seat to squeeze Martina's hand reassuringly. 'Don't worry. Remember, Görman and I are supposed to be business associates,' he smiled at her.

'It wasn't Görman I was thinking about,' Martina found she could not smile back.

Dorn nodded his understanding. Then he became the professional again. He slipped quietly from the car and walked quickly into the shadows of the house drive, his feet crunching away in the darkness.

Jessup looked at his watch. There was an hour left to midnight. He watched Dorn disappear then fished thoughtfully in his pocket for a tobacco pouch.

BALTIC INCIDENT

Lennart Feldt had been chosen for his skill rather than his looks. At thirty-five he was grossly fat and had a head of close-cropped blonde hair that looked more like an ill-fitting skullcap. But his ability to program and manipulate computers had persuaded even the tight fisted Görman that he was worth every penny of the hefty salary he'd been paid. For two years Feldt had sweated blood installing the most up to date computer equipment at the Karlskoga military headquarters. The work had been sub-contracted to Swedcom on the special recommendation of ASEA, the country's ultra-respectable home office equipment firm.

A single million-dollar payment into the Swiss account of ASEA's chairman, contributed by the Russians, had helped to seal the contract. The trickiest part of the computer link-up between Swedcom and Karlskoga had been to make sure that the engineer in charge knew all there was to know about both systems. With Feldt as the engineer in charge, their compatibility was perfect.

He dwarfed the console in front of him, his enormous paunch making it seem impossible for him to get close enough to the keyboard. Thick white and hairless fingers hovered now over the keys like the talons of a West Indian Turkey Vulture. Satisfied at last that the sophisticated machinery at Karlskoga – the computer he had himself chained to his command in the Swedcom warehouse – was prepared to receive only what he fed them, Feldt gave a sigh of relaxation and turned towards Stavrinsky.

The room was purely functional; no bigger than a large kitchen occupying one part of the warehouse complex. The single window facing outside had been heavily shuttered. Smudged whitewashed walls and two wire protected ceiling neon tubes indicated it had been used as a storeroom. Stavrinsky had seen to it that everything necessary for the operation was there. Three solid wooden tables, on which had been arranged the computer manual below an extra large screen, the feeder-box, printout machine and two telephones, one red and one green, stood in a corner of the room. Stavrinsky had furnished himself with a separate desk and chair, placed just behind Feldt's operating stool.

Stavrinsky lifted the black briefcase and placed it flat on the table before him. There was a coded lock on either side of the handle and the case was doubly secured by a separate key for each lock. He turned the dials as tenderly as he would have caressed a newborn kitten, for the explosives packed inside, a normal precaution against force or unauthorized attempts to open it, were sufficient to fragment anybody and anything within a ten yard radius. Without hesitation the powerful fingers efficiently and effortlessly reproduced the coded figures Stavrinsky had memorised weeks earlier. Satisfied with the codes, Stavrinsky then extracted a pencil from his pocket notebook and broke it carefully in half. The jagged ends of the pieces looked perfectly normal. It would have taken an expert with a magnifying glass to detect the smoothness of each projecting irregular splinter, pre-designed by the ballistics department of the KGB's 'M' section, to separate in such a way as to match the corrugations inside the briefcase locks. He inserted the broken pencil ends.

The briefcase opened easily on its greased hinges to disclose two rectangular boxes of bullet proof metal that would not have escaped attention had they been secretly ex-rayed by a curious customs officer. Which was one reason why Stavrinsky had chosen to enter the country by means of the Russian trawler that regularly surveyed the south coast of Sweden and the North Sea.

BALTIC INCIDENT

He took out the heavy box labelled 'program' and opened it. The five-inch square of black card that held the plastic disk weighed less than an ounce. He looked at his watch, then handed the disk to Feldt. 'For transmission in five minutes.' he said.

Stavrinsky reached across to the green telephone. 'All clear?' he asked. He listened briefly and a frown came to his leather-beaten face. He spoke abruptly, 'Coming', and replaced the handpiece. It took four long and urgent strides for him to reach a door on the other side of the room. A short passage led to a box-like office, transformed into a temporary kitchen and guardroom. A Krupp coffee machine and plastic cups littered a desk. On another table lay a black plastic-handled submachine pistol.

As Stavrinsky entered, a guard, dressed in night uniform of regulation tight black trousers and sweater, stood to attention.

'What is it?' Stavrinsky growled at him. The guard pointed to an outsized television screen positioned at one side of the room.

'A car with four occupants, Sir. Came past too slowly and stopped too close.'

Stavrinsky looked hard at the white on black infrared picture. He had expected to see Dorn arrive alone. Three passengers would be more troublesome. He could not identify features from the pictures. But the shape of the car was distinctive even if the outline was blurred, and he'd seen it somewhere before. What the hell was Dorn doing with passengers? At any rate he had been right about Dorn. Since an open approach to consulates and embassies was forbidden, and Dorn knew he would be at the operational base, Swedcom was his obvious choice. Besides, he could not forget just yet that he was supposed to be Dorn's immediate chief.

As Stavrinsky watched, he saw Dorn's figure leave the car and walk towards the drive where he left the view of the camera. Giving instructions to the guard, Stavrinsky went back to the operations room, dearly wishing Dorn had still been safely and uncomplicatedly in the hands of the Swedish security police.

He closed the door behind him, checked his wristwatch again, then returned Feldt's expectant look. 'Now.' he commanded.

Feldt pressed the release button. Immediately the screen showed the disposition of the Warsaw Pact invasion fleet. Feldt's smooth round face turned to Stavrinsky in a victory grin that made his eyes disappear in a roll of flesh. What was on the screen now, and was being duplicated in Karlskoga, represented the successful completion of many months' work in a highly technical field. The infatuation with computers he had nurtured both in the company he had worked for since the age of twenty and in the privacy of his own home, was paying off handsomely. It was not the first time he had keyed into computers of state importance. But this time he was being paid for it.

Stavrinsky did not particularly share Feldt's joy in technical know-how. He said, impatiently, 'Let me have a printout.' He knew that, within a time span of ten minutes or so, the synchronization had to be made precise. It was vital that, at the beginning, the information on the Swedcom disk should agree with that already available to the Karlskoga technical team. He need not have worried. Feldt was supreme in his work.

The Ukrainian took the long folded sheet Feldt tore from the printout machine and meticulously compared the figures with those he had received from Russian sources, via the Gothenburg consulate. They fitted. For the next forty minutes the real movements of the attacking force would be diagrammatically reproduced accurately on the Swedcom control disk. It was after that, at about midnight when the fleet reached longitude thirteen and thirty seconds, that the deception would begin. From then on, neither the Swedish air and seacraft which sent back reports, nor the Karlskoga technicians could know that the real signals were being blocked by the Swedcom master disk. Stavrinsky knew that, soon after midnight, somebody up there in the Karlskoga headquarters would be ordered to hit the panic button, the order 'Execute', which would put Sweden on an immediate war footing and open its Pandora box of highly secret defence positions, probable tactics, weapons, back-up code systems for troop movements and a host of other details, to his agents and their recording equipment stationed in a hundred different parts of the country.

The door behind him opened. Without looking up, Stavrinsky called 'Come in, Heinrich. You're just in time to see the results of your labours.' He turned, with a smile, to face Dorn. 'A celebratory drink,eh?' He ignored Görman who was standing in the doorway. Görman took the hint and left, closing the door behind him.

Dorn reciprocated the welcome. 'By all means, Boris. It's been a long drive, and that electricity cut's played merry hell with the traffic.'

'Very effective. Made my helicopter ride here a little more interesting, too.' Stavrinsky beckoned Dorn to the computer screen and told Feldt to take a break.

Dorn studied the figures while Stavrinsky reached into the deeper drawer at the bottom of his desk to bring out a half bottle of aquavit and two plastic beakers.

Feeling like a young reporter watching his first headline coming off the press, yet at the same time knowing he'd just entered the spider's web, Dorn was fascinated to see the Russian charts of the Warsaw Pact fleet movements he had himself worked with in Ljunghusen. Even as he watched, new figures replaced the old, tracking the fleet's movement, the numbers and types of vessel, as it closed on the 13°30" East longitude from the east. He took the proffered drink from Stavrinsky and emptied half the burning Scandinavian spirit down his throat without taking his eyes off the screen.

Stavrinsky said, 'You know, don't you? Or at least you've guessed. Or perhaps you pumped the old man before his sudden, er, departure?'

Dorn sat on Feldt's vacated stool and looked at his old chief. If Stavrinsky knew about Derringer, what more did he know? His eyes gave nothing away. He said, flatly, 'It was an accident.'

'Of course, of course.' said Stavrinsky agreeably. 'I don't know how you got to Helsingør or, for that matter, how you slipped away from the Swedish special branch, but I suppose Derringer tried to keep you quiet against your will. He had his instructions, too, you know.'

There was the hint of a question in Stavrinsky's slightly raise bushy eyebrows. Dorn ignored it. If Stavrinsky wanted to behave as if nothing unusual had happened that was all right by him.

Stavrinsky was not a vindictive person and, like many of his fellow Ukrainians, could feel a depth of compassion of the sort long suppressed in the West by the facade of its superficial glitter. 'Listen, Heinrich. Moscow didn't consult me when they chose you to lay the false trail. They make their own rules, there. You know that.' Stavrinsky was trying to assess Dorn's mood. He didn't want to upset him more than was absolutely necessary. He took another draught from the cup of aquavit. 'And what Moscow wanted was for you to give yourself up to the Swedish authorities. They knew you had been a good agent, even if you had become disposable. They didn't know you were a disciple of Houdini.'

Dorn looked away from the screen. He smiled ironically at Stavrinsky. 'The past tense, Boris? "wanted"? Is "M" section getting over anxious?'

The KGB colonel was genuinely sorry and he wanted no more discussion on the inevitable unpleasantness. He'd already said too much and Dorn needed no explanation. There were more immediate things to consider. In a way he was relieved to have Dorn in sight again. There'd been too much of a loose end with a man of his talent on the prowl at such an inconvenient moment. He didn't know how or why Jessup had remained in the picture, still less Dorn's other two companions, for he remembered now that the car had been an English make and belonged to Goddard's innocent recruit. That small issue had to be taken care of. But that should be no problem, not with MI6 and the CIA actively cooperating, and the Swedes dancing to everybody's tune. All he had to do was keep them on ice for a few hours. To take over where Derringer had failed.

At that moment, the door at the far end of the room opened and a black-clad KGB gunman entered. He ushered in Martina, Carol and Jessup. The guard Stavrinsky had spoken to earlier followed.

Dorn had to admit Stavrinsky infused his professional accomplishments with an uncommon charm. He watched as the big Ukrainian strode with open arms and smiling face to greet the confused and apprehensive looking trio. Dorn half expected him to clasp them in a Russian style bear hug.

'Dr and Mrs Jessup, I think, and Martina, if I remember correctly.' he said, raising his bushy eyebrows in a most convincing display of friendliness. 'Any friend of Heinrich is a friend of mine.' His courtesy belonged to the best of the old Tsar's salons. He waved away the guards with a sentence in Russian that made them quickly sling their machine pistols and retire. It was a performance, Dorn thought, incongruously like a host dismissing the attention of a waiter.

Dorn drank the remains of the burning spirit and waited for the subtle questioning that had to follow. He did not have to guess at the deadliness behind the little charade. He knew Stavrinsky; that his graciousness was not an act, yet still the means to a very positive end. He took a quick look at his wristwatch. There was one more vital thing to be done. Then, perhaps, they could all go home.

Martina, slightly ruffled in temper but immensely relieved to see Dorn safe, was both mollified and amused by Stavrinsky's welcome. She hadn't imagined that he had held her hand a fraction longer than was necessary. Dorn's boss, or was it ex-boss, now? was human after all. Then Dorn was at her side and she was in his arms for a brief moment.

Carol and Jessup followed Martina further into the room as Stavrinsky closed the door behind them. Both were acutely uncomfortable, despite Stavrinsky's welcome. Jessup knew he looked as uneasy as he felt. He decided to play up to the part of the passive and rather bewildered innocent he'd been taken for. That's what Stavrinsky would expect, anyway; had, perhaps, even helped Goddard in his choice of character. He saw the computer screen at once. There was the open briefcase, the same one he had seen in Dorn's house. It did not take a genius to add up the scene in front of him. Derringer and Dorn had already filled in many of the details. The great deception they called 'Operation Searchlight' was being controlled from this room. The movements of the Warsaw Pact invasion force, real and fictional, were already being programmed to Karlskoga. How long would the Swedish government wait before activating 'Execute'? If Dorn had a plan, then this was the moment to do something about it. How could Dorn look so calm?

Stavrinsky moved past him, as jovial as a grandfather celebrating the birth of his first granddaughter. Incredibly relaxed, Jessup thought. 'Come and join the party,' Stavrinsky was saying as he poured out a clear liquid into plastic cups.

Jessup smiled wryly to himself. No wonder Stavrinsky was so confident. He had the world on his side while the Swedish government was running like a well-trained Pavlovian dog along the scent of his false trails. With what seemed to be a small army, armed to the teeth, literally within shouting distance, there seemed to be nothing anyone could do to stop that program. He took the drink offered by the still voluble and obviously jubilant Stavrinsky.

Stavrinsky was saying, throwing a quizzical look at Dorn and Jessup in turn, 'I'm intrigued, gentlemen. I think we're all aware of recent events, you must tell me what brought you both together again. And in such charming company,' he added, including Carol and Martina in his question.

Jessup could see that Dorn was not fooled for a moment by Stavrinsky's lighthearted approach.

Dorn took his time in responding. He searched his pockets and brought out the Stuyvesant packet. He offered one of the extra long cigarettes to Martina then shook out another for himself, lighting both with a silver cigarette lighter. The smoke curled slowly upwards from the glowing end of his cigarette and Dorn, crossing one foot over the other, leaned casually on Stavrinsky's desk, a second drink in his smoking hand. His relaxed manner did not relieve the tension Jessup began to feel building up.

Jessup did not have to pretend nervousness. He brought out his battered pipe and reached in the deep pocket of his old grey overcoat for a tobacco pouch. Instead of the feel of soft leather, his fingers hit hard metal. In that moment he knew that whatever Dorn may have had planned, he himself had the means to force the issue. That disk had to be stopped. Right now. And there seemed no swifter way of doing it than to force Stavrinsky to take the disk from the computer. There was something else, too. One way or another, Heinrich would have to show his colours. There were too many odd things going on. Jessup's left hand, holding the plastic cup, trembled. He hoped desperately for Dorn to give some sign, or for the roof to fall in, or even that he himself might wake from this unreality. Anything that would make it unnecessary for him to take out that gun.

For seconds that seemed a hundred years' long, Jessup hadn't heard Dorn's partly fictional narrative in reply to Stavrinsky's gentle probing. His mind was racing ahead to the problems: would the threat of being shot be enough to make Stavrinsky comply? Would the guards interfere before the disk could be destroyed? One thing he realized immediately; with the disk out of the machine and made useless, there would be nothing more to do. He would hand the gun to Stavrinsky, or even Dorn, and surrender. There could be no thought of trying to escape the building with the responsibility of Carol and Martina.

BALTIC INCIDENT

It was extremely unlikely that Stavrinsky would harm them. He was a professional agent, not a gangster. As for Goddard and the British Secret Service, well, there was more to plain morality than a theoretical military advantage gained at the expense of an innocent country whose only weakness was a naive and very low pain threshold.

Jessup surprised even himself. He brought the small gun from his pocket, flicked off the safety catch simultaneously and sighted the barrel on Stavrinsky's chest. It was done in the blink of an eyelid. The women, standing on his left, gasped in unison; Dorn straightened from his casual stance at the table and instantly moved a pace from the side of Stavrinsky. Stavrinsky, standing in front of the computer layout, did not move a muscle. Even the smile on his face froze.

For a split second the tableau was still, and it crossed Jessup's mind that he probably looked ridiculous in that pseudo-cocktail atmosphere. For, while he held the gun in his extended right hand, the plastic beaker was still in his left and his teeth still clamped grimly to the stem of the pipe. Hell, this was no time for philosophical reflection. Without taking his eyes off Stavrinsky, Jessup simply dropped the cup, its fluid contents splashing over Carol's shoes, and removed his pipe.

'Thought you'd been paralysed, David. Why the delay?' said Dorn, and moved round the table towards Jessup. 'Okay, let me take over, we have to move fast.'

Jessup swung the gun quickly towards Dorn and back again to Stavrinsky. Dorn stopped, suddenly, on the far side of the desk. A look of surprise appeared on his face. Stavrinsky threw a sideways look at Dorn, his eyes narrowing.

'Not this time, Heinrich. This is my show.' He should not have doubted Dorn, but in the hours that had elapsed since the Elsinore castle incident, a number of items had been niggling away at the back of his brain, helping to create a strangely different image of Dorn from the one he had come to know over the previous months. Items as disparate in magnitude and significance as Dorn's overnight decision to defect to the West and the sudden urge to smoke a cigarette. If Dorn had known all along about the power-cut detail in 'Operation Searchlight', how come other details of the Russian plan had escaped his professional attention? Dorn had subtly changed character and, for the time being, the gun felt safer in his own hand.

Jessup raised his left hand to support the gun wrist. He seemed to have lost his nervousness somewhere along the line. He motioned to Stavrinsky, 'Take the disk out. Now!' He gave his voice a cutting edge.

Stavrinsky had lost none of his poise. If his origins in Odessa, or wherever it was Dorn said he came from, had been humble his natural intelligence had since been complemented by the quiet dignity and courage that Englishmen like Goddard could only associate with their own brand of culture. 'I'm afraid you misunderstand,' he replied calmly. 'That computer has been set up by the finest technician in Sweden. Only he can stop the program. On my instructions, of course. If you like we could fetch him. He's only in the next room. I could ring for him.' Stavrinsky half turned to the green telephone.

'Don't touch that!' Jessup commanded. 'There's another way to stop the program.' He moved the gun fractionally to point at the feeder box.

'Wait!' Dorn spoke sharply. 'If you want to keep the gun, that's alright by me. Believe me. But if you pull that trigger it'll bring the guards in.'

BALTIC INCIDENT

'Does that worry you, Heinrich? There's no way out anyway. You know the guards are patrolling the grounds and we haven't brought a machine gun with us. Besides, there's no more time. Might as well finish the thing off.' He knew his voice sounded harsh to Dorn, but that was no longer important.

'There's something you've missed, David.'

Jessup took his eyes off Stavrinsky long enough to glance at Dorn. He couldn't have picked a worse moment to have second thoughts about the German. 'Speak.' he said roughly. 'We're going to be interrupted at any moment by those guards.'

'If we destroy that apparatus, the Karlskoga computers will go dead for an unspecified number of minutes.'

'So?'

'No commander who fully expects an invasion could just hang around hoping his technician will be able to tie the wires together again. Without a doubt, the order will be given for "Execute", which is exactly what Stavrinsky is waiting for.'

Stavrinsky smiled broadly and tapped his hands together in silent applause as he looked at Dorn. 'Good thinking, Heinrich. I couldn't wish for a better pupil. But Dr Jessup is correct, is he not? What can you do? I don't really think I'm going to be shot. We all know it would serve no purpose at all. I believe, gentlemen, we've said all there is to say. It only remains for me to pick up this telephone.'

Jessup liked good theatre, and Stavrinsky was splendid. He wasn't playing for time. He didn't have to. He had all the time he needed.

His voice cut across Stavrinsky's mild tones like flame through a feather. 'That's enough, Stavrinsky. Heinrich, you've told me what can't be done. What can be done? Make it good.'

'We need this.' Dorn spoke firmly and stretched an arm over Stavrinsky's desk to take the remaining box from the briefcase. He held it up to make his point. 'The code that will cancel that program and allow Karlskoga headquarters to receive the Warsaw Pact forces "Exercise" signal. This is the only way. And since you don't want to give me that gun, use it on Stavrinsky's legs if he makes another move towards the telephone. Now, for God's sake let's get out of here.'

Jessup realized Dorn was right. Smashing the machine here would only bring about the disaster he was trying to avert. He hoped Dorn knew what he was talking about as far as getting out was concerned. He saw Stavrinsky's poise slip, the humour quite disappeared from his intelligent eyes as he stared at Dorn. That was all it took. Jessup knew a psychological disadvantage when he saw it, and the big Ukrainian was suffering from acute deflation. He hoped Dorn had a better idea than rushing four or five armed Russian commandos in an attempt to get to the Jaguar.

Carol and Martina had barely moved in the two minutes that had elapsed since Jessup had pulled out the gun. They were shaken from their momentary lethargy by Jessup's crisp command to them. 'Do what he says. Fast.' Jessup didn't move his eyes or the gun from Stavrinsky as Dorn, carrying the code box, rushed over to the door, waving the women to follow him. Dorn opened the door cautiously and looked out along the corridor.

Carol hadn't moved from the spot. 'You expect me to go and leave you here?' Her dark eyes sparkled with a determination Jessup knew only too well. This, he hadn't bargained for.

'Damn it! Go with the others! Nobody's going to hurt me.' All that was needed to give Dorn a sporting chance to get away with the code was for Jessup to keep Sta-vrinsky talking for a few precious moments. Carol was being loyally stubborn at the wrong time. Jessup took a step towards her, intending to urge her to the door where Dorn stood frantically beckoning.

Stavrinsky had been waiting for the amateur mistake, and this seemed to be it. For all his bulk, there was nothing slow about Stavrinsky in action. On the instant Jessup moved towards Carol, Stavrinsky placed his left hand flat on the desk behind him and began a vault in-tended to drop him into the hollow square next to the computer operator's stool where he would be out of Jes-sup's sight for vital seconds, giving him enough time to pick up the telephone receiver. But he had not reckoned on Jessup's own lightning reflexes. The Ukrainian was in mid-air when the bullet tore into the muscles of his right forearm. He was unable to prevent the bellow of pain that rose to his lips as he crashed heavily across the stool, unable to steady himself with the useless hand.

Jessup had had no time to think of Dorn's warning about aiming low. Nor did he remember the standard proce-dure about squeezing the trigger instead of snatching at it. If he had remembered, Stavrinsky would prob-ably be dead now instead of scrabbling blindly for the telephone with his good hand, his head well hidden by the desk and printout machine.

Jessup didn't wait to see if Stavrinsky pulled down the handpiece. It was hardly necessary to telephone, anyway. The shot had shattered the silence of the ware-house. 'Run like hell!' he shouted to Carol.

The crimson swirl of Martina's dress whipped from sight as Carol and Jessup ran to the doorway. Dorn had turned left in the corridor, towards Görman's villa and was four yards ahead of them, pulling Martina with him. Carol raced after them, Jessup bringing up the rear. A door was flung open behind them and Jessup turned to see a black clad guard, machine pistol held to his chest, step from a brightly-lit room.

'Keep going,' he yelled to Carol, and fired at the figure silhouetted against the light. The explosion in the confines of the corridor deafened him. There was a loud metallic smack as the lead crumpled against the hardened steel of the guard's breech mechanism and took away the top part of the surprised Russian's right thumb. Unable to bring his gun into a firing position, he ducked swiftly back into the room.

Jessup sprinted on, but the corridor was now empty. Carol's hand grabbed at him as he passed an open doorway.

'In here,' she cried breathlessly. 'That's enough heroics for one day.' She banged the door shut behind him.

Dorn had led them into what seemed to be an outsize barn, a cavernous room lighted, like the rest of the warehouse, by power from the independent generator. Three constructions of what looked like horseboxes were set against the wall. In the middle of a wide expanse of floor boarding were piled half a dozen bales of hay. The rafted ceilingless roof rose to a peak above them. There were no windows. By the aid of two weak light bulbs hanging primitively from the horse stalls by their electric cords Jessup could see the outlines of a closed double-doored loading bay at the far end of the room. He felt a current of fresh, moist air.

Dorn was hurrying, Martina in tow, towards the centre of the room. 'Here. Quickly,' he called to them, then disappeared behind the hay.

Jessup looked at Carol. 'This is a fine time for a practical joke. How do we get out of this? Is he aware that there are armed men out there whose business it is to get that code back at any price?'

BALTIC INCIDENT

There was a simple bolt on the door and Jessup pushed it home. 'That should keep them out for all of ten seconds.'

They heard running footsteps and shouting outside. Stavrinsky could be clearly heard not far away, obviously giving instructions. Nothing less than an armed company could get past the guards in the Swedcom yard. Dorn must surely be aware, Jessup thought, that Stavrinsky probably had every exit covered.

The footsteps stopped at the door. The latch was lifted forcibly and the door shook on its hinges. 'Come on.' Jessup grabbed Carol's arm and ran towards the pile of hay. Behind them they heard the wooden door splinter as someone rammed a foot or a gun butt against it. A staccato volley of automatic gunfire splattered bullets into the wooden wall on their right, probably fired blindly from the other side of the door. It sounded to Jessup like a small flock of sheep coughing into his ear, muffled by the wooden walls.

He shoved Carol violently into the doubtful shelter provided by the hay just as the wooden door crashed inwards. The next burst of gunfire sowed a row of holes, neat enough to satisfy the most fastidious bean-growing gardener, to pass within an inch of his right heel and spreading lethal wooden splinters in several directions. Someone had definitely been trained to shoot low.

CHARLES SMART
Chapter Ten

If ever Jessup needed a hole in the ground it was at this moment. And there it was, right in front of him. Before he could hit the floor, Jessup's outstretched hands were caught by Dorn. A large trap door was open and Carol was halfway down broad wooden steps as Dorn, standing on the same steps, yanked on Jessup's wrists. Jessup jackknifed his legs and half jumped into the gloom. Dorn was already pulling down the heavy trap door lid, and Jessup had only the faintest glimmer of the wide staircase with Carol and Martina below him before slithering to his knees beside Dorn. Then the weak glow from the room above was gone as the trap door banged down. He heard the rasp of metal as Dorn pushed home two bolts, and the darkness was complete.

It was barely seconds before heavy feet were thudding across the floorboards. There was shouting above. Jessup could imagine the first man's astonishment as he found empty space on the other side of the bales of hay. A second, then a third pounding of feet hesitated somewhere above their heads, before moving away. Whoever it was chasing them were not as familiar with the room's geography as Dorn.

'Where the hell are we?' Jessup asked in a loud whisper and breathing hard from the short but fast exit they had made from the computer room.

'Save your breath, friend, and let's move.' Dorn spoke in an urgent whisper. 'Everybody, get to the bottom of these steps. There're only a dozen of them. Keep close to the wall on your right and stay there.'

They needed no second bidding. Feeling their way carefully they shuffled downwards step by step.

BALTIC INCIDENT

Shouting was renewed on the floor above. Somebody had seen the iron ring attached to the staircase entrance. There was the scraping sound of feet on hay and a fumbling of the metal ring and grunts and curses as the trap door refused to budge away from the bolts that held it fast.

Dorn was carefully groping his way past the others when the first shots crashed into the wooden cover above them. The sound was muffled but no less dangerous when the heavy bullets thudded into the plaster and brick wall away on their left, and bits of wood from the jagged holes scattered on the steps. Jessup knew the shooting angle had been shallow, but once the holes were big enough and the bolts pulled back, or the trap door destroyed by gunfire then, with an almost vertical angle, he and the others would be like the proverbial fish in a barrel.

Martina stood with her back to the wall, holding Carol's hand. Both women were trembling from the past few minutes' traumatic experience. Their hands were cold and clammy and both were breathing hard from the exertion of clambering down the steps. Martina realized the darkness was no longer complete as, through a rapidly thinning black cloud, she became aware of light. Just below where she stood there were dots of dancing silver on black and the faintest greyness beyond them. Then she knew she was staring at the reflection of stars on barely moving water and the greyness was a sheen of cloth laid on a much vaster stretch of water. The others became aware of the light.

There was another burst of automatic gunfire from the room above. It made a sharper sound as the trap door began to break up. Again, Jessup had the fearful knowledge that their attempted escape was over and his own puny part in it worthless.

They could see one another's faces now, colourless death masks, animated but strangely featureless. Dorn spoke, whispering was no longer necessary. 'We're in Swedcom's loading shed on Lake Vänern' he informed them. He sounded authoritative and they knew at once that the temporary refuge Dorn had found for them had not been stumbled upon by accident.

Jessup was prepared to leave that question mark until later. He thought of the guards so thoroughly covering the grounds of the warehouse. Nobody had thought it necessary, apparently, to keep watch under the building. Why should they? They had no reason to think it important. They had been employed to keep snoopers out, not in. Yet Jessup still didn't see how they could get much further; there wasn't even a rowing boat. Had Heinrich known that, too?

Dorn said 'Now everybody do exactly what I say. We're standing on a ten yard long loading platform and if we stay alive for another five minutes we're going to be alright.'

The others had no idea what Dorn was talking about. But they hung on to the idea that they had a chance. Then Dorn ordered them to link hands and took the lead. Jessup brought up the rear as before and, as they moved slowly towards the lighter shadow of the lake, there was another frenetic chatter from the guns behind them. Pieces of wood and some of the bullets splashed into the water beside them. It was a clear sign that there were barely seconds left before the battered trap door was removed and the first man had an uninterrupted field of fire at their retreating shapes.

Jessup threw a quick look behind. Even as he did so, the light from the floor above shone from the opening that had been made for the bolts to be pulled back from above. The remains of the door were kicked aside and the legs of a crouched figure appeared. He loosed Carol's hand and took the gun from the pocket where he had thrust it as he had stumbled towards the trap door. There wasn't much point in waiting for the opposition. Once the first guard had covered the narrow platform on which they stood with a field of fire, it would be too late to hit back with a handgun. Jessup steadied the Walther with his left hand and aimed at the legs. The five inches of orange flame that came from the muzzle of the gun gave him a small shock. It was a spurt of violence more potent than the invisible bullet to Jessup who had never seen a gun fired in total darkness before. The shot thwacked into the wooden steps and the guard immediately disappeared upwards again. Jessup wasted no time watching. Three seconds later he had reached the end of the wall with the others. The loading platform extended to the right, jutting out two yards into the open lake. Together the four stood briefly out of the line of fire. But there was nowhere else to run. Their backs were against the farther wall of the storeroom they had originally entered. Above them were the closed double doors of the loading bay Jessup had seen when he had first entered the room. Now, at least, they were outside the building, and that in itself was a small miracle.

The lake stretched wide and dark all round them. Above, the sky was a clean cloth of black velvet with the stars sparkling like fixed fireflies. One of their pursuers, either from the steps or leaning through the trap door, let off another burst of automatic fire. The shots echoed and ricocheted from inside the darkened inlet. Then there was silence, and in the silence they heard the muffled whine of an electric motor. The sound came, increasing in volume, from the lake.

Again Dorn asserted command, making them feel he knew exactly what was going on. He seemed to know what they were thinking, too. 'Don't worry, with a little luck we won't have to swim for it.' he said, placing his arm round Martina's shoulder. Incredibly he was smiling as he stood there reassuring them, the code box still in his left hand. 'David, take a peek around the corner and if necessary put a shot down the length of the landing. It'll keep their heads down for a few vital seconds. There're only four shells left in that thing so don't try a massive barrage.'

Somehow, in the dangerous position they were in, his calm confidence warmed them. Carol and Martina were shaking with nervous fatigue. Carol's suit and Martina's red dress had not been designed for running gun fights, and the chill of a late night lakeside had pierced them to the bone. They fought the cold and the fear, their arms linked, hoping against hope that Dorn was as confident as he sounded.

Jessup knelt on the stone ledge at the turn of the building and looked into the darkness beyond. There had been no sound of running footsteps but, with the guards' obvious professionalism, he knew they could be within inches of the corner in a perfectly soundless rush from the trap door. At knee level he showed no more of his head than he had to. He was sweating and cold at the same time. A quick movement of his head, forward and back again. There was nothing to be seen, no hard shadows against the wall moving towards them. Only the glimmer of light from the square opening a dozen yards away.

Dorn was facing the lake, trying to pierce the darkness that surrounded them like the walls of a blacked-out room. The sound of the engine was much louder now. It was heading for the channel of the loading bay next

BALTIC INCIDENT

to where they stood. Martina and Carol saw it at the same time as Dorn. A pinprick of light from the lake, no more than ten yards away. Dorn gave a short, single cry with hollowed hands held to his mouth, directed towards the light.

Now the boat was a thick black blob, perfectly camouflaged on its black background of water. The Gemini dinghy, a Royal Marine inflatable with an outboard motor, manned by two black skin-suited shapes headed for them. The motor died to little more than a sighing throb. The figure at the rear of the boat shoved the tiller hard over and the craft, responding like a fast skier turning into the stop position, swung sideways and bounced against the stone platform on which they stood.

Jessup, Carol and Martina were reduced to a gaping silence at this totally unexpected apparition. It seemed like hours to them, but only a minute or so had passed since they had reached comparative safety at the angle of the Swedcom warehouse building. Jessup was acutely conscious that Dorn had known all along what he was about when he had run from the computer room.

The front figure in the dinghy leaned over to grasp the low wall. Clothed in the tight-fitting black uni-garment from head to toe, an automatic rifle slung across his back, the man's white face framed by the black cloth looked small and impish as he looked up unsmilingly at Dorn. He nodded towards Dorn's companions. 'Brought Uncle Tom Cobbleigh and all?' The dinghy was designed to carry four. It now had to hold six. 'Let's get on with it.' the white-faced man said.

Dorn handed the code to the second figure holding on to the short arm of the outboard motor's tiller and, with words of encouragement, assisted first Martina then Carol into the bobbing rubber bowl. The craft tilted dangerously as Jessup, too, climbed over the taut neo-prene. A crisp order from the steersman caused them to fling themselves down to the centre of the boat and Jessup got a strong whiff of synthetic foam and reinforced fibres from the dinghy's fabric as he obeyed with the others and buried his nose in the rubber floor.

The reason for the urgent command became clear a moment later. The loading bay doors above them were suddenly flung wide and two machine pistols were pointed at the dinghy. Stavrinsky's voice sounded un-naturally loud. 'Heinrich,' he shouted, 'don't be foolish.' He broke off, suddenly. He had known that, without a boat, and short of diving into the icy waters of the lake which would have been pointless, Dorn and his friends could get no further than the corner of the building. He had withdrawn his men from unnecessary exposure in the tunnel knowing that from the vantagepoint of the upper storeroom loading bay doors he could totally dominate the water exit. His intention had been to call on Dorn to give himself up. Once he had retrieved the code they could all go to hell, including Dorn, for all he cared.

Stavrinsky had not expected Dorn to have outside help, and he stopped, realizing the dinghy, just visible in the black water below him, was not there by accident. There were more than four runaways down there and the two skin-suited dark shapes manning the boat made him realize at once he was confronting something more organized than the four people he believed he'd caught in a corner. His first look had shown him the gun slung on the back of the slim figure at the front of the boat, and that made it quite a different ball game.

Immediately Dorn had dropped to the floor with the others, the dinghy's engine had increased to a high-pitched whine and, with astonishing acceleration, it swung away from the jetty.

Stavrinsky cursed loudly and spoke to the gunmen at his side. The first Russian volley swept the air above the lowered heads. Jessup felt the shock wave of low velocity heavy calibre missiles as they hissed inches above his head and bit deeply into the water. The taller figure in the dinghy, twisted at an impossible angle below the gunwale, arms resting on the rounded rubber, had already unslung his weapon and sent a burst of fire towards the lighted loading bay doors. The gunmen crouched there dived to left and right of the opening as the splay of slugs thudded into the wood and whined off the masonry. Even as the Russians swung back to return the fire the dinghy had merged with the blackness of night, leaving behind it only a widening turbulence of grey foam on the surface of the lake.

Stavrinsky clutched his injured arm firmly to his side in an effort to prevent the already excruciating pain from becoming worse by unnecessary movement. He knew the bullet had missed the bones of the forearm and the bleeding was not arterial, but the tendons and muscles had been badly ripped apart. He barked an order for the two gunmen to retire and continue to watch the Swedcom grounds then returned to the 'Operation Searchlight' control room.

Lennart Feldt sat on the swivel stool, hunched over the console, as though nothing unusual had had happened. As, indeed for him, nothing had. His technical brilliance with the construction and programming of computer equipment did not extend to the sphere of human activity. As soon as the rumpus had broken out minutes earlier, he had calmly carried his coffee from the rest room back to the screen. Despite their social and spiritual disabilities caused by the too rapid revo-

CHARLES SMART

lution from boorish farming communities, the Swedes could be relied on to master the mechanism of man-made instruments with the marked single-mindedness of the unimaginative.

Stavrinsky, still gripping his right arm, grunted his satisfaction. He sat down heavily at the desk behind Feldt and, releasing his right arm, reached out to pour himself a generous measure of aquavit. He thought about Dorn as the fiery liquid burned into the tissues of his throat. Dorn was not an idiot. He obviously knew or had guessed the code would enable the Karlskoga headquarters to receive the 'Exercise' signal from the Warsaw Pact fleet. It was just possible he intended to bargain for his freedom with it. But Dorn had badly miscalculated. What Dorn did not know, apparently, was that the code could not be received by the Karl-skoga computer until the false programme, now being run by Feldt, right here in this room, had been stopped. Not even Dorn, with all his trained ability, could mate-rialize again within the next five minutes.

Damn this pain. Stavrinsky ordered Feldt to dial the house number for Görman to bring bandages and an-tiseptic. The time factor was crucial. He checked his wristwatch. It was four minutes to midnight. He did not have to guess what was happening at Karlskoga headquarters. All the chiefs of the military and the Prime Minister would be there, watching the false in-formation fed to them by Feldt; the size of the Warsaw Pact force and its apparently inexorable progress west-wards towards longitude thirteen thirty East.

Stavrinsky knew, as they must know, that under normal exercise conditions the pre-arranged 'Exercise' signal would already have been sent by the fleet and should now be showing in the top right hand corner of their master screen. At that moment, thought Stavrinsky, and for once in his political life, the Prime Minister of Sweden must have felt the authentic heavy moral responsibility that other world leaders experienced every day. For he must even now, under acute mental strain, be calculating the effects of the 'Execute' order that he would have to give within minutes; an order that would expose to Stavrinsky's monitoring teams every major military counter-invasion plan Sweden had devised for its defence.

Stavrinsky frowned in annoyance at the closed briefcase lying on the desk in front of him. In snatching up the second box containing the code Dorn had accidentally knocked the lid of the case down so that the hardened steel prongs had again clicked home to complete the circuit of the detonator inside. He would have to use his key again and disarm the explosives, but he couldn't do a damn thing until that slimy Görman had brought the bandages. There was a discreet knock on the door and Stavrinsky turned to see Görman enter, carrying a first-aid box.

- - - - - - - - - - - - - - -

Jessup had pressed his forehead hard against the bouncing and vibrating rubber surface that comprised the floor of the dinghy. Somebody's leg lay across his neck and there was an undefinable weight on his ankles. His left hand was twisted painfully under his belly and the fingers of his right hand clutched the material of Carol's skirt. Five sets of limbs began to disentangle themselves carefully from the bottom of the boat as it pounded, seemingly at breakneck speed, across the water, held on its course by the shadowy black-clothed form of the helmsman.

Jessup's mind was in turmoil, and it had nothing to do with his physical discomfort. Slowly he lifted his hand

and shoulders and unwound the hand from its crooked position beneath him.

He was dimly aware that Dorn and the women were also straightening from the foetal positions into which they had flung themselves. It was the voice that had shocked him through and through. There was no moon, and very few lights were to be seen bordering the lake, but when Jessup finally managed to raise his head the starlight was sufficient for him to distinguish the pale features, made oval by the headpiece of the wet suit, of the slim man lodged precariously on the side of the dinghy. The man's right hand cradled the slung machine pistol. Jessup noticed, inconsequentially, the man rested his finger just outside the trigger guard while, with the other hand he steadied himself against the bucking boat, powering intensely towards an invisible destination. It was Goddard.

Goddard looked down at Jessup briefly, giving him a thin smile as he spoke above the sound of the engine, 'Welcome aboard, Dr Jessup.'

Before Jessup could formulate a coherent response from the series of questions that began to tumble about his brain, Goddard spoke again. 'Questions later, old chap. Rather busy just now. Worry not, you're among friends. Oh, and that's Bill McMahon at the driving end. American, but quite civilized.' Jessup was still gaping. 'One other thing, though. Let me introduce you to a member of our special European branch of Squawk.' He turned to look at Dorn who had struggled into a kneeling position next to Martina and had both arms round her body, hugging her closely against the piercing night air as it rushed like a localized gale over the speeding craft. His generous mouth was stretched in a grin, showing the whiteness of his teeth against the dark night.

BALTIC INCIDENT

For a long moment Jessup's face took on a simpleton's look of stupefaction. Amazement mingled with relief and a host of other, unidentifiable, sensations made Jessup even less capable of intelligent response. He croaked a single word that managed to express astonishment, disbelief, accusation, joy and relief all at the same time.

'You!'

'In person, old friend' said Dorn holding out a big hand in sham protocol. 'Greet the new Dorn!' he quipped.

Martina had corkscrewed her neck to look up at Dorn. Her eyes, black in the night, reflected the starlight in tears that welled up uninvited as she began to hope again. She could not speak, and simply drew his arms more closely about her.

Carol leaned across from beside Jessup and squeezed Martina's arm in silent understanding.

Dorn broke the moment of revelation with a thirty-second résumé, of the evening's events in the warehouse and the part played by Jessup. Goddard listened without comment until Dorn had finished then told Dorn how he knew that Jessup and the women were with him and of Svensson's disappearance from the face of the earth. 'My next order to Svensson,' Goddard added 'would have been to keep our friend Jessup out of the warehouse while you went in and made the plant.'

'In that case' Dorn replied 'I'm glad your order didn't get through. It looks as though Karjagin wanted to bend Moscow rules a little and I might not have got out alive if Jessup hadn't been there.'

Goddard cut off further explanations. The electric motor had reduced its low-pitched whine to a whisper and the dinghy suddenly lost way. Goddard announced crisp and precise instructions. The faintest strip of grey emerged from the darkness in front of them where the water lapped a sandy stretch of beach. A black wall of trees rose steeply beyond. The blunt nose ploughed fast into the soft sand and before the forward motion had stopped Goddard had leaped on to dry land. The others followed in quick succession. The man Goddard had introduced as Bill McMahon was on their heels steadying the slung machine pistol with one hand and clasping with his left hand the box containing the code. On Goddard's orders nobody spoke as they followed him stumblingly across the sand. They felt the urgency of the moment. Almost at once they were into the screen of firtrees that sloped upwards away from the lake. Against the blackness of the trees Goddard was an almost invisible figure in his skin suit, and only his orders that they should link hands prevented them crashing head-on into tree trunks. Within seconds, Carol's tights had been torn to ribbons and Martina's red dress made ragged by the lowest branches of the trees and brambles that reached out to them from the thick underbrush.

Goddard did not falter in his lead and Jessup realized he must have traversed this route in the darkness many times before in order to be so certain of his direction.

Then they were through the screen of trees and on a rutted track that crossed their path at right angles. A dark coloured Cherokee van stood to their left. They bunched round Goddard, breathless from the climb, as he unlocked the rear doors with a key taken from a small, nylon-zipped pocket on his thigh. It had taken no more than two minutes for them to reach the van from the beach.

Jessup took a quick look at their surroundings. The track had been cut into the slope of a steep, wooded hill some fifty feet above the lake. The forest continued upwards into the blackness beyond them. The beach below was hidden by the trees they had just struggled through, but from this higher point the vastness of the lake itself could be seen through gaps in the trees. The lake was quite black in the still and star-filled night, stretching away endlessly. Except to the right as they looked down, the direction from which they had just come. One or two lights, candles or hurricane lamps, flickered from houses on the lakeside like the dying embers of a burnt out Catherine wheel, giving a vague shape to the shoreline. Perhaps a lighted window from Swedcom was among them. It was impossible to tell. Beyond them the beams of a car's headlights moved along a road.

Goddard, smoothly unslinging his gun and pushing it in front of him, jumped into the van, urging the others to follow quickly. McMahon climbed in last and locked the double doors securely behind him. Goddard had gone forward to sit at the driving seat, turning a switch on the instrument panel as he sat down. The interior was immediately flooded with light.

It was a big vehicle, specially kitted out. A long, narrow workbench had been fitted to the length of one side and the American, who now appeared to take command, sat on a stool facing it. Dorn had climbed into the passenger seat next to Goddard and Jessup had the feeling that he himself, Carol and Martina had stepped unwittingly into the middle of a thoroughly planned and well-rehearsed operation. With the two women he sat as instructed on the foam rubber-covered floor with his back against the side opposite the workbench. With their legs tucked under them and maintaining the silence imposed on them by Goddard, they watched the movements of McMahon.

Immediately in front of McMahon was what looked like a portable black typewriter. It was, in fact, a mini version of the highly sophisticated Commodore computer. Only this portable set would cost about ten times the amount of the bigger models used by NATO's own secret service organization. Mainly because it incorporated all the same features but had been reduced to a fraction of the size. It was to the square transmitter on his right that McMahon turned his attention first.

He pressed a switch on a small control panel fixed to the wall of the van and they heard the buzz of antennae extending from telescopic roots somewhere on the external surfaces of the Cherokee. Then he held his finger over a red button on the transmitter. 'Time check.' he said abruptly to Goddard.

'Midnight minus two minutes,' replied Goddard instantly. 'And time to go, I think, Bill.'

'Where did you place the MEP, Heinrich?' asked the American.

'Same level and one yard away.' Dorn responded without hesitation.

'Right. Going now.' said McMahon, and pressed down hard on the red button. A red warning light disappeared from the transmitter to be replaced by a green operational light.

– – – – – – – – – – – – – – –

Stavrinsky, in the Swedcom control room he had chosen as the brain centre for 'Operation Searchlight', had his back to the computer console while Görman finished his inexpert bandaging of the injured arm. Feldt sat on the stool watching the constantly changing green figures on the screen fed to it by the false program disk in the machine at his side.

It was less than two minutes to midnight. On the instant McMahon pressed the red button, the micro electronic pulsator, so accurately tuned and housed in the compact shell of the stainless steel cigarette lighter

BALTIC INCIDENT

Dorn had left on the table, radiated its energy in all directions. An electric charge, powerful enough to put out of action the treble bank of computers in the main central room of Swedcom's telecommunications centre in Stockholm, instantly destroyed the delicate tracings etched on the plastic disk of the false program. Given enough time, Feldt would have seen, with dismay, the smudges of meaningless green splashed incoherently across the screen.

But at the same moment, time had ceased to exist for Feldt. For the stream of electronic particles that were transmitted from the cigarette lighter also activated the detonator in Stavrinsky's briefcase.

The rumble of the explosion travelled easily on the surface of the lake to reach the far shore fifteen miles away. Its frightful crashing sound echoed and re-echoed in the closer tracts of the surrounding forest. It penetrated even the walls of the small hospital outside the village of Sjötorp and infiltrated the single bedroom where Lieutenant Lars Dahl lay in a serious state of shock, received after walking back from his tank to be confronted by the smeared remains of Peter Svensson. The noise slipped through his sedated unconsciousness and his eyelids fluttered as though he dreamed again the nightmare of the bloody bones.

The Swedcom control room and everything in it split into an untold number of flying fragments of wood, metal and human flesh. A week later, the remains of a handless arm was found floating just below the surface of the lake by a local angler. It was to be identified, with difficulty, as that of Görman's. One of the guards in the nearby rest room was killed outright when the heavy wooden wall shattered on his head as he sipped from a mug of coffee. Three of the KGB guards patrolling the grounds outside were knocked flat by the blast, one of them pierced through below the ribs by the barrel of his own gun.

In the Cherokee's driving seat, Goddard had been looking at the dial of the special issue combat wristwatch. The flicker of light on the window at his shoulder caused him to turn and look towards the lake. The sound of the explosion followed almost immediately and the big Cherokee rocked slightly on its hydraulic suspension. 'My God, what the hell was that?' He stared, fascinated at the swirling flames.

Dorn leaned over from the passenger seat and they both watched from the window. A great orange flame, brighter and whiter at its base, rose from where they knew the Swedcom warehouse was situated.

Goddard looked at Dorn 'You were supposed to leave an MEP there. Did you have time to fix a nuclear device as well?'

'What's going on out there?' the American called. He left his stool to peer over Goddard's shoulder. 'Hell and incarnation' be breathed in his New England drawl. 'If the pulsator didn't put the program out, that little bang sure as hell did.'

Dorn was not smiling. 'Goodbye, Boris,' he murmured, as if he were at the funeral pyre of some loved friend. He shook his head slowly as if to let the past slip inevitably away, then he explained. 'I think it was necessary. We all know why we couldn't take chances with Stavrinsky's briefcase. Well, when I took the code box, I purposely knocked the lid shut again. It wasn't foolproof, but if that new pulsator you developed was as powerful as you said it was, Bill, I thought it might be worth the double insurance.'

Martina, Carol and Jessup hadn't moved from their sitting positions and their faces showed tense and white in the van's roof lighting as they looked towards the three men. On the drive from Gothenburg Dorn had told them, without going into detail, about the importance of Stavrinsky's briefcase and that it had undoubtedly been rigged with a self-destructive explosive against any unauthorized attempt to open it. Jessup understood exactly what Dorn was telling Goddard and the American, for he had already guessed the nature of the grey-coloured plasticine substance, held rigid by broad red tape, when he'd seen it on the inside of the open case on Stavrinsky's desk. But they had to contain their curiosity still further, for Bill McMahon had wasted no more time with the obvious.

He nodded curtly at Dorn's explanation then slipped back into his seat in front of the computer keyboard and picked up the metal container Dorn had handed to him on the dinghy. With strong, lean fingers he prised open the airtight lid. From the bed of its cotton wool padding McMahon took a strip of titanic alloy material and studied the code engraved deeply in its surface.

Jessup was holding Carol's hand and felt the pressure of her fingers increase. The faint trembling of her body was a reflection of the tension that had built up in the four minutes or so they had spent inside the van.

Goddard and Dorn had half turned in their seats to watch McMahon at work. Goddard's face looked paler and more pinched than ever. Like McMahon he had not taken off his frogman's suit and Jessup thought of the uncomfortable heat that must be building up in his body after his recent exertions. Dorn's thick dark hair was tangled and untidy, and the black stubble that covered much of his face made him look as though he was in permanent shadow. Neither took his eyes off the American as he bent over the computer in profound, professional concentration, for they knew that at this moment, and for a very short while afterwards, the Prime Minister and the military and state security heads at Karlskoga were staring at a blank screen while technicians were frantically searching for the unfindable fault. But no one was more aware than McMahon that the confusion would not last forever; that the Prime Minister would be forced to order 'Execute'. It would be irresponsible for him not to, since the false programme issuing from Swedcom had shown that the Warsaw Pact fleet would be just west of longitude 13'30º East at midnight. The internationally agreed 'Exercise' signal would not have been received. So much McMahon knew from Goddard's fruitful liaison with the Russians on 'Operation Searchlight' and from Dorn's accurate observations and calculations that had been passed on to Moscow.

McMahon began to tap out the Karlskoga recognition signal. Then, after a brief hesitation, began to copy on to the keys the characters and numbers of the code that would instantly unblock the information sent by Swedish naval and air craft shadowing the Warsaw Pact fleet.

Since it was barely midnight, the genuine position of the fleet would differ hardly at all from the destroyed false programme. Most critical of all information was the 'Exercise' symbol that would now appear on the Karlskoga screen, sent simultaneously from Moscow, Peenemunde and the fleet's flagship. McMahon depressed the transmission key.

With the passing of the explosion, the silence of a Nordic forest descended on them and the soft contact of fingers on keys sounded like the dainty hooves of a stray sheep clopping along an English country lane in mid-summer.

BALTIC INCIDENT

Goddard raised a fluted champagne glass to eye level and saluted Jessup with it, giving him the youthful grin Jessup remembered from the first time they had met in Derringer's room. 'To amateurs.' he said.

'And the bloody British who invented the breed.' McMahon added irreverently, his grey eyes twinkling. The others joined his merriment.

Dorn had his arm round Martina's shoulder as they sat close together on a comfortable sofa. She huddled up to him as though he might suddenly disappear. Carol sat on the thick-piled wine red carpet, her back was against the armchair on which Jessup sat and her head rested on his knees.

They were in the large sitting room of McMahon's house, a fifteen minutes drive north of the canal. Goddard, now in grey flannels and white sweater, stood with his back to the shiny white-glazed floor-to-ceiling stove common in older Swedish homes. McMahon had shared out the bottle and was standing near the cocktail cabinet. He, too, had changed into casual clothes and wore a large chequered red jacket over a pale blue, dapper, waistcoat with shirt and tie to match. An extraordinarily long cigar hung from his lips and perfumed the room.

The glow from the open panel in the stove threw out a genuine warmth into the room. Half a dozen red candles in elegant silver holders of different designs added their light to an intimate and relaxing atmosphere. It was past one in the morning and although all six were in various stages of near exhaustion they had unanimously approved McMahon's proposal to toast success.

They had had to wait an agonizing five minutes in the Cherokee after McMahon had put through the code to

Karlskoga. Only when the one word telephone call had come through on the Cherokee's special number did they know for sure that the Russian deception plan, 'Operation Searchlight', had failed. The call had come from Goddard's Säpo contact who had travelled to Karlskoga with Sorbron. They hadn't wasted time with cheering, for there had been a loose end Goddard had not forgotten to tie up. Too many questions would be asked if he had allowed the Jaguar to remain outside Swedcom. As soon as he had replaced the telephone receiver, Goddard had driven like a madman and it had taken only minutes along back roads to reach the Swedcom warehouse. As he had guessed, in the confusion of the night caused by both 'Red Alert' and the power cut, neither the police nor fire brigade had arrived. There had been no one to raise the alarm anyway. The two uninjured KGB men had fled in the helicopter with their wounded companion as soon as they realized the extent of the damage and discovered Stavrinsky had died in the explosion.

By the time the Cherokee arrived the flames had gutted the room in which Stavrinsky had set up the computer, and were already consuming the remaining parts of the warehouse. The covered passage leading to the house was still on fire. Jessup, with Dorn beside him as a precaution against the two vehicles becoming separated, had driven swiftly away. It had already been decided that everyone should spend the rest of the night at McMahon's secluded country house. Part of Goddard's detailed operational plan had involved renting a safe house north of the canal area. He wasn't the careless type.

Jessup thought he had found his bearings at last. But there were unexplained details. He felt the wine adding its relaxing effect to his overtaxed body as he sat deeply in the armchair. He responded to Goddard's gesture with wry acknowledgement. Then he looked at Dorn. 'So you were in this caper from the beginning, Heinrich?'

'Had to be, old friend. Part of the price I paid to the old firm back in West Berlin. I handed Dyson the platter of goods as soon as I was given the tip that Moscow intended to dump me. Got it from an old Leningrad student friend. There'd be no future for me in the East, would there? Besides, Moscow was right. I was contaminated, and enjoying every minute of it in West Berlin.'

They all saw Martina dig him hard in the ribs with her elbow.

Goddard took the opportunity to cut in on his explanation. 'Don't play yourself down, Heinrich.' He turned to Jessup. 'He'd had it rough before that, David. Both parents killed at the end of the war in Berlin. His father died leading a suicide attack – rifles against Russian tanks. Mother dragged from the rubble where she had died protecting baby Heinrich with her own body. Ate scraps as an orphan for the next ten years. Only natural he should jump at the chance of studying languages in Moscow once his ability had been noticed at school. It was easy for a KGB talent scout to spot him. After that, no boy of eighteen with his background could resist the offer of specialized undercover agent training in the competitive Leningrad College for West orientation courses. He'd been good at that, too. Got a good few bits of information from our side for a while.'

'Thanks for the back cover blurb, James.' Dorn laughed. 'As I was saying, David. Dyson had me flown to the American base in Mildenhall. Not that showpiece at Lakenheath, the one closer to the town. They put me through the proverbial hoop there. Eight hours a day.

That's where I met Colonel Bill McMahon, here.' Dorn used his left hand, the one holding the glass, to wave at the American. McMahon bowed to him mockingly.

'I lost fifty dollars to him on the twenty-lane ten-pin bowling alley they've got there. We played between the brain picking sessions. Come to think of it, I guess he was still working on me while I thought he was concentrating on the number one pin.'

'Right again, Heinrich,' said McMahon, chuckling, 'Dyson didn't stop pumping you for a minute. Not even when you were asleep. We had a low-pitched, low frequency pre-recorded tape on you all the time. After five minutes, seven out of ten lightly drugged sleepers come up with some sort of answer. One of the little devices I developed down at my place in North Miami.'

'Gott, and I thought the Russians were bad enough.' Dorn was slowly shaking his head in bittersweet amusement.

'I'd like a little talk with you about that,' said Martina, smiling mischievously at McMahon.

'So you're the electronics expert?' Carol queried, lazily re-crossing her outstretched legs.

'The best the CIA have,' Goddard answered for him.

'Stow it, James,' said the grey haired man good humourdly. 'I just get lucky with my ideas sometimes.'

'That little cigarette lighter Heinrich had to place near Stavrinsky's computer was something Bill's been working on for a few years. The CIA got very interested in using it in a real live situation,' Goddard said.

'A pulsar, you called it, or something like that, wasn't it?' said Carol wrinkling her nose at the technicality.

'A micro electronic pulsator, the boffins call it. Makes a terrible mess with reception on car radios,' Goddard explained.

BALTIC INCIDENT

'We tried an early model in the middle of Hawaii about five years ago,' said McMahon. 'Every car with a fuel injection system stopped dead. There was one hell of a pile-up in Honolulu. The local garages did a roaring trade re-adjusting the tuning.'

Jessup asked Goddard 'Was it really necessary to involve Derringer?' He had already outlined to Goddard the events at Kronborg castle.

Goddard gestured as though to push back the hair from his brow, but the long fair hair was still damp from his recent shower and had remained smooth and sleek on the top of his head. ''fraid so. The whole point of Dyson's plan for squawk's involvement with the Russians was anti-deception. They were getting far too cocky in the north – if you'll forgive the expression – especially in Sweden. Our aim was to destroy Russia's credibility here for a long time to come. We think we'll have done that when the Swedes have finished assessing all the angles. Heinrich, of course, will be given a new identity.' He looked at Martina with a smile, 'Not too new, my dear.'

'And we've already planned a slot for him in West Germany.' McMahon added.

'Anyway' Goddard went on. 'We had to appear to go with them all the way. We knew Derringer worked both sides of the fence and made damn sure he would convince his other masters that we really did want to share the Russian spoils when Sweden ordered "Execute".'

'I suppose you had to keep me in the dark for similar reasons.' Jessup said.

'Absolutely. You had to be quite innocent. Had to be convincing with Sorbron and the Reds. But we had to keep you out of trouble as well. That was almost as bad. You really worried me with that little excursion to Rødvig. But it paid off with Derringer. Getting yourself into a scrape with Dorn must have made Derringer certain sure that we did intend to expose Heinrich according to Moscow's plan. I've no doubt he reported that news to the right source.

'However, I became a bit over-anxious and made the mistake of ordering Derringer to watch you more closely.'

'That's when he got too big for his boots.' Dorn interjected.

'That reminds me, Martina,' said Goddard. 'How did you guess Heinrich was lying low in Elsinore castle?'

'I didn't have to guess.' Martina smiled broadly and ingenuously as she snuggled her blonde head on Dorn's shoulder. 'The castle guns were firing in the background when he telephoned me to say he was alright.'

Dorn shook his head in mock amazement as he spoke to Goddard. 'She has a fantastic memory for romantic places. She's absolutely right. They fire those guns every afternoon for the benefit of the tourists. We'd watched the ceremony together only a month earlier.'

'Talking about guessing, James' said Jessup, removing his pipe from his mouth. 'Surely, not even you could have guessed those workmen in Frihamn would have a hole in the wall at the right time and in the right place?'

'Indeed not, David.' Said Goddard as he moved a step sideways from the heat of the stove. 'If Heinrich hadn't made it, then I should have had to get the MEP into Swedcom myself, which would have been deuced tricky at that stage of the game. But no. Those workmen you saw were loaned by the West German special operations branch. The Frihamn works department uniform and identification cards were as easy to get as yours had been. They were just two more invisible labourers. Except that they had landed from an earlier German ship with a bottle of corrosive acid strong enough to eat through that wall, if that had been necessary.'

'James himself had rehearsed the way I was to go aboard the Helsingør ship.' said Dorn. 'Only he'd done it the hard way. He wore just an ordinary suit to see what sort of challenge he'd get going up the car ramp.'

'You must have had a back-up story for that.' said Jessup.

'Simplest is best' Goddard replied. 'Obviously I'd bought a boat ticket to get into the Frihamn area. The trick was not to use it. Of all the people walking down the ramp, it was the captain I had to bump into. No bother at all, though. Told him I'd left my copy of the Financial Times in the ship's restaurant. Charming fellow. Hoped I'd had a pleasant crossing from Kiel and bade me good day.'

'After that kind of security we knew Heinrich had a better than even chance of getting aboard as a loader,' said McMahon. 'We'd watched the loading gangs often enough, so we knew how they worked and what they looked like.'

'But what if it had not worked?' Martina insisted, her big blue eyes coming suddenly alive at the thought. 'You would have left him in prison?' The south German accent rolled the "r" sound round her tongue.

'Hell, no, darling.' said McMahon with humour. 'You wouldn't read about it in the papers, but after a few diplomatic exchanges he'd have been in London or Bonn within a week.'

Jessup put his hand on Carol's head and fondled the rich darkness of her hair. He said, loud enough for all to hear. 'Well, my love, bedtime, I think. I have to arrange for a meeting tomorrow.'

'Oh, you didn't tell me. Is it important?'

CHARLES SMART

Jessup bent to her ear and spoke in a stage whisper. 'Slipped me mind, sweetheart. Somebody rang me the other day. Apparently collects antique machines. You know, typewriters, cash registers and the like. Seems he'd like to buy my old Nordiska radio.'

BALTIC INCIDENT
EPILOGUE

Five miles to the north of Stockholm city centre on the edge of a suburb of modern communal concrete blocks of two-storey flats lies a tiny, discreet Jewish cemetery, 'Fredsgården', the garden of peace.

David Jessup took a taxi from town, paid off the driver and stood before the wrought-iron gates set in the low brick boundary wall of the cemetery. He felt the silence of the place as much as the warmth of early summer sunshine. He opened the gate and began along the loose-stoned path between carefully manicured plots.

He found the square of granite he was looking for. Facing the small mound of well-kept grass, edged with blue and yellow pansies – the colours of the Swedish flag – he saw the newly engraved Star of David. Would this man still be alive if he had dealt more robustly with Moscow? If he had roundly condemned the submarine infringements? If he had declaimed more furiously and less diplomatically with Soviet Communist Party Central Committee member Georgij Arbatov? Could the British involvement with the Russian plan have contributed to his death?

Not least, Jessup pondered, would he still be alive if he had thoroughly investigated the stranded trawler incident at Falsterbo instead of actively assisting the Russians, without a single protest, to refloat the SHISHAK? Had that apparently minor event led to this premature plot, the resting-place of the assassinated Prime Minister? Jessup read the simple inscription under the six-pointed star.

SVEN OLOF JOACHIM PALME
1927 – 1986

237